28.95

DEADLY NIGHTSHADE

This Large Print Book carries the
Seal of Approval of N.A.V.H.

DEADLY NIGHTSHADE

CYNTHIA RIGGS

Thorndike Press • Waterville, Maine

Published in 2001 by arrangement with St. Martin's Press, LLC.

Thorndike Press Large Print Senior Lifestyles Series.

The tree indicium is a trademark of Thorndike Press.

The text of this Large Print edition is unabridged.
Other aspects of the book may vary from the original edition.

Set in 16 pt. Plantin by Minnie B. Raven.

Printed in the United States on permanent paper.

Library of Congress Cataloging-in-Publication Data

Riggs, Cynthia.
    Deadly nightshade / Cynthia Riggs.
      p. cm.
    ISBN 0-7862-3754-6 (lg. print : hc : alk. paper)
    1. Women detectives — Massachusetts — Martha's
Vineyard — Fiction. 2. Martha's Vineyard (Mass.) —
Fiction. 3. Aged women — Fiction. 4. Large type books.
I. Title.
PS3618.I394 D43 2001b
  813′.6—dc21
                                  2001053457

FOR

DIONIS COFFIN RIGGS
POET

1898–1997

\\ Acknowledgments //

Thank you, Arlene Silva, for urging me to go back to school. And thank you, Jonathan Revere, for suggesting, once Vermont College accepted me, that, since all the other students would be writing the great American novel, I should write mysteries instead. Thank you, Dan Sharkovitz, for drumming into me the importance of character in fiction.

Thank you, Vermont College, for accepting a student who was *not* writing the great American novel, and for insisting I write five hours a day. Bret Lott, my first advisor, said it was okay to use real settings and real people fictionally. The real people will be flattered, he said. Advisor Mary Grimm assured me mysteries can be good literature. Thank you, Francois Camoin, for working with me through two semesters and two books. And for writing "Texture! More texture!" in the margins of my typescripts. Thank you, Phyllis Barber and Sena Jeter Naslund, two of many outstanding faculty members in the Vermont

College MFA program.

My writers' group saw me through the throes of school and beyond. "Not clear!" they told me. "Too many 'saids.'" "More body language!" Thank you, Lois Remmer, our leader; Wendy Hathaway, who has thought of just the right word to make a sentence sound right; Brenda Horrigan, who knows the right phrase to make things clear (and who brings me chicken soup when I feel discouraged); and Vicki Kennedy, who spent a summer being writer-in-residence at my house.

Thanks to loyal friends, still with me even though every time they see me I proffer them a manuscript to critique. Among them are Fred Simons, who fixes my words as well as my furniture; William Stewart, who has an impeccable sense of taste and grammar; Pat Suarez, a mystery lover, who pleased me when she said, "Shit, I like it!"; Ruth Grupper, a B and B guest who read my books instead of going to the beach; and Janet Atherton and Don Ziegler, B and B guests, who read my books in bed instead of . . . (never mind).

Don't ever show your books-in-progress to your family, I was told, but I did anyway. Cousin Carlin Smith was my very first reader. When she told me she didn't fall

8

asleep over my book, I knew it was safe to move on to my big sister and brother-in-law, Alvida and Ralph Jones, who said, "That last chapter is awful. Cut it out," which I did. Then on to sister and brother-in-law Ann and Bill Fielder, who said, "The first chapter might be okay in a great American novel, but . . ." So I cut that out, too. Daughters Mary Wilder Stoertz and Ann Ricchiazzi and daughter-in-law Fiona Harris Stoertz spotted inconsistencies, repetitions, and faulty logic. To make it easy for me, they wrote notes on Post-its, four to a page in places.

For technical advice, thanks to geophysicist son-in-law Douglas Green, astrophysicist son-in-law Paul Ricchiazzi, Brendan O'Neill of the Vineyard Conservation Society, computer consultant Douglas Jones, and Ramon Suarez, retired New York City police detective.

Thank you, Nancy Love, my agent, who seems to know what every publishing house in New York is — and is not — looking for. Thank you, Ruth Cavin, my editor at St. Martin's Press, Julie Sullivan, assistant editor, and Carol Edwards, my copy editor.

The West Tisbury Public Library must be one of the best libraries in the Commonwealth. Librarian Mary Jo Joiner located a research volume that the Boston Public Library couldn't find, let me take it home, and didn't hassle me when it was overdue.

I hope Police Chief Beth Toomey, West Tisbury's real police chief, will forgive me for the liberties I have taken with our town's police procedures. My fictional Casey, like Chief Toomey, is an off-Islander working in a traditionally male job on a fairly small island. That's as far as the resemblance is meant to go.

To wind up everything, thank you again, Jonathan Revere, who, after getting me into murder in the first place, has stuck with me through it all as my plot doctor. When my characters get themselves into implausible situations, which happens frequently, Jonathan thinks up wickedly ingenious solutions. And gives me psychological chicken soup when I hit a writers' block wall.

Thanks not only to all of you, but those others — you know who you are — who've taken my writing seriously.

10

\\ Chapter 1 //

When she heard the scream, Victoria Trumbull had been waiting for her granddaughter Elizabeth to return from the outer harbor, where she and the harbormaster had gone to check boats. The scream sent prickles along the back of her neck. She had never heard anything like it before.

She had waited almost an hour after a friend dropped her off at the harbor. She didn't mind waiting. As long as she had paper and a pen, she could always work on her poetry.

She watched sunset colors dance in the tidal ripples of the channel leading into the harbor basin, bold splashes of orange and red and purple. The incoming tide created a stained-glass mosaic of fractured color that washed against the boats tied up in the harbor.

The incoming tide rocked sailboats on their moorings, set shrouds to slapping against aluminum masts with a mournful bell-like clang, a sound that repeated itself from boat to boat, until the whole was a

11

cacaphony of bells tolling.

Across the narrow channel, an osprey returned to its untidy nest of sticks on top of a telephone pole. Victoria watched it circle, wings spread wide. She could see its markings, gray and black and white. Colors flickered off the scales of a large struggling fish that the bird held in its talons. The osprey's chicks set up a greedy clamor, and Victoria could see their heads over the rim of the nest, beaks open wide. The osprey landed on the edge of the nest, feet extended, wings out to the sides. The fish flipped violently, its tail flicking sunset sparks, and the chicks' shrill peeping stopped abruptly.

She rummaged in her old leather pocketbook for something to write on. An envelope would be fine, the ComElectric bill she had forgotten to give Elizabeth to mail last week. She turned it over to its blank back. She found a purple-and-green pen with stars, gold glitter, and the words *Victoria Trumbull has just won $25,000!!!*, and started to write in her loopy backhand scrawl.

The osprey lifted up from its nest, its wings spread wide. The darkening sky, now drained of fluorescent orange, silhouetted the bird. It cried, a mournful peeping cry, too feeble-sounding for the strong wings, talons, and beak.

The wind was picking up, a brisk breeze from the northwest. She was vaguely aware of the sound of men's voices across the harbor on the East Chop side, could almost make out words.

The scream jolted her out of her reverie. It echoed across the inner harbor and reverberated against the moored yachts, ricocheted off the shingled side of the harbormaster's shack. Suddenly, it cut off. She stood up, and the pen fell out of her lap, rolled toward the edge of the deck, and plopped into the water six feet below. She heard grunts, a scuffle, a splash, then nothing. The commotion came from across the harbor, near the yacht club's dock, where she thought she had heard men's voices earlier. But the light was fading quickly and Victoria couldn't be sure. An engine whirred, coughed, and caught. Was it a boat or a car? She thought she saw a plume of exhaust in the darkness on the other side of the dock. Tires skidded on sand, bit into a hard surface, and squealed as a vehicle turned. A sound came off the water. Was it an echo? Had the vehicle turned left or right? She couldn't tell.

Stillness settled again. It was as if no scream had ever spoiled the peace of the evening, no splash.

No one moved on the boats. No curious heads poked out of cuddies; no one stood up in cockpits. None of the strollers along the bulkhead paused to point and shout. Was she the only one who had heard the scream and splash, the sound of a motor, the squeal of tires?

Victoria looked at her watch. Not quite 7:30. What the devil could she do?

She hadn't the foggiest notion of how to use the radio in the shack to call the harbormaster and Elizabeth, tell them about the commotion, the scream and the splash.

She picked up the envelope on which she'd written the first line of her poem and put it back in her pocketbook. She paced the deck in front of the shack, no more than eight feet. She paced down the side of the shack, no more than twelve feet. She turned and paced back again.

Night was settling on the harbor. The bright sunset colors had faded and now dark purple wind clouds scudded across the darkening sky.

Finally, she heard, dimly, an outboard motor heading into the channel. The entry

14

lights had come on, triggered by darkness, a flashing red on the right of the harbor entrance, green on the left. Victoria eased herself down the ramp that led to the floating dock where Elizabeth would tie up the harbormaster's launch. She held the railing tightly with both hands. She was not going to act like an old lady, slipping and falling and breaking something. She had to tell the harbormaster what she had heard, what she might or might not have seen, and she had to tell him immediately.

The launch turned into the channel and slowed, its bow settled down, leveled, and its wake dropped behind it in a long, curling vee that broke in small combers against the rock sides of the channel. Elizabeth, lanky as a boy in the fading light, was in the stern, holding the tiller. Domingo sat in the bow seat, facing her, his arms folded over his broad chest, his dark baseball cap squared over his brow. Victoria knew that cap, the navy blue one that read NYPD in faded gold letters.

"Hey, Gram!" Elizabeth idled the engine and let the boat drift into the floating dock. "What's up?" Victoria could see her granddaughter's bright eyes in the dusk, her short gold-streaked hair tousled in damp curls.

Domingo turned, careful not to upset the boat's balance, and doffed his cap. "Sweetheart," he said to Victoria. "Be careful. Watch yourself." He remained seated.

"Grab the line, Grammy." Elizabeth reached for a cleat with slender fingers, held the boat against the floating dock, and passed the stern line to Victoria. Domingo still remained seated. Victoria, who'd been reared around boats, flung the line around a cleat and secured it. Elizabeth got out carefully and stood up straight, a tall young woman (thirty was young to Victoria) in tan shorts and white uniform shirt. The bow of the boat dipped lower in the water with the weight of the harbormaster. Domingo uncrossed his arms long enough to hand her the bow line.

"Don't put the boat away yet." Victoria stood up and backed toward the railing on the ramp so she could hold on to something.

"What's up, sweetheart?" Domingo pulled his cap down over his close-cropped hair and adjusted it over his heavy black brows. The boat bumped gently against the fender of the floating dock.

"I heard something on the other side of the harbor." Victoria pointed toward the

East Chop dock with her gnarled hand. "A scream. Then a splash." She held the railing and braced herself against the slight movement of the dock. "I thought I saw someone before I heard the scream, but I'm not sure."

"Get in," Domingo ordered.

Elizabeth held out her hand for her grandmother, and Victoria took it and settled herself onto the middle seat, her back to Elizabeth, who sat down again in the stern seat and started the motor. Domingo undid the lines and gave the dock a small shove with his hand. He leaned toward Victoria. "Show us where, sweetheart."

Elizabeth steered away from the floating dock, as much at home on the water as Victoria had been at her age. She piloted the launch among the sailboats moored in the center of the harbor, slowly, so the wake would not upset dishes or cocktail-hour glasses. Victoria heard music coming from the cockpits and cabins, music that varied from boat to boat. Rock, reggae, Bach, mostly contained within the boats. She could see the soft light of kerosene lamps, the glow of battery-operated lanterns.

"The scream was loud enough to wake the dead," Victoria said to Domingo. Eliza-

17

beth shifted slightly in the stern seat.

Domingo unfolded his arms long enough to gesture toward the music wafting from the boats. The whites of his eyes contrasted with his dark face, made it look still darker. He shrugged, hands out, pale palms up, opened his eyes wide. His expression seemed to say, What do you expect? Victoria hadn't realized how loud the music must be inside the boats. Domingo peered out from under the peak of his cap, dark eyes watching her. Victoria, who had gotten to know him well during the two months Elizabeth had worked for him, saw an expression of pleasure she had never seen before. Retired New York cop back in action, she thought.

Behind her, Elizabeth was quiet as she steered the launch slowly among the boats.

"Where did the sound come from?" Domingo asked. Victoria pointed toward the far shore. He lifted his chin at Elizabeth. "You," he said. "Slow down. You're making too much wake."

Elizabeth grunted and slowed the boat. The wake trailed off gently, met and broke against the whitecaps that wind and tide had stirred up in the harbor. The bow of the launch slapped small breaking waves, sending sprays of water over the harbormaster's uniformed back, an occasional spray over Victoria. Her face glistened with salt water, her beaklike nose dripped water, and diamonds of moisture sparkled in her white hair in the light from shore.

Above them, the sky had become black velvet, punctuated with stars so bright, the lights from shore couldn't drown them out.

"The tide's changed," Domingo said. "The current will be full flood in another ten or fifteen minutes."

The launch's red and green running lights reflected off the darkening surface of the harbor; the stern light trailed a path of white glitter behind them.

Victoria lifted her right hand from the gunwale, gingerly, so as not to upset the balance, and pointed toward the dock, now dark. "More that way."

Elizabeth changed direction slightly, and the bow slapped the choppy water.

"Slow down," Domingo ordered Elizabeth. "There's no rush." Elizabeth cut the speed to bare headway. "Sweetheart, let me have the searchlight under your seat." Victoria felt around until she found the plastic-encased light and handed it to him. "You." He gestured to Elizabeth. "Back and forth, starting here."

Elizabeth gave the boat more power.

"What's your hurry? Slow down." He turned back to Victoria. "Sit still, sweetheart. Tell me if you see anything." He swept the searchlight across the dark surface of the water. The light reflected on foamy white wave tops.

Elizabeth turned the boat and steered slowly toward the light on the Harbor House. When she was even with the last of the moored boats, she turned again and steered toward the barely discernible osprey pole, a line against the pinkish gray evening sky. They were broadside to the waves now, and the launch rolled, shipping water with an occasional slurp, until an inch or so sloshed around in the bottom of the boat.

"The bailer is under the seat, Gram."

Victoria fumbled until she found the Clorox bottle scoop tied to a thwart with a length of fishing line. She spread her knees apart and leaned over to scoop up the water at her feet. She heaved it over the side, careful to toss it away from the wind.

"Your grandmother's a better sailor than you are." Domingo nodded at Victoria. Elizabeth snorted, a sound Victoria interpreted as a muffled laugh.

Domingo swept the light back and forth

as they moved closer to shore. Victoria bailed. The Clorox scoop scraped against sand in the bottom of the boat. As they neared the shore, the harbor surface, sheltered by land, calmed, reflected the stars, the lights from the hotel. The boat steadied.

"Whoa!" Domingo said. "I see something."

Elizabeth idled the motor. Domingo held the light on a floating dark mass a couple of boat lengths from them. They drifted past, and Elizabeth steered the launch toward it, letting the boat's momentum carry them.

Victoria rose slightly in her seat.

"Watch it!" Domingo said, balancing the boat. "Looks like we found the source of your scream." He held the light high and aimed down at the dark mass.

"My God!" Elizabeth gasped.

"Careful!" Domingo ordered.

Victoria sat back. "How awful." She stared at the object. "He's not dead, is he?"

"Doesn't look too good, sweetheart."

"I heard him scream." Victoria stopped, then continued. "He screamed for help. And I did nothing."

"There was nothing you could do, sweetheart. Don't start thinking that way."

Domingo turned to Elizabeth. "You!" he said. "Get the boat hook."

Victoria moved slightly so Elizabeth could slide the boat hook out from under the seat. She stared at the mass bobbing in the light from shore.

"Are you okay?" Domingo asked. "You're not cold, are you?"

"No," Victoria replied. "I was thinking about that man."

Domingo nodded and looked beyond Victoria to Elizabeth. "Pull it in. Get it next to the boat. That's it," he added as Elizabeth leaned out and hooked the neck of the dark sweatshirt, navy blue or black, although Victoria couldn't tell which. "Go easy. That's it."

"For Christ's sake, Domingo," Elizabeth said, exasperation in her voice. "You don't need to tell me every single thing."

The body was that of a heavyset man. He was floating facedown, arms spread over his head. His jeans were pulled down, so his plump bottom was exposed, two pale, gelatinous globes. His legs had sunk into the water, out of sight. It was difficult to tell much about him in the dim light. His wet hair seemed to be gray, held back in a short ponytail with an elastic band.

"Don't rock the boat." Victoria had

leaned over to get a better look. "You," he said to Elizabeth, "get a line out of the box and secure him. That is," he added, "if I'm not telling you too much." The sound Elizabeth made was the same noise Victoria had heard her make as a little girl when her mother told her to clean her room.

"Get the line under one of his arms," Domingo ordered. The boat shifted as Elizabeth unlatched the box, took out a length of line and reached out toward the body bumping against the right side of the boat. Victoria leaned slightly to her left for counterbalance.

Domingo unclipped the handheld radio from his belt and switched it on, twisted the dial until the static stopped, and spoke into the mike.

"Oak Bluffs harbormaster on channel sixteen to Coast Guard."

"Coast Guard on sixteen, sir," a woman's voice answered. "Switch to channel twenty-two."

Domingo entered the numbers, two small beeps of sound. "We have a floating body in the harbor near the yacht club."

"Yes, sir." The Coast Guard woman repeated what Domingo had said.

"We're taking it to the dock."

"You're taking it to the dock, sir."

"I'm calling the state police and the Oak Bluffs police on channel four oh four."

"Yes, sir." The voice repeated that information.

"Switching back to sixteen, and standing by," Domingo said.

"Standing by channel sixteen, sir."

"I've got his arm tied," Elizabeth said in a thick voice. "The other end of the line's around the thwart."

"Start her up and take the boat to the dock. We can secure him to the pilings until the police get there."

He radioed Communications on channel 404. "Send the hearse." He refastened his radio to his belt. "Not that I expect much from them." He adjusted his cap and sat back in the bow seat, folded his arms over his chest again. "Hope you don't have to go anywhere, sweetheart. This might take awhile."

Elizabeth geared up and headed toward the shore, where the dock was barely visible.

"Not so fast. Slow down." He looked down at Victoria. "Recognize him, sweetheart?"

Victoria looked at the body tied alongside, dragging through the water with a sloshing sound, and shook her head. Water washed over the head, lifted the ponytail, rippled down the back, dividing into three streams when it reached the pale, round buttocks.

"Who is it?" Elizabeth said from behind her grandmother.

Domingo didn't answer immediately, and Victoria looked up at him. "Bernie Marble," he said finally.

"Oh no!" Elizabeth gasped. "Are you sure?"

"Yes," Domingo said.

"How can you tell?" Victoria, one hand on each side of the boat, kept gazing at the body.

"Ponytail and fat ass," Domingo said.

Sirens whooped in the distance. Vehicles with blinking emergency lights sped toward the dock, then stopped on the road leading to it, red and blue lights still flashing.

Domingo turned around in his seat, his hands on the gunwales. "Ambulance and police cruisers." He turned back to Victoria. "I told them we needed a hearse. Watch Chief Medeiros's reaction when he sees whose body it is."

Domingo's face was hidden in darkness. Behind him, the strobing red and blue emergency lights backlit his chunky torso, framed his capped head.

"I mean it," he said to Victoria. "Watch the chief's face carefully. See what he does when he recognizes his crony."

Elizabeth throttled down the outboard engine, and the launch drifted toward shore. As they got closer, the dock loomed over them. Five or six figures — Victoria couldn't tell exactly how many — stood on the end of the dock, silhouetted by the eerie red and blue strobe lights that swung round and round on the vehicles.

A voice came down from the dock, five feet above them. "That you, Mingo?"

"Yo!" Domingo said.

"What the hell have you done now?"

"Come and see." Domingo turned to Victoria. "You okay, sweetheart? Can you get up that ladder?" He paused. "You'll have to go to the police station to give a statement."

"There's nothing I can tell anyone." Victoria's eyes avoided the floating corpse a foot from her.

"I don't trust that chief," Domingo said under his breath. "But there's a procedure we have to follow."

"I can get up on the dock." Victoria looked up over her head. "Where's the ladder?"

"Yo, Chief!" Domingo shouted up to the man on the dock above them.

"Yo, yourself," Chief Medeiros said.

"How about giving Mrs. Trumbull a hand up, like a gentleman?"

"What the hell's she doing here?"

"She's a witness." Domingo turned to Elizabeth, who was attempting to secure the left side of the launch to the piling while the harbormaster and police chief talked. The body was outboard. Victoria looked up at the dock far over her head. Of course she could climb up there. She simply had to make sure she had a firm handhold and move slowly.

Elizabeth looped a line around the barnacle-encrusted piling.

"You," Domingo said to her. "What are you doing?"

Elizabeth looked up at him. Victoria had turned slightly so she could see her grand-daughter.

"Tying the boat up, of course."

"Those barnacles are razor-sharp." Elizabeth retrieved the line quickly. "You come back and the boat would be in the middle of the harbor, with crabs feeding on the corpse."

"Ugh!" Elizabeth said.

"Nice fat crabs," Domingo said. "Tasty."

A voice came from above them. "I'll take the line." Elizabeth, balancing herself cautiously, passed lines up to an extended hand. Someone tied the lines around dock cleats. A young man, his hair blond in the lights from the vehicles, scrambled down the ladder and got in the boat next to Victoria, then helped her to her feet. When she had straightened her legs, she reached for the uprights of the vertical wooden ladder. She looked up and saw faces peering down at her from the dock. Thank goodness I don't wear old-lady shoes, she thought. Her hiking shoes with the hole cut in the top of one to ease the pressure on her toe had lugged soles. She put her right foot on the ladder, slick with seaweed, and held tightly to the sides. The blond boy was behind her. Left foot on the same rung. Right foot on the next rung. Left foot. She looked up and could see the top of the dock, hands reaching out to her.

At the top, two more people, another young man and a stocky woman Victoria recognized as an emergency medical technician at the hospital, helped her onto the dock.

Chief Medeiros stood off to one side, waiting for Domingo to climb the ladder.

"You," Domingo ordered Elizabeth, "stay there until I tell you to move."

"Asshole," Elizabeth muttered under her breath.

Chief Medeiros looked down at her and grinned. "You got that right, girlie."

Domingo's cap appeared at the top of the ladder, the faded gold NYPD showing clearly in the light from the vehicles.

Victoria realized how short the harbormaster was when she saw him next to the police chief on the dock. He was even shorter than the woman, whose name she couldn't recall. Domingo was probably five foot seven, a squat, dark man with broad shoulders. His chest widened to an ample stomach that hung over his belt buckle, then narrowed to slim hips.

"What've you got for us, Mingo?" Chief Medeiros said when Domingo walked over to him.

"The body's tied up to the launch. Want to see it from down there?" Domingo hooked his thumbs into his uniform pockets, stood with his feet slightly apart, toes out. "We brought him in the way he was, floating facedown. Didn't turn him over."

"Any idea who it is?" The chief placed his hand on Domingo's shoulder, which was damp from the ride across the choppy harbor.

"You tell me."

The chief turned to go down the steep ladder and disappeared from view.

"Want me to go back down to watch his reaction?" Victoria asked, looking anxiously at Domingo, who shook his head.

"I think we'll find out what we need to know," he said, so softly that only Victoria could hear. "You can sit on the bench, if you want, sweetheart. It's going to be awhile."

"Shit!" The police chief's voice exploded up from the launch. "Jesus Christ!" Domingo looked at Victoria and raised his eyebrows, moved his lips in a faint smile. The chief appeared on the ladder again.

"Bernie," he said to Domingo. "You knew it was Bernie, didn't you?"

"Who, me?" Domingo opened his eyes innocently. He spread his right hand across his chest, fingers splayed out. "How can I identify a corpse in the dark, a body floating facedown?"

"Shit," the chief said again. "Excuse me, ma'am." He turned to Victoria, then back to Domingo. "What's her role in this?" He jerked his thumb at Victoria. "Witness, you said? We need to get back to the station as soon as we get him into the ambulance."

"You need the hearse, Medeiros, not the ambulance."

The chief ignored Domingo and turned to one of the patrolmen. "Call Toby, will you? You know, the undertaker," he said when the patrolman looked perplexed. Then, impatiently, he added, "He's dead, fool. He doesn't ride in the ambulance. Toby knows what to do." The patrolman walked quickly back to the police vehicle, and Victoria heard a burst of static as he got on the radio.

"Can you get the launch up to the beach?" the chief asked. Domingo nodded, his thumbs back in his pockets, his feet apart. "Be easier to get him out there than to lift him up to the dock," the chief said. "Jesus Christ. What timing."

Domingo raised his eyebrows at Victoria.

Elizabeth started the motor, and a patrolman and medic passed lines down to her. She eased the boat toward shore, then lifted the outboard motor into the boat as the water shoaled. The corpse grounded in the shallow water, and water sloshed over his head, ponytail, back. His bare buttocks shook.

Victoria looked down from her perch on

31

the dock. She counted six people altogether, not including the harbormaster, her granddaughter, and herself. Lights circled around and around on top of the three vehicles — two police cruisers and an ambulance. Victoria thought of strobe lights in the disco she had once gone to with Elizabeth and her granddaughter's now ex-husband. People seemed to flick in and out of visibility, red, blue, red, blue. Someone moved a vehicle to light up the scene with headlights, illuminating the launch and Elizabeth, the body and its exposed bottom.

Victoria watched Elizabeth untie the body from the thwart. The medics and police waded into the water to turn it over. She supposed so they could load it onto the stretcher they had wheeled next to the shoreline. She couldn't see what they were doing because their backs shielded the body from her sight. She heard a splash. They must have turned it over, she realized. At the same instant, she heard mingled shouts, curses, grunts. She saw Elizabeth stand up in the boat, then sit down again quickly. Elizabeth leaned over the side of the launch, the side away from the corpse, put both hands on the port gunwale, and vomited into the harbor, over and over. She continued to heave even after nothing more came out.

Victoria stood up and walked stiffly down the dock, stepped down onto the boardwalk that crossed the sand, stepped off into the sand, and headed toward the group. Domingo blocked her way.

"No. You don't want to see this," he said. "You don't want to see what they did to him. No, sweetheart. Sit on the boardwalk until they load him into Toby's hearse. Then you'd better take care of my assistant back there. She needs you." He jerked his head toward the launch. "We've got a long evening ahead of us."

\\ Chapter 2 //

"I've put a password into the computer program." Howland Atherton peered down his nose at Elizabeth, who was sitting next to him in the harbormaster's shack. Sunlight reflections danced off the water, glistened on Howland's high cheekbones, and flickered on the computer screen.

It was two days after Victoria, Domingo, and Elizabeth had found Bernie Marble's disemboweled, emasculated corpse floating in the harbor. Elizabeth was back at work, although nothing seemed normal to her anymore.

She could tell by Howland's expression — his turned-down mouth and the way he sneered at the computer — that he was irritated, probably with himself.

"Domingo pretends he's Denny the Dunce." Howland leaned back in his chair and ran his fingers through his hair, silvery on the sides, dark on top. "Then when you agree to help the poor guy, he springs the trap — *snap* — and you're caught up in whatever scheme he's got going." He keyed in a few numbers with his two forefingers. "And I fell for it. I did exactly what he wanted. He wanted to computerize the harbor."

Elizabeth shook her short hair off her forehead. She was dealing out a handful of receipts like a deck of cards.

"I'm sorry I got you involved in this job," Howland continued. "He can't be much fun to work for."

Elizabeth looked up from the receipts in surprise. "I love working here. It's what I needed after getting rid of my creepy husband." She returned to the receipts. "Domingo's hard to take sometimes, but I like him, sort of."

Howland's smile made his mouth turn down, not up. "Two mature people, you in your thirties, me in my fifties, groveling before a Latino tyrant."

Elizabeth laughed. "You didn't know my ex."

The harbormaster's shack, set high on pilings driven into the harbor floor, moved gently in the tidal current. Water swashed past clumps of seaweed on the shack's footings.

The two worked quietly. After several minutes, Howland said, "If it weren't such a challenge to design this program, I'd be tempted to walk away." He moved the monitor slightly to cut glare from the harbor. "It's more complicated than I thought it would be, and Domingo doesn't make things easier."

A powerboat came through the channel into the harbor. Elizabeth went out on the deck, cupped her hands around her mouth, and yelled, "Slow down! No wake!"

The sunburned man at the wheel, his nose blistered and peeling, waved at her and slowed. The boat's wake trailed off.

"I hope the password you're putting in will keep the dock attendants from messing it up." Elizabeth came back in and sat down again. "Those kids think they know everything there is to know about computers."

The shack trembled, and Elizabeth looked up, to see a couple in their sixties coming up the catwalk to the window.

"Customers." She got up again to greet them, slid the window open, exchanged pleasantries, and handed the woman a clipboard with a form to be filled out. The man signed the credit-card receipt and put his part in his wallet. The woman gave Elizabeth the completed form, and they left.

"The dock attendants know only enough

about computers to screw up my program," Howland said after they'd gone. He typed in a series of words. "Maybe the password will keep them out, but who knows."

"What's the password?" Elizabeth picked up a receipt and placed it on one of the piles. The wind blew through the open south window, which looked out over boats in slips around the edge of the harbor, fluttering the papers on Elizabeth's desk. She brushed away tendrils of hair that blew into her eyes.

"The password is the harbormaster's wife's nickname in Spanish." Howland keyed another set of words into the computer, then moved the monitor again to shade it from flickering reflections.

"That should be easy to remember," Elizabeth said wryly. She looked up from the receipts. "I have no idea what Mrs. D.'s nickname is in English, let alone Spanish."

" 'Woman.' " Howland glanced at Elizabeth with his turned-down smile.

" 'Woman'?" Elizabeth slapped the receipts down on the counter. "That's what Domingo calls his wife? 'Woman'?"

"Yes." Howland returned to the keyboard, held his hand over the monitor. "Still too much reflection."

37

"That pig!" Elizabeth leaned back in the rickety chair. "I don't see how Noreen puts up with him. 'Woman'! He's not in Colombia now."

"He never was." Howland pushed his chair away from the counter with both hands. The chair scraped on the sandy floor, and he stood up, gradually unfolding his tall frame. "He comes from Brooklyn; his father came from Colombia. The password is *'Mujer.'* Write it down somewhere safe."

"Believe me, I'll remember that." Elizabeth picked up the receipts from the countertop and started to sort them again. After a few seconds, she threw them down. "I can't think straight. I can't concentrate on anything. I keep seeing that obscene corpse."

A sailboat came into the channel under power, and when Elizabeth saw the skipper, she waved.

"They're here for a week, all the way up from the Virgin Islands, and this is their first stop." The sailboat turned, under power, and backed toward a slip. "They've got a glorious day, and tomorrow is supposed to be just as beautiful."

"They clear U.S. Customs before they get here, don't they?" Howland asked.

"Technically, they're supposed to, in Miami or Washington or New York or Boston. But most don't. That boat can carry enough fuel and provisions to cross the Atlantic easily." She stood up and looked out the sliding window toward the boats and the Harbor House beyond them. "Where the devil are the dock attendants? They need to help with lines."

"How is your grandmother taking the murder?"

"You know the way Victoria is." Elizabeth turned to him. "She's more like a ten-year-old than a ninety-two-year-old. She loves action of any kind."

Howland moved the chair back under the counter, and it scraped again, fingernails on slate. Elizabeth winced.

"I might as well sweep the sand out of this dump." She got up. "The dock attendants are supposed to keep this place clean, but look at it." She gestured around the small office.

The shack had windows on all four sides. The window on the south, now open, could be pushed to one side, so the staff could take in money or give information to boaters. From that window, Elizabeth could look over the harbor with its moored and docked yachts, could see the activity of

39

guests at the Harbor House. Through the window to her right, she could see the narrow channel leading into the harbor, and, across the channel, the osprey nest high on its pole. On weekday evenings, when the harbor was quiet, she liked to watch the ospreys. She had seen the male arrive early in the spring, even before she had taken the job in the harbor, and had watched the pair fix up the nest, watched them sit on their eggs, had seen the hatchlings when they emerged.

To the north, beyond the channel, she could see ferries coming and going on Nantucket Sound, from Woods Hole on the mainland to the Oak Bluffs wharf. The computer and printer were on a counter that ran under that window.

The fourth window faced the parking lot to the east. Across the lot, pastel-colored Victorian houses, festooned with wooden gingerbread, faced the harbor. A desk under the window looked out at the catwalk that led from the shack across a hundred-foot stretch of water to the parking lot.

A grimy T-shirt hung limply out of an open desk drawer, and a torn chips wrapper and a crushed soda can lay on the floor.

The windows made the shack feel larger than it actually was. Elizabeth had measured it, and it was smaller than Victoria's upstairs bathroom, which was only eight feet by twelve.

"Those hotshot kids can't even hit the wastebasket." Elizabeth gestured at the rubbish on the floor, and Howland ducked to avoid her arm.

"Try to keep them away from the computer at least." Howland leaned over the monitor and, still standing, entered a couple of numbers. "I have more work to do on the program before it's safe from them."

"The program will never be safe from them. They've been playing with computers since kindergarten." Elizabeth moved the aluminum lawn chair that served as office furniture to one side and reached behind the door for the broom. She pulled the T-shirt out of the open desk drawer and tossed it, the soda can, and the chips bag into the trash container.

Footsteps pounded on the catwalk, shaking the small building. Elizabeth looked up, to see two teenage boys tossing punches, hopping from one foot to the other, dancing toward the shack.

"Cut it out, you guys," Elizabeth

shouted at them. "Go back and get the sailboat's lines. Go on!"

"He don't need help," the kid with green hair said.

"Go!" Elizabeth said.

"We need to get a pad of receipts," the taller kid said.

"I already checked out a receipt pad to Louie." Elizabeth nodded her head at the green-haired boy. Both were wearing khaki shorts and blue knit collared shirts with DOCK ATTENDANT across the back. Except for the hair and the difference in height, they looked identical.

"I don't know where it's at." Louie avoided Elizabeth's eyes.

"Help the sailboat; then keep looking until you find the receipts. They're numbered. If you've lost them, you're fired."

"Shiiit," said Louie. "C'mon, Dewey. Creepy old lady."

"Watch your mouth, or you're fired."

"You can't fire me. You ain't my boss. My father is on the Harbor Advisory Committee."

Elizabeth grabbed the broom and wrenched the door open, fire in her eyes.

"He didn't mean nothin'," Dewey said, backing away from Elizabeth, who was brandishing the broom. Both kids put their arms over their heads.

"Let's get outta here," Louie said, and they turned and sauntered down the cat-walk. When they got to the bulkhead, they looked back at Elizabeth, and the green-haired kid jerked his head toward her in an insolent way.

"Dewey and Louie, hey?" Howland said.

"There's a third one we call Huey," Elizabeth said. "I've forgotten their real names."

Elizabeth leaned the broom against the door and dusted off her hands. "That's that."

"I doubt it." Howland watched the kids move as slowly as they could toward the sailboat. A crew member on the stern of the boat held a line, prepared to jump ashore and tie it off as the boat backed into the slip.

"Lazy bastards," Howland said of the kids, who were still too far away from the sailboat to help. "They need Domingo to get after them. New York cop meets Island bumpkins."

"Even Domingo can't handle the kids. 'You can't touch me; my father is . . .' " Elizabeth mimicked the teenager, high voice and a wiggle of slim hips. "I almost feel sorry for Domingo." She straightened papers on the desk. "My grandmother thinks Domingo is wonderful, courtly, considerate, charming."

"He is, to her."

"Victoria flirts with him as if she were a girl." Elizabeth smiled. "She admits he might be difficult to work for. That's not exactly how I'd put it. 'Impossible' is more like it, much as I love the job and respect him." Elizabeth set the two chairs outside on the deck, then swept the sand into a heap mixed with paper scraps, dust balls, and twisted paper clips. "At times, I get fed up with the way he wants me to document every teensy-weensy thing. I go to the bathroom. 'Document it,' he says."

"Really?"

"Almost. And those dock attendants! If I had anything to say about it, I'd fire every single one of them. All they do all day long is show off for one another, boys flexing muscles, girls tossing their snaky hair."

She opened a lower desk drawer, took out a piece of cardboard, and swept the dirt pile onto it. "Every one of them is related to someone — a selectman's niece, a Harbor Advisory Committee member's girlfriend's son's girlfriend. Honestly, you can't say anything around here. It's as if we're surrounded by a pack of kid spies."

44

She slid the pile of dirt off the cardboard and into the trash, then stepped out the door and slapped the cardboard on the railing, shaking off the remaining dust. A breeze eddied around the shack, flicking a cat's-paw of disturbed water across the harbor, rocking sailboats on their moorings.

For a few minutes, Elizabeth remained on the deck. She leaned her elbows on the railing and watched the wind on the water. Then she went back into the shack and swept vigorously.

Howland sneezed, then sneezed again. He reached into his pocket for his handkerchief.

"And to think" — he gestured around the small shack — "instead of all this, you could be gardening and taking care of Victoria."

"Victoria does not need taking care of," Elizabeth said. "She thinks she's taking care of me, and she's right." She changed the subject abruptly. "How did Domingo ever talk you into designing a harbor-management program?" She nodded at the computer.

"He's trying to convince me I can sell the program for a million dollars." Howland put his handkerchief back into his pocket. "He's wrong, of course, and he knows it. It's a game he plays. I'm simply using off-the-shelf software and adapting it to the harbor." Howland leaned back against the desk and crossed his right leg over his left, half-sitting. He was wearing worn boat shoes with no socks, and Elizabeth could see the big toe of his right foot through the broken stitching at the seam.

"He tells me it's a challenge, which it is, a challenge to design a simple, foolproof program that deals with a lot of variables."

"He's not thinking about you, though, is he." Elizabeth made it a statement, not a question. "He thinks there are leaks in the money-handling system, and he wants you to seal them off."

"Exactly," Howland said. "He's convinced that someone has been skimming money from the harbor receipts, a hundred thousand dollars or more a season."

"From mid-June to Labor Day?"

Howland nodded. "Two and a half months."

Elizabeth whistled. "Not bad! Forty thousand a month."

"From what I see so far, he's probably right. The harbor seems to be taking in about that much extra this year." Howland opened one of the desk drawers and started to put his foot on it. He looked in and shut the drawer quickly. "Good heavens! You know what's in there?"

"No. Let me see." Elizabeth leaned forward to look. Howland opened the drawer a crack, and she saw a loose pile of twenty-dollar bills.

"Yeah. We have to take that to the bank tonight. Would you put it in one of the green bank bags? Second drawer down on the left side."

"No," Howland said. "I don't work here, remember? I don't want my fingerprints on anything." He shut the drawer again. "What were you saying?"

"I was going to say, before he took over the harbormaster job, the town had a sloppy way of keeping records."

Howland raised his eyebrows. "Oh?" He opened the drawer.

"No, really. That money is all accounted for with receipts and paperwork. When your program is up and running, we can turn it over to the town accountant, but Domingo wants all the data entered into the computer before we do."

"In the meantime, we have how much in that drawer?"

"I think it's about fourteen thousand dollars."

"What!" Howland choked. "Fourteen thousand, you think? In a drawer? Loose?"

"No one's going to take it."

"They're eviscerating people right and left, and yet the money is safe in that drawer?"

"Don't remind me of that." Elizabeth turned to her work.

"We've got to enter that into the computer right away, even though the program isn't foolproof yet," Howland said. "Domingo suspected something funny was going on here at the harbor even before Bernie was killed."

"You think Bernie's death is related?"

Howland nodded.

"How?" she asked.

"Domingo seems to think the hundred thousand is, or was, a payoff for someone to keep quiet. He thinks he's a threat to somebody, and he's not sure who." Howland turned to look out the window. "How were they handling the money before?"

"The dock attendants would bundle up loose cash and loose checks and take the whole mess, uncounted, over to Town Hall."

"So between the time boaters paid their money and the treasurer counted it, no one had any control over it?"

"That's right. And a lot of the money was cash." Elizabeth straightened papers on the counter.

"The computer program will seal up most of the loopholes," Howland said. "Once we have all the boat names and owners' addresses entered, it will be easy to track the money. I'm not sure this is going to help Domingo, though. It's as though some town officials hope he fails, as though they're setting him up." He looked out the window again toward the parking lot. "Here he comes now with Victoria."

Elizabeth put the broom back behind the door and glanced out the window. Domingo was parking his white convertible in the harbormaster's slot. Victoria sat on the left side of the front seat, her face shaded by a large floppy straw hat.

"Look at that car of his!" Elizabeth said. "If that isn't conspicuous consumption!"

"Rolls-Royce Corniche," Howland said. "Right-hand drive. He claims it fell off a truck when he was a New York cop."

"He's driving it for my grandmother's benefit. He usually drives Ernesto's pickup truck."

Domingo got out of the right-hand side

and slammed the door shut with an expensive *thunk*. He reached into the backseat and retrieved a manila folder and a basket covered with a Black Dog napkin, walked around the back of the car, looked at the rear tires, walked down the left side, and opened the passenger door.

"Look at that, will you?" Elizabeth put both hands on the desk and leaned forward for a better look. "He's pretending he's a gentleman. Watch this!"

Domingo had taken off his navy blue cap. He bent slightly at the waist in a courtly bow and offered his right arm to Victoria, who took it and smiled up at him. Howland laughed.

Still holding the folder and the basket, Domingo put his cap back on, and with Victoria on his arm, he walked toward the catwalk leading to the shack. She swept her straw hat off with a girlish gesture, her smile revealing a complicated set of wrinkles upon wrinkles. She was wearing a lavender-colored pantsuit, the pants riding high on her still-shapely long legs. The ends of the yellow ribbon she'd wound around the hat brim fluttered in the breeze. Victoria had tucked a bunch of black-eyed Susans into the ribbon, and the flowers were beginning to droop. She

50

looked up at Domingo with her hooded eyes and gave him a smile.

"Trapped," Howland said. "I'd hoped to get away before he got here. Are you finished sweeping?" Elizabeth nodded, and he moved the two chairs back into the shack from the deck.

"You'd think she'd act her age." Elizabeth watched her grandmother and Domingo.

"If you're her age and still have it, you can act any way you want," Howland said.

Outside the shack, Domingo escorted Victoria to the bench where she'd sat two nights before, then set the basket beside her.

Water lapped gently around the pilings. A seagull flew overhead, soaring on the air currents rising from the harbor's surface. The osprey circled; a plane droned overhead.

Domingo shaded his eyes with his hand.

"Won't be long before the president arrives," he said to Victoria. "Then we'll have planes and boats everywhere. Secret Service, the press. It's going to be a mess." He looked at Victoria, who was searching for something in her pocketbook. "Your lunch won't spoil, will it?"

"I didn't pack anything that would," Victoria said.

She took an envelope out of her pocket-book, then continued to search for something. Elizabeth, who had been watching her from inside the shack, reached into the cup of pens and pencils on the counter and found a thick pen inscribed with the words *This number qualifies Victoria Trumbull for the final round of the Million-Dollar Sweepstakes!* She walked outside and gave it to her grandmother.

Victoria pushed her straw hat back on her head, reached up for the ribbons floating in the breeze, and tied them under her chin. "Thank you," she said, taking the pen.

As soon as Elizabeth stepped back into the shack, Domingo followed her. He pointed his index finger at her. "You," he said. "Did you get all those receipts entered into the computer?"

"Not 'You.' I have a name," Elizabeth said. "No, I didn't enter them. I haven't even sorted them yet."

"Is something holding you up?"

"I am," Howland said. "I'm installing your million-dollar computer program."

"We're working against time." Domingo thrust his hands into his trousers pockets and set his feet apart. "The selectmen are getting impatient."

"To hell with the selectmen. I can only go so fast."

"That's very well for you to say." Domingo looked up at Howland with dark eyes. "They're not paying you."

"No kidding." Howland's mouth turned down. He put his head back and looked down at the harbormaster through half-closed eyes. Reflections from the water flickered across his high cheekbones, gave his hazel eyes a leonine appearance.

"You don't understand," Domingo said. "They're setting me up, I tell you. Especially now, after what happened to Marble." He patted his shirt pocket, where he kept his pack of Camels.

"Surely they don't think you had anything to do with Bernie's death?" Elizabeth said.

"They're looking for a reason to fire me. Not turning over the receipts to the treasurer is reason enough, to their way of thinking." Domingo stood in the doorway and looked out at the Harbor House. "I'm not handing that loose cash over to the treasurer without getting a receipt. They won't give me a receipt unless we have the money accounted for on one of their forms. And we can't generate a form until Atherton gets the bugs out of his program."

"Debugging a new system takes time," Elizabeth said.

"They're not giving me that time."

"What can they fire you for?"

"They'll call it mismanagement, mark my words."

"But they hired you. Why would they want to fire you?"

"They hired him because they thought he was a dumb black cop who would do what they wanted him to do," Howland said.

"Yas," Domingo replied.

"They'd be crazy to fire you." Elizabeth looked steadily at the harbormaster. "You've tightened up the money-handling system, closed loopholes, installed high-tech mooring systems. Why would they fire you?"

"Because they don't want the money-handling system tightened up," Domingo said. "Money is leaking out of the system into somebody's pockets; I've suspected that for months." He turned and looked directly at Elizabeth. "Get those receipts entered into the computer if you have to stay here all night." He patted the cigarette pack in his shirt pocket.

Elizabeth shrugged and turned to Howland. "What about it?"

"Go ahead. The database is ready. I'll enter some of the data for you, give you a break. Domingo's right — we have to get everything into the system before we can turn the money over, and we have to do it as soon as possible."

"Don't put your initials on it," Domingo said to Howland. "You don't work here, you know."

"Thank God."

Outside, Victoria was scribbling on the back of an envelope. Occasionally, she looked up as a boat came into the harbor, rocking the shack, or at the osprey nest, the birds bringing an endless supply of food to their chicks. The ospreys' plaintive cries echoed across the harbor.

Domingo looked out the window at Victoria. He pulled the pack of Camels out of his shirt pocket, shook one out, and started to light it with a battered Zippo.

"Not in here," Elizabeth said sharply. "No smoking. Don't you dare smoke in here."

Domingo put the cigarette back into the pack. He turned to Howland. "They're all alike."

"Yeah, yeah."

"Ms. Elizabeth" — Domingo stretched out the "Ms." — "I need to tell you something, and I don't want your grandmother to hear."

Elizabeth looked up, concerned at the harbormaster's tone.

"No one knows what she saw two nights ago. She says she saw something — four people, maybe. She isn't sure." He put his hands in his pockets and continued to look over the harbor. "No one knows whether she can identify the vehicle she heard leave the scene. She doesn't think she can. She forgot to tell the police she thought she heard a boat. She's not sure. But as long as someone out there thinks she might have seen someone, recognized a voice, recognized a vehicle, she is in danger." He stopped.

Elizabeth stared at him, her face paling under her tan. Howland, who was leaning against the desk, put his hand up to his chin, stroked it. Elizabeth heard the slight scratch of afternoon whiskers.

"What can we do?" she said.

"I, for one, am going to talk to your West Tisbury police chief, have her or one of her patrolmen watch your house." He turned and looked at her, then at Howland. "I'll go by your place as often as I can." He thrust his hands deeper into his pockets. "I still have a valid gun permit."

"Gun?" Elizabeth turned back from the counter.

"Your car is not exactly inconspicuous," Howland said. "A white Rolls-Royce convertible?"

"The more conspicuous the better." Domingo patted his pocket. "I don't trust the Oak Bluffs cops. I don't trust the selectmen. I don't trust anyone on the Harbor Advisory Committee. The recently deceased Bernie Marble had ties to all of them. Owned a bar on Pequot Avenue, in partnership with two of the selectmen."

"The Good Times?" Elizabeth said. The radio in the shack crackled with static, and the three listened until it cut off.

"That's another of his properties. Meatloaf Staples is part owner of that. The two selectmen were partners with Bernie in the Sand Bar, two doors down from the Good Times."

"Meatloaf," Howland said thoughtfully. "He was always with Bernie, almost like a bodyguard."

"That is correct," Domingo said. "He knows how to spot power and cozy up to it."

"The advantages of not being in power." Howland moved away from the desk, headed toward the door. "I need to get home to feed my dogs."

"You better keep them hungry." Domingo moved out of Howland's way. "You never know when someone may find his way into the duchy. You want them hungry, ready to attack."

"Tigger and Rover, attack dogs?" Elizabeth said. "I don't think so."

"Damnation!" Howland halted at the door, his hand still on the knob, and looked toward the parking lot. A van had pulled into a slot. The door opened and an obese man slid out of the driver's seat. His two small feet touched the macadam. He faced the van and slammed the door, pushed his glasses back up his small nose, tugged his baseball cap down on his forehead, pulled his tan jacket over his gut, pulled his pant legs away from his crotch, and looked over at the harbormaster's shack.

"Meatloaf," Howland said. "What's he doing here?"

"Get going with those entries, Ms. Elizabeth." Domingo turned to her. "We're running out of time."

\\ Chapter 3 //

Meatloaf Staples stepped onto the catwalk, holding the railings on either side with small hands that seemed out of proportion to his body.

As he approached Victoria, who was sitting on the bench outside the shack, Elizabeth, still sitting at the computer, watched her grandmother's reflection in the computer screen.

Victoria looked up from her writing and shaded her eyes. "Good afternoon," she said. Meatloaf turned his head toward her without answering. He pushed his sunglasses back onto his nose. Drops of sweat ran off his forehead in rivulets, traveled down the side of his face, and dripped onto the wooden catwalk, where they made fat dots that spread out on the boards. Sweat blotched the armpits of his tan shirt.

"How rude," Victoria said softly, although clearly enough that Meatloaf must have heard. Inside the shack, Elizabeth laughed.

"Watch yourselves." Domingo glanced out the window.

Meatloaf stepped over the doorsill and into the shack.

"How can I help you?" Domingo said civilly.

Elizabeth turned back to the computer and began to enter receipts she hadn't yet sorted.

Howland leaned back against the desk and folded his arms across the chest of his thrift-shop shirt.

Meatloaf removed his sunglasses, took a crumpled handkerchief out of his pocket, and wiped his glasses. He lifted his baseball cap with ARAUJO SEPTIC SYSTEMS and mopped his forehead. He put his sunglasses on, stuffed the handkerchief back into his pocket, and straightened his baseball cap. Elizabeth watched his reflection in the screen, heard his heavy breathing.

"I'm here about a complaint," Meatloaf said finally.

"Won't you sit down?" Domingo indicated the empty aluminum lawn chair. Meatloaf pulled the chair to the end of the shack, scraping it along the floor. He turned around, his back to the chair, put his hands on the armrests, and eased himself into it. Aluminum rubbed against alu-

60

minum; the synthetic webbing squeaked. He faced the three of them, Domingo standing beside the door, Howland leaning against the desk at the end of the shack, and Elizabeth at the computer on the side.

"What's she doing out there?" Meatloaf looked at Domingo and jerked his head toward Victoria. He clasped his hands together on top of his belly.

"Writing poetry," Howland said.

"I asked you, Mingo, not him." Meatloaf turned his head toward Domingo, his eyes hidden by his sunglasses.

"It's public property. She can sit there if she wants." Domingo folded his arms over his chest like Howland. Elizabeth made soft clicking noises on the keyboard as she watched the reflections of Meatloaf and Domingo on the screen.

"What's the complaint?" Domingo said.

Overhead, a seagull cried, a long, mewling call ending in a series of short squawks.

"Seems you have one of the selectman's nieces working for you as dock attendant. Is that right?"

"That's correct." Domingo remained next to the door, his arms still folded. Water splashed gently against the pilings. A small motorboat went out of the harbor.

Domingo narrowed his eyes at Meatloaf. "Allison Phipps."

Elizabeth paused briefly, then continued typing. The osprey cried. Wind lifted papers on the counter next to her, and she put a rounded beach stone on top of them to hold them down. The telephone rang. She got up from the desk and answered it.

After a long wait, Meatloaf continued. "Her aunt lodged a complaint against you."

"What for?"

"You pretend you don't know?" Meatloaf laced his hands high on his belly. Water reflections, stirred up by the passing boat, danced on the ceiling of the shack.

The radio crackled, and a man's voice came over it. "Oak Bluffs Harbor — this is — yacht —" Static garbled the message. Elizabeth pushed her chair back, got up, and lifted the radio mike off its hook on the wall next to Domingo.

"Vessel calling the Oak Bluffs harbormaster," Elizabeth said in her low voice. Domingo, Meatloaf, and Howland held their poses as if for a time exposure. "This is the Oak Bluffs harbormaster on channel nine. Your radio message is breaking up. Please repeat. Over."

"She's not the harbormaster." Meatloaf's

voice was high-pitched, almost a soprano. He moved his head slightly to look at Elizabeth as she spoke into the radio mike. "You got her taking over your job?"

Domingo said nothing.

The voice came through more clearly. "This is the sailing yacht *Sea Slide*. I reserved a slip for five nights."

Elizabeth directed the boat into the harbor and told the skipper how to pay. She hung up the mike and sat again, where she could watch Meatloaf's reflection.

"*Sea Slide*, eh?" Meatloaf moved in the chair. "Where's she coming from?"

"I can tell you in just a sec." Elizabeth keyed something into the computer.

"The program can track boats from the time they first contact us until they leave here." Howland moved toward the screen, which was showing a list of boat names. "*Sea Slide* called us several weeks ago to request a slip."

Elizabeth scrolled down to the boat's name while Howland stood over her, one hand on the top of the computer monitor, the other in his pocket.

"It's all in here," Elizabeth said. "*Sea Slide* left the Turks and Caicos four weeks ago, stopped at Saint Croix, and then sailed directly here to the Vineyard."

After a long silence, Meatloaf spoke, as if the information Elizabeth had given him meant nothing. He glanced toward Howland, then back at Domingo. "Looks like you need some better operating procedures." He wiggled his laced fingers.

"What was the selectman's complaint?" Domingo asked.

Meatloaf turned his sunglass gaze to Domingo. "Harassment."

Howland coughed, then sneezed. He took his handkerchief out of his pocket and blew his nose.

Elizabeth turned from the computer, her lips parted.

"Harassment?" Domingo scowled.

Meatloaf shifted in his chair, and the aluminum frame creaked. "I'm only reporting what Liz Tate said. She's the one who filed the complaint against you, not me."

"How am I supposed to have harassed her?" Domingo leaned against the wall next to the radio. Looking at the computer screen, Elizabeth could see his jaw clench, could see Howland sit against the desk again, holding his chin in his right hand.

The telephone rang. Elizabeth answered, "Oak Bluffs harbormaster." She listened. "Let me get your boat's name, its length and beam." She listened. "And the date you'll be arriving?" Howland, Domingo, and Meatloaf didn't move. Elizabeth clamped the telephone receiver next to her ear with her shoulder, filling out a form as she spoke. "Call on channel nine when you get here." She hung up the phone and returned to the keyboard.

Howland crossed one foot over the other.

"How am I supposed to have harassed the young woman?" Domingo repeated. He took his cigarette pack out of his pocket, shook one out, stuck it in his mouth, and put the pack back in his pocket. He reached into his pocket for his Zippo, flicked it a couple of times without lighting up, put it back in his pocket, took the cigarette out of his mouth, and held it, unlighted, between his index and third fingers.

"According to Liz Tate, her niece left work last Friday night in tears. She claims you abused her. Verbally."

Howland grunted, and when Elizabeth looked up at him and saw his expression, she suspected he was holding back some inappropriate witty comment that had occurred to him.

"Verbal abuse is not harassment," Domingo said.

"Harassment, abuse, same thing." Meatloaf unclasped his hands and pushed his sunglasses back with his forefinger.

"Tell Liz Tate to make her complaint to me in writing." Domingo put the unlighted cigarette in his mouth and let it dangle from his lower lip. "She set up the procedure."

"She's going to love this." Meatloaf hoisted himself out of the chair, stretched his arms, and yawned hugely. "She's no lady when you get her upset. Don't say I didn't warn you."

"Thanks." Domingo's cigarette danced on his lower lip.

The radio static crackled. The telephone rang. Howland leaned down and scratched his bare right ankle. A suntanned couple wearing identical madras shirts and khaki shorts came to the window. The woman held a credit card.

Elizabeth got up from her chair. "I'll be right with you," she told the couple at the window. She picked up the phone and said, "Please hold; I'll be with you in a moment." She lifted the radio mike. "Vessel calling Oak Bluffs harbormaster, this is the Oak Bluffs harbormaster."

Meatloaf shook his head. "I feel sorry for you, Mingo. Wouldn't want to be in your shoes." He lumbered out the door and squeezed past the couple in madras shirts. "Pardon me," he said, then walked down the catwalk to the parking lot.

Howland turned to Domingo, while Elizabeth finished giving directions on the radio. She filled out a charge form for the couple at the window, and took the telephone message.

"Allison Phipps is that skinny blond girl, isn't she?"

Domingo nodded.

"She's sneaky. I wouldn't trust her," Elizabeth said.

A boat whistled. Elizabeth looked up and saw the small passenger ferry *Cuttyhunk* heading into the channel. People in bright summer clothes leaned on the rail. In the parking lot, three tour buses lined up, doors open. The drivers stood together in a small cluster, talking.

Howland pulled a chair out from the desk and sat facing the others. He crossed his right leg over his left.

Domingo unclenched his hands and thrust them into his pockets. He watched Meatloaf, his large dark eyes half-closed.

"Do you have a special reason for not trusting her?" he said to Elizabeth finally.

"A couple of times, I've come into the

shack and she's been sitting at the desk, as if she'd been looking through stuff."

"Did you actually see her looking through something?"

The ferry's engines went into reverse, and the water in the channel foamed and bubbled. The ferry pulled alongside the bulkhead. A crew member on deck tossed a line to a darkly tanned man on shore, who dropped the end loop over a bollard. A young woman with red hair turned an iron crank that ratcheted the gangplank from ferry to shore. Then the tanned man secured the gangplank with lines.

"No, I didn't actually see her; it was just a feeling."

"A feeling," Domingo said. "A feeling. Can you document a feeling?"

"To hell with you." Elizabeth felt her face flush. "I don't trust her. That's all."

"Keep an eye on her, then," Domingo said. "If you see her doing anything she shouldn't be doing, doc—"

"Document it," Elizabeth replied, interrupting him.

On the shore, passengers from the ferry called to one another as they loaded into the tour buses. Meatloaf opened the door of his van and hoisted himself up onto the driver's seat with a small jump. His feet dangled above the pavement, the toes of his shoes pointed at each other. He wrote something in a notebook held high on his stomach. Elizabeth looked from Domingo to Howland to Meatloaf and then back at Domingo.

The unsmoked cigarette flipped up and down on Domingo's lower lip as he spoke. "That's the start of it."

The last passenger had walked down the gangplank and onto a tour bus. Blue smoke puffed out of exhaust pipes as bus engines started up. The buses backed out of their parking spaces and left. The parking lot was quiet again.

"What do you want us to do?" Howland watched Meatloaf through the window as he spoke to Domingo.

"Document everything." Domingo took the cigarette out of his mouth. "Dates, times, names, everything that transpires. Everything. Document going to the bathroom."

"Told you so," Elizabeth said to Howland.

A sailboat entered the channel under power. A crew member stood on the cabin roof, tying the loose mainsail onto the boom with long white ribbons. Elizabeth reached for the radio mike and directed the boat to a slip. A slim Cigarette boat followed the sailboat, powerful engines so loud, Elizabeth could barely hear the radio. The phone rang and she answered it. She saw the masts of two sailboats heading for the harbor entrance. A man walked up the catwalk toward the shack, a couple following him, and, behind them, a woman with two small boys. Elizabeth went out onto the deck, leaned over, and shouted above the engine noise, indicating a slip number for the Cigarette boat and pointing to the slip.

Back in the shack, she told the man how to find the Laundromat, informed the couple about where they could take a shower, and directed the woman with children to the carousel.

Domingo stepped out onto the deck, where Victoria was still sitting, and leaned his back against the rail, facing her. He took a deep breath and let it out again. He put the limp cigarette back in his mouth. "How're you doing, sweetheart?"

"What a rude man." Victoria looked down the catwalk to the parking lot and Meatloaf's van. A breeze flicked the ends of her yellow hat ribbon. A seagull mewed. "I hope you're not going to tell me I'm supposed to know who he is."

Domingo laughed and took out his

Zippo. "You mind? Your granddaughter won't let me smoke."

Victoria shook her head. "Go ahead."

"How's the writing?" He lighted the cigarette and inhaled deeply, held the smoke in.

She nodded.

"Finding that body was heavy stuff. Sorry you had to go through that, sweetheart." He let the smoke out slowly and leaned back, both elbows on the railing.

Victoria again looked toward the parking lot, where Meatloaf's van was pulling out of its space. "Who is he? I've never seen him before."

"Meatloaf Staples. He's fairly new to the Island. He's on the Harbor Advisory Committee."

He took another drag on his cigarette and threw it into the water, where it went out with a hiss.

"I couldn't help overhearing. Why is he accusing you of harassment?"

Domingo paused before he answered. He leaned back again, resting his elbows against the railing, and looked over at the osprey nest across the channel. The osprey returned with a fish in its talons. The chicks set up a shrill peeping. "I'm not sure yet. Something's going on that involves town officials — the selectmen, the Harbor Advisory Committee, the Oak Bluffs police. I haven't sorted it out."

"I know you think someone has been skimming money off the harbor receipts." Victoria watched him quietly, her hooded eyes shaded by the straw hat.

"Money they were skimming off the harbor receipts is small potatoes compared to something bigger that's going on," he said.

"A hundred thousand dollars, small potatoes?" Victoria reached into the pocket of her lavender jacket with her gnarled hands, brought out a used paper napkin printed with fluorescent frogs, and dabbed at her nose.

"Yes, small potatoes," Domingo repeated. "You don't understand the scope of what we're dealing with." He turned, facing the Harbor House at the head of the harbor, his back to Victoria, elbows on the railing, hands clasped. "Someone is not pleased with Howland's computer program." He turned to face Victoria again, one elbow still on the railing. "The more loopholes I close up, the more frantic someone is getting."

"Who?"

Domingo shrugged.

On the shore, another set of tour buses pulled up to the *Cuttyhunk*'s dock; these passengers got off the buses, boarded the ferry.

"But you're doing such a good job." Victoria tugged the brim of her hat to shade her eyes as she looked up at him.

"You don't understand, sweetheart. They don't want me to do a good job. They want me to go along with them. If I don't go along with them, who knows what they'll do?" He looked intently at Victoria, who was watching him, her hand on her hat brim.

Inside the shack, the phone rang. Elizabeth answered. A small sailboat came in the channel under sail. Domingo waved.

"How you doing, Cap'n?" he said to the small girl who was at the tiller. She grinned, big front teeth bright in the sunlight.

He looked at his watch. "Your granddaughter will be off in fifteen minutes. Tell her to be careful, will you? She's on duty again this evening, eight to midnight."

"Domingo's car has leather seats," Victoria said as she settled onto the frayed pink towel that covered the exposed foam of the passenger seat in Elizabeth's VW convertible. The car had been parked in the sun in front of the gingerbread houses, and the black surfaces of the dashboard and armrests radiated heat.

"His car is a Rolls-Royce," Elizabeth said, as if that explained it. She straightened the pink towel on the driver's side, sat, and swiveled her legs into the car. "At least my seat covers match."

The ferry's engines revved up and the whistle sounded. The crew ratcheted the gangplank back. A crew member lifted the hawser off the bollard and tossed it aboard, and the ferry moved out of the channel.

"They'll probably try to blame last year's missing money on Domingo." Elizabeth turned the key, and the engine caught with a metallic rattle. "Probably say he bought his car with the harbor money." The engine coughed and the convertible shook.

"Domingo's car is much quieter," Victoria said.

Elizabeth snorted. She looked behind her and backed out of the parking spot.

Victoria braced her hand on the dashboard. "I'm sure he's exaggerating the problem. He has a sense of the theatrical."

"He didn't exaggerate Bernie Marble's murder." Elizabeth drove slowly through the crowded street that ran next to the

74

harbor, avoiding mopeds, bicycles, and tourists. "I wonder, by the way, who'll run the Harbor House now. He and Chief Medeiros were partners, but Bernie managed it."

"He let that wonderful hotel get rundown," Victoria said after a few minutes. "I remember when my grandparents used to take me there for Sunday dinner, all of us dressed up. It was so elegant. Now look at it." She indicated the weathered shingles and peeling paint. "And do you remember the time we went to the selectmen's meeting, and some woman said the five dollars he was charging boaters to take a shower at his hotel was too much?"

"I remember," Elizabeth said grimly. "It is too much. He hassled that woman, made her look foolish. Embarrassed her."

Elizabeth turned right onto the main road, which went past the harbor. Power yachts fringed the harbor on the right, their sterns facing the bulkhead. Tourists strolled past, viewing the boats; they stopped to talk with boaters sitting on deck chairs in cockpits, drinks in hand, bare feet propped up on transoms.

"Some of the boats that stay here have come a long way." Elizabeth stopped to let a couple wheeling a baby stroller cross the road. "Bermuda, the Caribbean. They come from all over. They go up to the Harbor House with their toilet-article kits and towels, wanting a hot freshwater shower, and have to pay a fee, on top of what they pay to keep their boat here." She started up again slowly, watched out for a boy and a girl wobbling next to the road on purple-and-pink bikes. "It's a rip-off."

On the left side of the road, a row of gingerbread houses faced the harbor, their window boxes full of flowers that matched the pastel trim. Guests sat in rockers on the big front porches, drinks in hand, watching tourists walking along the bulkhead past the boats, watching boaters with their drinks in hand watching them on their porches. Teenagers sat on porch railings, sandy bare feet swinging, sunburned faces, arms, and legs bright against sleeveless T-shirts and faded cutoff jeans. Guests rocked and talked. The women wore floral-print sundresses; the men sported slacks embroidered with whales.

Beyond the row of gingerbread houses, the Harbor House stood by itself, a sprawling gray-shingled Victorian hotel with cupolas, archways, carpenter's lace, balconies, and wraparound porches. Banks of

76

bright blue hydrangea, yellow marigolds, and red salvia lined the front walk.

As they passed the hotel, Victoria said, "Remember how he spoke to that woman? Said he was sick of the females in Oak Bluffs telling him how to run his business."

"I remember." Elizabeth slowed the car to let a truck pull out of the parking lot next to the Harbor House.

"And he pointed at all the women there, each and every one of us, including me, and I hadn't said a thing."

"As I recall, you were carrying a sign that read JAIL, NOT BAIL," her granddaughter said.

Victoria ignored her and went on. "Chief Medeiros was standing next to him, grinning like a baboon."

After they passed the Harbor House, they came to the far side of the harbor, next to the liquor store.

"Want to go the long way, around East Chop?" Elizabeth asked, her foot on the brake. "We can eat our sandwiches at the lighthouse."

"Maybe we can stop by the yacht club's dock, where all the action was."

"I thought so." Elizabeth looked over at her grandmother, saw the eager look in her hooded eye. Victoria's nose lifted, as if she would find the perpetrators by sniffing them out.

"It's hard to believe it was only two nights ago," Victoria said. "It seems longer. There was nothing in the *Enquirer*."

"You wrote it up for your column, didn't you?"

"Yes, but Skelly called, said it was Oak Bluffs, not West Tisbury, and edited it out."

"They don't want to print anything that might mar the luster of this paradise, the president's vacation isle." Elizabeth turned onto East Chop Drive. The harbor was on their right. "Seems to me that's pretty important West Tisbury news, that the West Tisbury columnist for the *Enquirer* witnesses a murder."

"I don't know that I witnessed anything." Victoria looked straight ahead, her face shaded by her hat, the black-eyed Susans drooping. "I heard a scream, then a car or truck start up." Victoria looked over at Elizabeth. "I told them that at the police station when they took my statement."

They turned right onto the sandy road that led to the dock. "You'd think this would be roped off with yellow tape as a crime scene, the way they do in movies." Victoria sat up straight in her seat. "I

78

forgot to tell the police I thought I heard an outboard motor right about the same time."

"You told Domingo, didn't you?"

"Yes."

"They've finished doing whatever they think they needed to do here." Elizabeth parked the car by the side of the rutted road, next to a hedge of wild roses. "Domingo said they took down the crime-scene tape the day after it happened."

"So we don't need to worry about destroying evidence," Victoria said. "Tire tracks or whatever."

"I don't think so." Elizabeth got out of the car. "We can walk from here."

When Victoria opened her door, it pushed aside a branch of wild roses, dropping pink petals onto the ground.

"There've been all kinds of vehicles in here." Elizabeth pointed at the ground. "That night, there were two police cruisers, the ambulance, and Toby's hearse." She reached into the backseat and lifted out the lilac branch she had carved into a walking stick for Victoria.

"We may find something that wouldn't mean anything to anyone else," Victoria said. "Sometimes it's just as well if you don't know what you're looking for."

Victoria walked around the front of the car, bracing herself on the hood, brushing between the rose hedge and the convertible. Elizabeth handed her the stick.

They walked up the beach toward the yacht club. Victoria flicked over pebbles and bits of seaweed with her stick, shells, driftwood, a piece of glass, a plastic bottle. Elizabeth walked next to her, watching the objects her grandmother uncovered.

They'd gone a couple of hundred feet toward the yacht club when Victoria stopped.

"A boat pulled in here," she said. "It's not a fresh mark, and it's not where you landed with the body the other night. That was closer to the dock." She examined the long, straight mark in the sand. "It's well above the high-tide line." Elizabeth saw the distinctive trace of a keel, footprints that were mere indentations in the sand, leading from the keel mark into the tall grass and wild roses on a slight bluff above the beach.

"No one ever uses this beach," Elizabeth said. "The yacht club people swim on the Sound side, where the water is deeper."

"I suppose we should look through the shrubbery and see if we find anything. You go." Victoria sat on a driftwood log and handed her stick to Elizabeth. "You can

80

use this to go through the brambles."

"Thanks. You're as bad as Domingo." Elizabeth took her grandmother's stick and stepped up onto the two-foot-high bluff. Pebbles and sand slid down the face. Black roots showed at the top, holding clumps of dark soil onto the top of the sandy bank. "There's a sort of beaten-down way here," she called down to Victoria. "As if someone has been through here recently."

"Do you see anything on either side?" Victoria called back.

"No. The rosebushes and grass are thick. It's hard to see through them. I'll look down low, under the tops."

"I suppose they might have thrown something off to one side," Victoria said.

"If there's anything here. What am I supposed to find, a knife or something?"

Victoria heard her brush through the growth of wild rose, stiff bayberry, huckleberry, muttering an occasional "Ouch!" as the branches slapped her bare legs.

"Something like that." Victoria could see Elizabeth moving brush aside with the lilac stick.

"Why wouldn't they have tossed it overboard, instead of dropping it here?" Elizabeth was making slow progress. Branches snapped; dry leaves rustled.

"It's too shallow," Victoria called back to her. "At the end of the dock, it's only four feet deep, and the water is quite clear."

"Found something." Victoria heard her scrabbling through the rosebushes. "Never mind. It's a broken bottle."

"Bring it out," Victoria said. "Do you have a paper in your pocket you can handle it with?"

"A paper towel. I'll lay it in the path and keep looking."

"What does it look like?" Victoria said.

"The bottom is broken off," Elizabeth said. "It's wicked-looking. Jagged."

"A whiskey bottle?"

"Rum. Strange brand. Coulibri?"

"Never heard of it," Victoria called back.

"Me, neither. The top's still got the seal on it. Want me to keep looking?"

"Go to the end of the path, just in case there's something else. But I think we found what we came for."

Elizabeth carefully carried the broken bottle back to the car, laid it on the backseat, protected it with the pink towel from the driver's seat. Victoria walked slowly along the beach, turning seaweed over with her stick.

"This is interesting." She bent over to pick something up.

"What is?" Elizabeth went over to her, her face alert.

"A plastic cover of some sort." Victoria stood the lilac stick in the sand. "The cover for a checkbook," she said. "No checks in it, but there's something under the flap."

Elizabeth had come abreast of her grandmother.

"It must have been in the water, drifted ashore with this clump of eelgrass." Victoria opened the flap carefully. Inside was a soggy deposit slip with a water-blurred name and account number, and a yellow deposit receipt, also water-blurred.

"I can't make out the name or numbers." Elizabeth peered over Victoria's shoulder.

"I can't, either. I think we need to show it to Domingo, see what he has to say." She reached into her pocket for the frog-printed napkin and wrapped the plastic cover in it. "It may be just a piece of flotsam, but who knows."

"I'll put it in the car with the other evidence." Elizabeth held out her hand.

"Handle it carefully," Victoria said. "Maybe when it's dry, we can read the lettering."

Elizabeth put it on the backseat of the

car, next to the broken bottle, and laid the frayed pink towel over both.

"While we're here, we might as well go out to the end of the dock." Victoria started toward it.

They walked along the boards laid across the sand and onto the weathered dock.

"You were right." Elizabeth looked down into the water. "You can see right to the bottom. The water is crystal-clear."

Below them, a school of tiny fish swam in unison, abruptly changing direction with a flash of silver, as if the hundreds of fish were a single organism.

"Look how clearly you can see the harbormaster's shack from here." Victoria put her hand up to shade her eyes from the glare. "I can even see Domingo leaning over the railing."

Elizabeth followed her grandmother's gaze. "My God," she said. "No wonder he's worried."

"What?" Victoria lowered her left hand and looked at Elizabeth.

"I didn't realize you could see across the harbor so easily, that's all."

\\ Chapter 4 //

After supper, Victoria had returned to the shack to help her granddaughter sort receipts. At sunset, she went out on deck for a few minutes to watch the osprey chicks, fledglings now, poised on the edge of their nest, their strengthening wings spread wide for tentative flight. The parents hovered above the nest, flying in circles, plaintive cries echoing around the harbor.

Darkness closed in around the shack. Victoria and Elizabeth worked quietly, commenting occasionally on a boat name, or asking each other to interpret handwriting.

Victoria heard the click of the wall clock above the east window and looked up. "Eleven-thirty. Only a half hour to go."

"This evening's gone fast." Elizabeth entered a few more receipts into the computer. "I should be finished in another fifteen minutes, Gram. Thanks a million for helping me."

"Is it always this quiet?" Victoria, at the desk at the end of the shack, turned to face her granddaughter.

"Pretty much so. Most of the boats get in before dark. Not much happens after dark — usually, that is." She looked at her grandmother and frowned.

The window that faced the parking lot and the gingerbread houses was a black mirror, reflecting the shack's brightly lighted interior. Victoria peered into the dark surface and saw herself, her white hair softly disarrayed, saw Elizabeth sitting in front of the computer, half-turned toward her, her hair wisping around her forehead. Elizabeth was as lean as Victoria had been at her age, and taller. Her uniform was still sharply creased after a full day.

"There's a nice feeling of privacy at night." Victoria smoothed her hair in the window mirror and looked at her granddaughter's reflection.

"It's deceptive." Elizabeth picked up a receipt and studied it. "I can't read the writing on this." She put the paper to one side. "Everybody in the world can see us, but we can't see them."

At that moment, there was a knock at the sliding window.

"Who's there?" Elizabeth asked; then to Victoria, she said, "I didn't hear anybody coming."

Victoria glanced up at the clock. Eleven-forty-five. She had not heard or felt anything, either.

Elizabeth stood up, and her chair fell over with a metallic clatter. Victoria turned toward the sliding glass window. On the other side of the reflections, she could dimly see someone. "Who could it be at this time of night?" Elizabeth moved toward the window and slid it open a couple of inches. A tall man, half-hidden in the darkness, loomed on the other side.

"Frightened you, didn't I?" The man moved closer to the window. His shoulders filled the frame. Elizabeth stepped back.

"Can I help you?" Her voice was higher than usual. Victoria got to her feet.

"Two large vessels are coming in," the man said in a deep voice. "They need berths."

"Who are you?" Elizabeth slid the window open a few more inches. Victoria could see the man had a huge head of fluffy black hair stuck with osprey feathers, and a huge black beard that covered the lower half of his face. He was wearing a black mesh muscle shirt that exposed dark, hairy upper arms tattooed with intricate designs. Around his neck, he wore a black scarf printed with what looked like white skulls.

"Who am I?" He grinned at Elizabeth, teeth white against the blackness of his beard and the night. Victoria could see that his upper-right-front tooth was missing. "I am the Wind and the Rain. I am the messenger for the sheik of Qatar. It is the sheik's vessels that are arriving."

Victoria moved closer to the open window. Elizabeth glanced at the door. Victoria assumed it was to make sure it was locked. Elizabeth looked behind her. Victoria could tell she was wondering how to handle this situation.

"The vessels will be here in an hour," the apparition at the window said. "Two vessels, each one hundred and twenty-five feet in length."

Elizabeth's mouth opened slightly. Her hands were on the windowsill.

"They're coming from the Persian Gulf." He sounded impatient. "The sheik needs two berths for the night."

"Berths!" Elizabeth said. "We can't take boats that size; the channel isn't deep enough. We don't have slips large enough."

"The sheik expects you to find something." The Wind and the Rain scowled, and his dark hair, dark eyebrows, and dark beard almost met. His eyes showed a ring of white around dark irises. Victoria saw the tattoos on his upper arms writhe as he crossed his arms over his chest.

Victoria moved to the window. Elizabeth stepped forward to stop her, but Victoria slid the window open as wide as it would go. "You look familiar." She looked intently into the man's hairy face. "You're a Gay Head Indian, aren't you?"

"I am a Wampanoag." He flexed and unflexed his arm muscles and scowled, uncrossed his arms and put large grimy hands on the windowsill. "I am a Native American from Aquinnah." His raggedly bitten nails were rimmed with black. Elizabeth moved back, as if she thought he was going to vault through the window.

"I know you," Victoria said in a conversational voice, the voice she used at garden club meetings. "Aren't you one of the Minnowfish children?"

The man stared at Victoria. His dark irises floated in the glistening whites of his eyes. His pink mouth opened in a pale O. He leaned forward into the window. Elizabeth stepped backward again and fetched up against the computer keyboard. Victoria heard a humming noise and looked over to see a string of x's march across the screen. Victoria put her knobby hands on the sill between the Wampanoag's heavy calloused hands, his nails bitten to the quick. The man continued to stare. Victoria heard Elizabeth's breathing. She heard the x's continue to march.

Victoria turned to Elizabeth. "Hadn't you better do something about that?" She indicated the screen. Elizabeth stepped away from the computer and the x's stopped.

Suddenly, the Wind and the Rain sagged. His muscles relaxed and his eyes closed partway.

"Yes, ma'am, I'm Bessie's boy. The youngest Minnowfish."

"I thought so." Victoria stood up straight, her hands on the sill, her arms extended. The man moved back from the window a half step, fingers with bitten nails still holding on.

"Your great-grandmother was Charity Minnowfish."

"Yes, ma'am." He opened his eyes and the irises floated.

"Charity must have been your father's father's mother."

"Yes, ma'am." He let go of the windowsill.

"I went to school with Charity." Victoria leaned forward. "She was one of my pals. We looked for birds' nests together."

"Yes, ma'am." He shook his head, and Victoria heard the string of bones around his neck rattle. "That was a hundred years ago," he whispered. The osprey feathers in his hair quivered. His black skull-printed scarf moved in the night breeze coming off the harbor.

"Not quite." Victoria leaned out the window toward the man, who had backed up as far as he could to the railing. She put her elbows on the sill so she could see him better.

"You must be Dojan, the youngest boy, aren't you?"

"Yes, ma'am," he whispered.

"Well, Dojan," Victoria said in her Sunday school teacher's voice, "tell the sheik to come back tomorrow. We don't have room for him tonight." She leaned farther out the window, and Dojan moved to one side. "Give the sheik my respects."

"Yes, ma'am." Dojan moved along the railing, sideways like a crab, eyes fixed on Victoria. "A hundred years," he whispered.

"I remember when you were a little boy." Victoria pointed at him. "You haven't changed a bit. Do you still lobster?"

"Yes, ma'am," Dojan said. "I fish some, too."

"Wonderful!" Victoria said brightly.

"You like lobster?" he asked suddenly in a loud voice. A startled night bird flew up from the water, beating its wings, squawking.

"Of course." Victoria saw the breeze lift the ends of Dojan's skull scarf.

"Will you be here tomorrow?"

Victoria turned to Elizabeth, who was staring from her grandmother to the apparition beyond the window and back to her grandmother again.

"Will we?" Victoria said to Elizabeth.

Elizabeth nodded.

"I'll bring you a lobster." He moved his hands apart to indicate to Victoria the size of the lobster he would bring to her. "I'll bring you two lobsters tomorrow."

"How's Bessie?" Victoria still leaned partway out the window into the darkness.

"She's well, ma'am. Touch of arthritis."

"I know all about that." Victoria lifted her knobby hands. "Tell her hello from me, Victoria Trumbull."

"Yes, ma'am." Dojan raised his hand in a movie Indian's salute and sidled away from the window. His black hair, black shirt, black jeans, and bare feet faded down the catwalk.

Elizabeth let out her breath in a long sigh.

Victoria spread her hands in front of her and looked at them. "I'm glad you don't bite your fingernails, Elizabeth."

Elizabeth slid the window shut, locked it. Locked the window over the desk. Shut the two windows that looked out over Nantucket Sound. Deleted the strings of x's on the computer screen and turned it off.

"Dojan comes from a good family. He's quite bright. He can be a bit strange, but he's harmless. He's like his father, who was strange, too." Victoria gathered up her papers and dropped them into her pocketbook. "Did you finish what you were doing?"

"No way I can do it now," Elizabeth said. "I'll finish it tomorrow." She opened the desk drawer and rummaged around for the bank bag, stuffed it full of bills from another drawer.

"Wouldn't it be nice if he actually does bring us lobsters?" Victoria looked at her reflection in the window and patted her hair, turned her head to one side to examine her great nose.

"I don't see how you do it." Elizabeth looked in the bank bag and zipped it shut, locked it. She took a flashlight out of the top desk drawer, waited for Victoria to step out of the shack, then turned out the lights and pulled the door shut.

They drove the short two blocks to the bank, past the Steamship Authority dock, at night only a suggestion of a structure that faded into the distant deep water to their left. Waves lapped softly on the deserted beach below the bluff. Some creature swam beneath the surface of the water, trailing a stream of phosphorescence. A line of white foam lingered where waves broke onto the dark shore. A lone night bird cried. The breeze blew in from the sea.

Elizabeth parked in front of the closed bank, and Victoria watched as she unlocked the night deposit box, put in the bank bag, relocked the drawer, and got back into the car.

"That was harbor revenue we haven't turned over to the town treasurer yet." Elizabeth looked behind her and pulled out into the deserted street. "Domingo is determined to have every penny accounted for on the new computer forms, and he wants a receipt from the treasurer to prove he did."

The Flying Horses had closed for the night. They could hear laughter and shouts on Circuit Avenue, music coming out of the open doors of the Sand Bar on Pequot Avenue. The rest of the town was quiet.

Elizabeth drove along the route they had followed earlier in the day, past the gingerbread houses, past the boats. No one sat on the porches now or walked along the bulkhead. No one sat in boat cockpits with feet up on transoms. They passed the Harbor House and the road to East Chop.

Victoria looked in the side mirror. "There's a car behind us. It came out of the road next to the Harbor House."

"Can you make out what kind of car it is?" Elizabeth moved her head to one side. "The headlights are blinding me."

"It looks high, like a truck or a van."

"Wish they'd switch to low beam." Elizabeth moved the mirror to cut the glare. "I hope they turn off before we get to the curve near the hospital."

The vehicle stayed close behind them. Elizabeth slowed at a wide place in the road, where it could pass them easily, and the vehicle dropped back.

"I'm going to turn left onto the road that goes to the lobster hatchery, Gram." Elizabeth switched on her left-turn signal. "See if I can shake him."

"He's turned on his left-turn signal,

too," Victoria said, looking into the side mirror.

"Damn." Elizabeth stepped harder on the accelerator.

"Why don't we stop at Domingo's?" Victoria said. "We can pull into his drive and wait there, let him pass."

"Good idea." Elizabeth moved her head so the lights behind them were not reflected into her eyes from the side mirror.

She signaled a right turn onto Barnes Road, and the other driver did, too.

"I suppose it's possible that he happens to be going the same way we are." Elizabeth adjusted the mirror again.

"Unlikely this time of night." Victoria leaned forward to look into her side mirror again. "It's after midnight."

They halted at the stop sign by the fire station and the vehicle behind them stopped, too. No other cars were in sight.

"We're almost at Domingo's," Elizabeth said. "When I turn into his drive, see what kind of car it is, if you can." She passed the boxy privet hedge in front of the de los Fuerzos's and made an abrupt turn, without signaling or braking until she'd turned into the drive. Brakes squealed on the vehicle behind them before it accelerated and sped into the night.

"A Ford van," Victoria said. "Light color, gray or tan, not white. The license plate was muddy, but it started with 'FU.'"

"Nice going, Gram!" Elizabeth said with admiration.

"Mr. D.'s lights are on. I suppose midnight isn't too late to call on someone."

"I think it's a good idea, under the circumstances." Elizabeth opened the car door.

"Besides, we need to tell Domingo about finding the bottle and checkbook cover."

Noreen and Domingo were sitting in wicker armchairs at the glass-topped table in the living room, watching a late-night rerun of the selectman's meeting on Channel 9. The room was dense with cigarette smoke. Elizabeth knocked on the sliding door and pushed it to one side.

Noreen stubbed out her cigarette and stood up. She was small and blond, almost a foot shorter than Elizabeth, who was six feet tall. She was wearing white sweatpants and white socks and a magenta T-shirt printed with exotic blue-and-gold flowers.

"Yo," Domingo said to Elizabeth, and remained seated. As soon as Victoria came through the door, he stood up and took off his baseball cap.

"Is everything okay?" Noreen turned down the volume on the TV with the remote and moved a chair over for Victoria.

"We were being followed and decided to stop here," Victoria said. "Besides, we found something."

"Did you identify who was following you?" Domingo put his cap back on and sat down again.

"Light-colored Ford van, license starting with 'FU,' " Victoria said.

" 'FU.' " Domingo laughed. "That's not Meatloaf. I don't know who it is, but I'll find out." He waved the smoke away from Victoria. It drifted toward Elizabeth, who cried, "Hey!" and fanned at it.

"They didn't try anything smart, did they?" Noreen asked.

"No," Elizabeth said. "They came out of the road next to the Harbor House and followed us here."

"Was the harbor busy tonight?" Noreen asked Elizabeth, who was sitting on the couch under Domingo's display of antique harpoons.

"Did you get all the receipts entered?" Domingo asked.

"Will you let me talk without you butting in?" Noreen turned to him, hands on her hips.

"Okay, honey, okay." Domingo took his cap off and placed it over his heart, then looked up at the ceiling with liquid brown eyes.

"No." Elizabeth yawned, then covered her mouth with her hand. "It was quiet until almost midnight. Then this weird, creepy man came by, saying a couple of huge boats were arriving."

"Oh?" Domingo looked at her.

"It was only Dojan Minnowfish," Victoria said. "I went to school with his great-grandmother."

"He frightened the hell out of me." Elizabeth stretched her arms over her head. "Black hair, black beard, black eyes, black clothes, rags and feathers and bones rattling and blowing in the wind." She looked up at Domingo's harpoons. "I hope those things are wired in place. Some weaponry."

"Dojan lives here in Oak Bluffs, doesn't he, Domingo?" Noreen said.

Behind them, the TV showed two of the selectmen gesticulating at the third, Liz Tate, whose back was to the camera.

"I think he lives in the Camp Meeting Ground, behind Harbor House." Domingo paid no attention to the selectmen. "His family owns one of the wooden tents off Pawtucket Avenue."

Noreen turned to Victoria. "You went to school with his great-grandmother? She must have died twenty years ago."

"Yes," Victoria said. "In fact, I wrote a poem about her. I must find it and give a copy to Dojan." She watched the selectmen on TV. "It's better without the sound. Looks as if they're saying things I'd rather not hear."

"That is correct, sweetheart," Domingo said. "You know where the name Dojan comes from?" he asked suddenly, leaning forward in the wicker chair, his hands clasped between his knees.

"No. Where?" Victoria said, interested. "Is it Wampanoag?"

"It's ancient Norse. It means 'dead.' " He looked first at Victoria, then cut his eyes at Noreen and then at Elizabeth.

"Christ!" Noreen sat up straight in her chair. "You're making that up."

Domingo shook his head. "His name means 'dead.' "

"Where do you get this stuff?" Elizabeth said.

"He's full of it." Noreen turned to Elizabeth. "What did Dojan want?"

"He told us a sheik was going to bring two huge boats into the harbor tonight." Elizabeth kicked off her shoes and put her

100

feet up on the couch.

"He does that a couple of times a season," Domingo said.

"It's the first time I've seen him." Elizabeth yawned again.

"Why didn't you warn her, Domingo?" Noreen said. "He'd frighten anyone, sneaking up to the window at midnight."

"I assumed they had him locked up somewhere," Domingo said. "That nice jail in Edgartown. Country club."

"Cut out that shit, Domingo," Noreen said. "You're not funny." She turned to Victoria. "I'm sorry, Mrs. Trumbull."

"A couple of months ago, before you came on board, he got into an altercation with a drunk," Domingo continued.

Elizabeth waved her hand to direct his cigarette smoke away from her face. Domingo opened the window.

"When I arrived at the scene, this drunk was lying on the ground. Dojan was hitting him over the head with what appeared to be a leg."

Noreen got up. "I've heard this before. Want some coffee?"

"Yes." Elizabeth covered another yawn.

"Then what happened?" Victoria said.

"There was blood all over the place," Domingo continued. "I thought Dojan had torn the guy's leg off." He looked at Victoria, who was watching, enthralled. "He had."

Victoria sat forward in her chair.

"It was an artificial leg," Domingo added, and sat back with a smirk.

"That's sick," Elizabeth said.

"It's the truth," Domingo said.

"Domingo, you're full of it," Noreen said.

"Come to think of it, Dojan drives a light Ford van."

"Talk about nightmares!" Elizabeth said. "Would you rather be tailed by Meatloaf or by some crazed Wampanoag named Dead."

"You said you found something." Domingo turned to Victoria. "What did you find?" He leaned forward again, bright eyes fixed on her.

"We stopped by the East Chop dock on the way to have lunch at the lighthouse."

"You went to the crime scene. You couldn't help yourself. Go on."

"Let her tell her story her own way, Domingo," Noreen said.

Domingo reached for his pack of cigarettes and lighted one.

"Why don't you just light it from the old butt?" Elizabeth said. "Save lighter fluid."

She waved the smoke away.

"We walked along the beach toward the spit that goes out to the osprey pole," Victoria said.

"Go on." Domingo watched Victoria.

"Someone had pulled a boat above the high-tide mark."

"A lot of people do that." Domingo watched Victoria's face.

"Let her talk, Domingo," Noreen said.

Elizabeth held the mug in both hands, sipped her coffee, and looked at her grandmother over the rim.

"Not many people," Victoria said. "It's a kind of backwater. Flotsam washes up on the beach there, plastic oil containers, sunblock bottles, eelgrass. I would think boats would prefer to land on the beach near the dock, where it's cleaner. No one would want to swim there."

Domingo's expression never changed. "Do I understand you to say, sweetheart, you think that a boat landing several hundred feet north of the dock has something to do with the killing?"

"For God's sake, Domingo," Noreen said. "Shut up."

"Footprints led from the keel mark to a sort of path. . . ."

"A path?" Domingo said.

"Not exactly a path, a trodden-down place at the top of the bank, where the rosebushes and bayberry were disturbed, and the grass was crushed down."

"Go on." Domingo took another drag on his cigarette.

"I sent Elizabeth along the path — the stepped-on place — to look for anything she could find that might seem unusual."

"Go on," he said. "She found something."

"Yes. A broken rum bottle."

Domingo slapped his hand on the glass tabletop. The vase of flowers clattered.

Noreen stood up. "You can't let anyone else say a word, can you? Don't pay any attention to him, Mrs. Trumbull."

"No, no, honey," Domingo said. "Do you understand what my girlfriend is saying? Three-quarters of the men on the New York force — men and women, that is — wouldn't have thought to do what she did. You realize that?" He looked at Noreen, then back at Victoria. "Go on, sweetheart. Where was the bottle?"

"Off to the right side, under the rosebushes. Elizabeth picked it up with a paper and put it in the back of the car."

Domingo stared at her, his expression wavering between admiration and horror.

"You've got to remember, I'm an ex-cop. You don't mess casually with evidence."

"We had no reason to think it might be evidence."

Domingo shook his head.

"That's not all," Elizabeth said. "Tell him the rest, Gram."

"What else?"

"We were walking back to the car; I was turning things over with my stick, looking for interesting stones or shells. . . ."

"Go on," Domingo said.

"She's telling you just as fast as she can, asshole," Noreen said. "Give her a chance to talk." She turned to Victoria. "Sorry, Mrs. Trumbull."

"I turned over a clump of eelgrass, and found a plastic checkbook cover. No checkbook inside, but there were a couple of deposit slips that had not been filled out and a deposit receipt."

"What makes you think that had anything to do with the events of two nights ago?"

"The plastic was still pretty fresh-looking," Victoria said, "and the paper deposit slips and receipt were soaking wet, but not turned to mush by being in the water. I would guess it was in the water less than two days, maybe washed up yesterday." Victoria looked at Domingo. "It probably has nothing to do with the murder. But who knows?"

Domingo stubbed his cigarette out in the full ashtray and looked intently at Victoria. Noreen took the ashtray from him and went into the kitchen, then brought it back clean.

"Where are they now?" Domingo said.

"In the backseat of the car," Elizabeth said.

"The proper procedure is to turn evidence over to the police," Domingo said.

"But we have no reason to believe this is evidence," Victoria said again.

Domingo nodded. "Yas," he said. "That is correct."

Noreen sighed.

Elizabeth got to her feet and stretched. "I need fresh air. I'll bring the stuff in."

Victoria watched her lanky granddaughter slide the door open and head toward the car.

The papers in the plastic cover were still soggy. Domingo carefully peeled the plastic flap away from them.

"Get me a knife, honey." He reached out his hand without looking at Noreen, and she went back into the kitchen. She returned with a thin-bladed knife, making a gesture for Victoria's benefit, as if she were going to impale her husband with it before she put it in his outstretched hand.

"Thank you," he said, eyes bright.

Noreen went back into the kitchen and returned with a clear plastic cutting board and a handful of paper towels. Domingo looked up at her. Their eyes met. There was a faint smile on his face. Victoria felt a touch of electricity in the air. Noreen gave him a soft slap on his cheek and sat down again.

As carefully as a surgeon, Domingo slid the knife under the corner of the top paper and carefully separated it from the one beneath. He laid paper towels on the cutting board and gently set the two deposit slips and the yellow receipt on top.

"Can you make out any printing?" Victoria got up and leaned over Domingo's shoulder.

"Still too wet, sweetheart."

Noreen left the room again and came back with a clear piece of glass, a small windowpane. Domingo made a kissing sound in her direction, and Noreen punched him on the shoulder. He sandwiched the wet papers between paper towels and the glass and set a dictionary on top.

"It's probably nothing," Victoria said.

"Kept us entertained for a half hour," Domingo said. "By tomorrow morning, we may be able to see something."

Elizabeth yawned.

"I've got to get my granddaughter home." Victoria looked at her watch. "Good heavens, it's one-thirty."

"You want to spend the night?" Noreen said. "We have plenty of room."

"No thanks," Victoria said. "We'll be fine. I'm just curious to know what's on the papers we found today, that's all."

"They need to dry slowly," Domingo said. "The glass will keep them from curling as they dry. Air can get in around the edges, so it won't mildew."

"I guess we'll know tomorrow," Victoria said.

On the way home, Victoria looked in the side mirror.

"There's a car following us. A different one. The lights are lower and closer together."

"It must be Domingo." Elizabeth frowned, and Victoria could see her face in the reflected light from the car behind, high cheekbones and wide mouth. "Funny, he didn't say anything about seeing us home."

The car followed them along Barnes Road, turned right when they did onto the Edgartown Road, followed them past the airport, and when they turned into the driveway, it continued on past them, turned right on Old County Road, and Victoria could see its taillights disappear into the night.

\\ Chapter 5 //

"I haven't seen much of Victoria since the murder," Chief Casey O'Neill said to her sergeant, who was sitting at the desk across from hers, which he shared with the two patrolmen. Casey leaned back in her chair and lifted coppery hair away from her uniform collar. "She knows who's related to whom, so I don't make insulting jokes about someone's third cousin twice removed." Junior grinned, eyes turned down, mouth turned up. His pale mustache seemed to have been pasted on to make him look grown-up.

"That was my father's sister-in-law's second cousin," he said. "It's okay to insult 'connections.' "

"I'm learning. After I've been here a few more years, maybe I'll understand the politics of this town."

Junior was filling out monthly reports. He erased something vigorously, then brushed eraser crumbs off his desk with the side of his hand. "Since Victoria heard that scream, she feels personally responsible for the investigation."

"She would," Casey said.

Junior scooped a handful of blunt pencils from his desk and took them over to the pencil sharpener screwed to the frame of the window that overlooked the pond. "She also feels she needs to protect her granddaughter after the divorce. I guess it was pretty messy."

"Tell me about it." Casey leaned back in her swivel chair. "How's your dad these days?"

"He's got a one-man show of his landscapes this fall."

"All right!" Casey said.

When Ben Norton, Junior's father, retired as chief of police, Junior assumed he would succeed his dad. Instead, the selectmen hired Mary Kathleen O'Neill, from off-Island.

After the first buzz of astonishment, the village settled down and waited. Casey was not one of them; she was trained in big-city crime. Wait and see, the village said, see how her graduate degrees equip her to handle wandering grandfathers, missing bicycles, farmer's market parking, and emergencies down unmarked dirt roads.

Junior had been ready to quit and move off-Island. But he, too, waited. The new chief was making an effort to understand

111

her new town and its people. After six weeks, Junior stayed on.

He lined the pencils up on the windowsill and inserted them one at a time into the hand-cranked sharpener. In the pond, the pair of swans and their three half-grown cygnets were feeding, their long necks immersed in the shallow water, their tail feathers in the air. The cygnets' white adult feathers showed raggedly through gray baby down. On the other side of the pond, tall stalks of joe-pye weed had opened mauve blossoms.

"I suppose we won't see much of Victoria until she solves the murder?" Junior turned from the window to the chief.

"There's not enough action in West Tisbury for her at the moment." Casey keyed numbers into the computer. "These were supposed to save paperwork, not make more," she muttered.

"How's she getting to Oak Bluffs, now she's lost her license?" Junior blew shavings off a newly sharpened pencil.

Casey looked over her shoulder. "She hitchhikes. I picked her up on Old County Road the other day. Thumbing."

Junior laughed. "It's those long legs of hers," he said. "The first car that passes picks her up. Every time."

The phone rang. Junior put the pencils down and picked up the receiver. "West Tisbury Police Department, Sergeant Norton speaking."

The chief, who had turned back to her computer, could hear a man's voice and make out an occasional word. She heard the name Victoria a couple of times.

"That was Domingo," Junior said when he hung up the phone.

Casey sighed and stood. She wiped the dust off her polished boots on the back of her trousers, left foot, right foot.

"Sounds as if we've put a stop to her hitchhiking," Junior said. "Domingo asked us to keep a watch on her."

Casey paced the small area in front of the two desks. "We don't exactly have a lot of manpower to spare."

"We don't need police watching her," Junior said. "She's got friends. What about the guy who lives behind her?"

"Winthrop Lodge." Casey picked up a yellow pad and pen.

"He's like one of her grandkids." Junior brushed the top of his tidy desk. "How about the artist who lives in her attic?"

Casey felt her face redden. "Angelo Santellini." She turned her back to Junior, pushed her chair under her desk, tucked

113

her uniform shirt firmly into her trousers. "You know, don't you, that Victoria was trying to play matchmaker?"

"You and Angelo?" Junior grinned.

Casey nodded.

Junior laughed. "In a way, her matchmaking worked. Angelo and Winthrop."

"I wasn't looking anyway." Casey leaned over, turned off her computer, and sat again. She straightened papers on her desk, put them in manila folders, opened her bottom desk drawer, and set the folders in it. "Let me see the schedule." Junior handed her a yellow sheet. "Josh or Adam can cruise past her place on a regular basis. I'll drive by when I can."

"My father has a thing for Elizabeth. I'm sure he'd like to help. Get back in action," Junior said.

"Your father?" Casey said, surprised. "Elizabeth is your age, isn't she?"

"Younger." Junior grinned. "He's only thirty-five years older. Lotta life in the old man yet."

Casey shrugged. "Well, sign him up." She made some notes on her yellow pad. "Among us, we should be able to cover her for a couple of weeks."

Junior scribbled with his newly sharpened pencil, occasionally moistening the lead with his tongue.

"Elizabeth is with her at night. If we include Domingo, that makes nine."

"I'll talk to Elizabeth," Casey said. "Victoria doesn't lock her doors, of course. I doubt if they have keys." She sighed. "No one in this town locks doors. The selectmen acted as if I was out of my mind when I demanded a lock for the station door."

"You're not in Brockton now."

"That's for sure," said Casey.

"It's a relief to have a morning off." Elizabeth was on her hands and knees next to Victoria, both of them pulling weeds in the iris border. "Domingo gets on my nerves after a while."

Victoria knelt on a padded kneeler with handles that Elizabeth's mother had given her.

"I'd like to stop by his house sometime today to see if we can read those bank slips," Victoria said.

The weeds rustled under the peonies, and McCavity stalked through the tall growth of red clover and sorrel. He settled on a patch of weeds directly in front of Victoria, ones she was about to pull, and began to wash himself, reaching around

115

with his long pink tongue to clean his shoulders. Victoria laughed, roughed his head with her grimy hand, levered herself up with the handles on the kneeler, and shifted to a new spot. The cat cleaned his head where she'd patted him, then moved again.

"Here's some catnip for him." Elizabeth pulled up a fuzzyleafed plant and tossed it to McCavity, who scooped it up, rolled over onto his back, and pawed the catnip with his back feet.

"The ground is nice and soft. Last night's rain was just what we needed," Victoria said. They pulled weeds companionably, a gentle cropping sound, like animals munching. "I'll pull up this poison ivy. It doesn't seem to affect me."

"Do you want it on the burn pile?" Elizabeth got to her feet. Her jeans had a long rip in the right knee, worn through from kneeling in the garden.

"No." Victoria tossed the shiny-leafed plant to one side. "The oils get carried in the smoke, and if you breathe it in, you may have a problem."

"In your lungs, ugh." Elizabeth tossed grass clumps and lamb's-quarter and purslane and red clover, feverfew and mint and digitalis seedlings into a pile at the side for the compost heap. "What's this purple flower?"

"Which one?" Victoria asked.

"It's star-shaped, with yellow centers." Elizabeth moved peony leaves aside so Victoria could see. "Is it something you're trying to grow on purpose?"

"Nightshade," Victoria said. "Pull it out."

"It's poisonous, isn't it?" Elizabeth tugged the plant out by its roots. "Deadly nightshade."

"Same family as tomatoes and eggplant," Victoria said, shaking the dirt off the roots of a bunch of grass. "Better wash your hands right away. People have gotten sick from touching it."

"I'll put it on the burn pile. Guess we don't need it to seed itself any more than it has already." As she passed McCavity, who was lying on his back like a limp toy, the catnip resting on his soft belly fur, he suddenly reached out and swiped at her jean-clad leg.

"Whoa, McCavity! You crazy cat." She stepped over the iris spikes onto the grass. "There are enough weird weeds in this border alone to give everyone on the Island itchy rashes, or make them sick, or drive them crazy."

"Or worse," Victoria said.

"I can watch Victoria an hour or so a day." Noreen and Domingo were sitting at the glass-topped wicker table and she was making a list on a pad of legal paper. They were watching Court TV in a desultory way. A black woman lawyer with heavy horn-rimmed glasses and a red dress gestured at something on an easel. Occasionally, Domingo would look over at the television.

"All right!" he would say. Or "Yas!" Or he would shake his head and say, "Don't do that!" Sometimes, he would laugh.

"Would you pay attention?" Noreen said. "This is serious."

"I am paying attention, honey. Who do you think called Chief O'Neill?"

"Ernesto can drive by on his way to and from work," Noreen said. "He could stop in for coffee. Victoria likes him."

"Glad somebody does." Domingo leaned back in his chair. "Keep him out of my way for another half hour."

"Don't talk that way about your son-in-law." Noreen wrote Ernesto's name. "He's married to your daughter, remember?"

"Yes, honey." Domingo took off his cap and blinked his eyes.

"You are full of it." Noreen shook a cigarette out of the package on the table near her, lighted it with a disposable green lighter, and inhaled.

"What about your friend on the board of selectmen?" She looked at Domingo through a screen of bluish smoke.

"Liz Tate is no friend of mine." He got to his feet and went up the step into the kitchen, poured himself a cup of coffee. "She accused me of harassing her niece."

"You're shittin' me!" Noreen's blue eyes opened wide. "Allison, the scrawny blond kid? Liz Tate claims you harassed the kid? You?" Noreen started to laugh. "What did you do?"

"I told her to pick up a candy wrapper on the dock. I can't even tell a female employee to pick up a candy wrapper?"

"You told her?" Noreen put her pen down. "How did you tell her, Domingo? With a pat on her fanny?"

"No, no," Domingo said. "I was very polite. Maybe my voice was a little forceful."

"Yeah, sure. 'Forceful.' You yelled at her, right? She probably went home in tears and told her auntie."

"Liz Tate is a scheming broad." Domingo looked at his wife with his wide-set dark eyes. "Excuse me, honey. Liz Tate

119

is a scheming person. Meatloaf delivered the complaint."

"What does Meatloaf have to do with all this?"

"He was her messenger," Domingo said. "I told him — politely, of course — to have Liz Tate put the complaint in writing. I did call him a 'lackey.' "

"Cross her off the list." Noreen swiped her pen across the name she'd written. "We know a bunch of people who would be happy to watch Victoria."

"We can't trust half of them."

"What about your deputy harbormaster? He's out of jail now, isn't he?" Noreen said. "What's his name again?"

"Aggie. Victoria knows him. Add his name to the list."

"That's what I just said," replied Noreen, clearly irritated. "How about listening to me occasionally?"

"Yes, honey," Domingo said.

Victoria opened the cabinet above the stove. "We're running low on coffee. Also, we've run out of coffee cake and cookies." She closed the cabinet and went from the kitchen into the cookroom, a small room that had served as a summer kitchen when Victoria was a girl.

The afternoon sun poured into the room, touched the bouquet of black-eyed Susans that blazed like orange flame against the red-checked tablecloth. Sunlight touched the pine woodwork and the wide floorboards. Victoria's baskets hung from the hand-hewn beams. Pots of spider plant and Swedish ivy and philodendron curtained the windows. Victoria stepped down carefully into the cookroom, her hands braced on the doorjamb, and sat in her caned bentwood armchair. She fished an envelope out of the trash, then took a pen out of the marmalade jar on the windowsill.

She was starting to write, when McCavity stalked in, sprang into Victoria's lap, turned around, and settled himself, paws curled under him. Victoria patted him absently, and he purred, head up, eyes closed.

From her seat, Victoria could look through the west windows across the field, across New Lane, across the Doane's pasture. She could see the West Tisbury town center a half mile away, the church spire with the sun glinting on the weather vane on top, the roof of the new library above the trees.

"I've never known a time when we had

so many callers," she said to Elizabeth. "While you were at work, Ernesto stopped by. He had a cup of coffee with me and one of your rum raisin muffins. Two, actually. And Howland stopped by. He had two cups of coffee and a muffin. Ben Norton dropped in."

"Two cups of coffee, two muffins." Elizabeth pulled another caned bentwood chair up to the table, eased the ripped part of her jeans over her knee, and sat.

"I think he's set his cap for you," Victoria said. McCavity opened his yellow eyes and stared at Elizabeth. "I've started a grocery list. We'll need to go to Cronig's before it closes."

"For heaven's sake, Gram, he's older than my dad. Pair him up with Mom, not me." She ran slender fingers through her hair. "Besides, it's women who set their caps, not men."

"He's awfully nice," Victoria said.

"He is. His paintings are glorious, and it's fascinating to watch him at work. But no thanks."

"You could do worse." Victoria stroked McCavity. "Do we need more Bisquick?"

"Yes, large size. Why not set him up with Casey? They're closer in age, only twenty years' difference. Then Casey would be her

122

sergeant's stepmother." Elizabeth laughed.

Victoria got to her feet and checked the soil in the philodendron in the west window.

"I'll water it." Elizabeth filled the teapot and watered the plants until they dripped onto the floor.

"Would you please move my pocketbook?" Victoria said.

"Sorry." Elizabeth took a paper towel out of her pocket and wiped the water spots off Victoria's leather pocketbook and put it on the table.

"Then Winthrop stopped by after work, had a cup of coffee and a muffin. Angelo joined us. Then Junior Norton."

"How weird." Elizabeth took the teapot back into the kitchen and put it on the counter next to the stove. "Do you have everything we need on the list? Bananas. We always need them."

When Victoria finished the list, they went out through the entry to the car. A long shelf in the entryway was covered with treasures generations of children had brought back from the beach. Victoria took her wide-brimmed straw hat from a nail next to the windows. The black-eyed Susans she had stuck in the ribbon hatband the day before had dried to brown crisps. She tossed them into the garden at the top of the steps, where the well used to be.

"Maybe they'll seed themselves. They'd be pretty against the shingles."

The convertible's top was down, and a brown leaf had drifted from the Norway maple onto the seat. Elizabeth shook out the towel seat covers, and then Victoria got in and slammed her door shut.

Elizabeth backed the car out of the spot under the tree and headed out the driveway, past the iris and peony border they had not finished weeding. Brown pointed tips of the iris leaves marked the close of the dry summer. A vee of Canada geese flew overhead. They passed the west meadow with its ancient lilacs, so old and so large, they were more trees than shrubs.

They drove under the ailanthus tree Victoria's grandfather had brought back from China in a pot 150 years ago. "Tree of Heaven," he'd called it. Every year, the tree produced hundreds of offspring, and when Elizabeth and her sister were children, her grandfather would pay them a penny for each seedling they uprooted.

"With the president about to visit, traffic will be awful in Vineyard Haven." Elizabeth checked the road to the left. A van with a dish antenna on its roof was coming toward them.

"They're going much too fast." Victoria watched the van as it disappeared down the small hill to their right. "Ever since they widened the road, it's been like a speedway."

"CBS News," Elizabeth said. The van left a stream of dust swirling in its wake.

"When is he due?" Victoria tied her hat ribbons under her chin as the brim of her hat flopped in the breeze from the van.

"Next week, I think." Elizabeth pulled into the road and turned left. "The Oak Bluffs Harbor is in a dither." They passed the police station, the small shingled building that had once been a one-room school. Victoria waved at Junior, who grinned back. They passed the old mill on the left, now the home of the garden club, the mill pond across the road from it.

"The Coast Guard came into the harbor to check out places to keep their cutters," Elizabeth said.

"Cutters! Imagine that," Victoria said.

"They're bringing in two cutters. A state police boat came in yesterday. The marine conservation officer will be in the harbor the whole time he's here. The Secret Service are all over the place, dressed the way they think Vineyarders ought to look, thinking they'll blend in, only they've forgotten to take off the price tags. They all have microphones in their lapels."

"Why do they need all that security in the harbor? He's not staying in Oak Bluffs, is he?" Victoria put her hand on top of her hat as Elizabeth turned right past the mill pond and the breeze eddied from another direction.

"He's staying in Edgartown. But I guess they need to be ready for anything, from a plane crash to a fishing trip."

"That poor man. What a life, having someone watching you all the time."

"Hmm," Elizabeth said. "Yeah."

\\ Chapter 6 //

The siren whooped once as the ambulance backed up to the hospital entrance, its beeper warning anyone behind it. The EMT in the passenger seat opened her door, dashed around to the back of the vehicle, and yanked open the doors.

"Is he still with us?" she said to the technician inside, who was sitting next to a stretcher with a figure laid out on it like a corpse, hands folded over a large belly.

"He's still breathing." He unstrapped the stretcher from the ambulance floor. "Can you hear me, sir?" There was a moan from the stretcher. "It's okay, sir. We're at the hospital."

A hospital tech flung the emergency room doors open as the EMTs wheeled the stretcher with the limp figure out of the ambulance and hurried him inside.

A small gray-haired man in a pink-and-blue-plaid shirt and open white coat came from behind the admitting desk, where he'd been filling out paperwork. He took a pair of glasses from his pocket, put them on, and inspected the man on the stretcher.

"Damned if it's not you, Meatloaf," he said. "I told you this was going to happen if you didn't stop stuffing yourself."

Meatloaf moaned, eyes slits in his puffy face.

The doctor took his glasses off and put them back in the pocket of his lab coat. "Bring him in here. Might be his heart."

"Yes, sir, Dr. Erickson," the tech said.

Dr. Erickson gestured to another tech. "Get the portable cardio machine, stat." While the techs rushed off, Dr. Erickson unveiled Meatloaf, peeling off the light blanket the EMTs had placed over him, unzipping his windbreaker, unbuttoning his shirt, lifting up his undershirt to expose an expanse of pink belly with a smattering of hairy curls.

"If it didn't get you this time, it will the next," Dr. Erickson said unsympathetically. He slapped the side of Meatloaf's belly, and Meatloaf moaned.

A tech wheeled in the portable cardiograph machine and two techs, a nurse, and Dr. Erickson attached the wires to Meatloaf, first rubbing on splotches of jelly at each point where the wires were to be attached. Meatloaf shifted slightly, and the stretcher creaked.

"Don't move," Dr. Erickson ordered.

Meatloaf made bubbling noises through his pursed lips. His skin was a grayish green. His face sagged like a day-old balloon.

"Start 'er up." Dr. Erickson motioned like a conductor, and the techs switched on the machine.

"Odd." Dr. Erickson, his glasses on the end of his nose, held up one end of the paper, which showed regular, even peaks and valleys. "Curiouser than hell."

"Indigestion?" Noreen said. "Indigestion?" She had pulled her rusted red Volvo up to the emergency entrance of the hospital, where Victoria was waiting, her string bag of poetry books in one hand, her broad-brimmed straw hat in the other.

"That's what I heard as I was going through the emergency room." Victoria set her books on the floor of Noreen's car and swiveled herself in.

Noreen waited until Victoria was settled. "I heard on the scanner they were stopping at Meatloaf's place. I figured Domingo had jinxed him."

As Noreen pulled away from the grass strip in the emergency entrance's parking lot, Victoria indicated a lemon yellow pickup truck. "That's the new surgeon's car, a 1956 Jeep."

Noreen looked over at it. "That's the year he was born."

"He's younger than most of my grandchildren." Victoria shook her head. "It's amazing what children can do these days."

Noreen pulled out of the parking lot and waited for a string of cars to pass before she turned onto the main road. On their right, they could glimpse salt marsh, before trees closed in and the road veered away from the water. On their left, stone walls and fences had been moved back from the road to make way for the new bicycle path, and the gray lichen-covered sides of the stones no longer lined up the way they had for a century or more.

"I suppose the road by your house was dirt when you were a girl." Noreen braked at the stop sign by the fire department.

"It was sandy, with wagon ruts on either side of a high center." Victoria looked in the side mirror, where the road spun out behind them. "One night, a boy from Edgartown who was courting one of my sisters, and my cousin Leonard from West Tisbury, who was courting an Edgartown girl, both fell asleep on the way home," she continued. "When their horses met at

Deep Bottom, they stopped, nose-to-nose. The boys slept on."

Noreen laughed. "Imagine that happening today." She waited for cars coming from her left, then turned right. "It must have taken a couple of hours to go the eight miles or so from Edgartown to West Tisbury."

"Now we get in a car and think nothing of driving from one end of the Island to the other. We used to go to Oak Bluffs two or three times a year, a great occasion. Now, Elizabeth commutes, drives there every day."

"Domingo told me Liz Tate accused him of harassing her niece, one of the dock attendants."

"Domingo's too refined," Victoria said.

"Domingo, my husband?" Noreen turned to Victoria in astonishment. She swerved and a car horn honked. She moved back to her side of the road. "You gotta be kidding me."

"He has such courtly manners," Victoria continued.

Noreen raised her eyebrows. "Are we talking about the same person?" She sneaked a quick look at Victoria.

"And he knows so much about poetry." Victoria looked straight ahead, her nose lifted. "He appreciates it. Not many people do these days." She moved slightly in her seat.

"I'll give you that." Noreen turned into her drive. "Domingo likes Elizabethan poetry because the guys who wrote it were sneaky, plotting, and conniving, and wrote in code."

Noreen stepped outside the car and leaned in through the driver's side to talk to Victoria. "He identifies with that shit. Excuse me, Mrs. Trumbull." She opened the back door to take out the groceries. "Come in and have a cup of coffee."

Victoria carried one of Noreen's bags of groceries into the house and dropped it onto the couch. She sat in the wicker armchair in front of the glass-topped table while Noreen brought in the rest. Sunlight filled the large, sprawling room. At one end, opposite the table, a wall of mirrors reflected green plants and sunlight, and the couch with Domingo's harpoons above it. Afternoon light poured through two skylights on either side of a brick chimney behind a large black wood-burning stove.

Noreen stepped up into the kitchen, returned with two mugs of coffee, and sat across from Victoria. Sunlight filtering through the plant-filled window lit up Victoria's face, made her wrinkles stand out in strong relief, hummocks and gullies of time. Her eagle's beak of a nose cast a long shadow on her cheek. Her eyelids drooped over her bright brown eyes. She put a knobby hand up to her face to brush back a loose strand of hair that waved naturally around her face in a white halo.

"You and Domingo have a thing going with that poetry." Noreen stirred her coffee. "If I didn't know my husband pretty well, I'd worry about you two."

Victoria looked down modestly. "The best thing about getting old," she said, "is that you can flirt with the men and their wives don't mind."

Noreen sipped her coffee and watched Victoria's face. "I'm not so sure about that, Mrs. Trumbull."

A car pulled into the drive. Noreen pushed the plants aside and looked out.

"Elizabeth. She's early. Domingo must have gone softheaded." The white Rolls-Royce pulled in next to Elizabeth's car. "And here he is. Wonder who they left in charge?"

Elizabeth pushed the sliding door aside, came in, and dropped onto the couch.

"What a day!"

"Domingo giving you a hard time?"

Noreen poured a cup of coffee and handed it to her as Domingo came into the room.

"Thanks." Elizabeth took the cup and sniffed the fragrance. "No, it's not so much Domingo, for a wonder." Domingo rolled his eyes. "It's the dock attendants, the treasurer, the selectmen, the Harbor Advisory Committee. The harbor is busy, but that's okay. It's just the whole atmosphere."

"Did you enter the harbor receipts you were worried about into the computer?" Victoria asked Domingo.

"All done, sweetheart."

"Except for a bunch we can't read," Elizabeth said. "We've got enough entered so Domingo can fill out the paperwork and get that cash to the treasurer."

"You mean, *I* can fill out the paperwork." Noreen stepped down from the kitchen. "I'm the one he's going to get to do it."

"You heard what Howland's code word is, didn't you?" Elizabeth looked up at Noreen.

"I'm not sure I want to know."

"It's your nickname in Spanish."

"He calls me 'woman' when he thinks he's being cute. What is it, *'mujer'?*" She tugged on a strand of Domingo's hair.

"Ouch!" he said. "You know I love you, honey."

134

"You're full of shit." Noreen gave him a swat with the back of her hand.

"At least one good thing happened today," Elizabeth said. "Meatloaf Staples didn't show up." She kicked off her shoes and wriggled her toes in the soft carpet.

"You heard he was taken to the emergency room?" Noreen said. "Suspected heart attack."

"No!" Elizabeth sat up.

"It was indigestion," Victoria said.

"Shucks." Elizabeth leaned back against the couch cushions again. "Since Allison's aunt filed the complaint against Domingo, the dock attendants are acting surlier than usual. Domingo walks by and they put on this big act of being terrified."

"They ought to be terrified of him," Noreen said.

Elizabeth said, "I don't see why Domingo can't fire all of them. We're trying to institute controls on money transactions, and the kids lost one of the receipt books, fifty numbers' worth. That could easily translate to five thousand dollars."

"How can you lose a receipt book? They're not exactly small." Noreen picked a yellowed leaf off a plant in the window.

"We designed them so you couldn't slip the book in your pocket and take it home by mistake," Elizabeth said. "I don't think you do lose them."

"Here he comes, Mr. America!" one of the lunchtime regulars at the corner table in the ArtCliff Diner sang out as Meatloaf lumbered through the door. The diner was on Beach Road, across from the Mobil Mart and down the road from the shipyard.

"Whaddaya say, Cap'n?"

"Hey, Dorothy!" a bald guy with a fringe of sandy red hair and bushy coppery eyebrows shouted to the woman in the kitchen. "Bring Meatloaf a double order of sausage and gravy."

"With fried potatoes and onions," said a cadaverous-looking man with prominent cheekbones, who was wearing a greasy red baseball cap with GEORGE'S AUTO BODY printed on it.

"Add a couple of rashers of bacon to the order, Dotty," said Red, the guy with the bushy red eyebrows. "Put it on my tab."

Meatloaf shambled over to the round corner table. Lunch patrons in the diner looked up and moved aside to let him pass. The diner had five small tables in addition to the big corner table, and a counter with five stools that ran partway across one side.

Meatloaf squeezed past the counter, pushed his baseball cap up on his forehead, and took off his sunglasses.

"You guys cut that out," Dorothy, a sturdily built woman in her forties, called out from the kitchen. "You wanna kill him?"

"Yeah," said one. "Why not?" said another. "Who'll know the difference?" asked the third.

Meatloaf pulled out one of the captain's chairs around the big table and sat down with a grunt.

"So, you're dieting, I hear," said Red. "Have a carrot stick, Meatloaf."

"It wasn't funny." The three men at the table laughed. The one sitting to Meatloaf's right slapped him on the back.

"How many EMTs did it take to carry you in?" asked the first man, a graybeard wearing the ubiquitous baseball cap, this one emblazoned with MARTHA'S VINE-YARD SHIPYARD.

"One to screw in the lightbulb and four to turn the stretcher," Red said.

Shipyard brayed with laughter.

"Wrong joke," said Meatloaf, his mouth turned down.

More raucous laughter.

"Whatsa matter, baby?" Beanie, the cadaverous man, who was sitting on Meatloaf's left, asked solicitously, putting his arm partway around Meatloaf's broad back. "Can't take a joke anymore? Diet getting to you?"

"Lay off me." Meatloaf's face was getting red.

"Temper, temper!" sang out Shipyard.

"Yeah, lay off him." Dorothy set in front of Meatloaf a plate with a hamburger patty, a tomato slice, and a dab of cottage cheese.

"Oooh, girls!" Shipyard looked at Meatloaf's plate.

"I mean it," Dorothy said. "Lay off. The guy almost died."

"Almost died, my aunt Fanny," Beanie said.

"Almost killed the EMTs who had to carry him in is more like it," Red said.

"You about finished with your witticisms?" Meatloaf stabbed the hamburger with his fork held tines down and carried a chunk of it to his mouth. "Real funny guys, you are." He chewed the bloodred meat. "Real funny."

"What's the news at the harbor with that nigger spick?" Beanie leaned forward, bony elbows on the table.

Dorothy scooted out from behind the counter, grabbed Beanie's collar. "You watch your goddamned mouth around here." She shook him. "Hear me? Nobody talks like that in my place."

"Awright, awright." Beanie shrugged her off and straightened his collar.

"I mean it." Dorothy scrubbed the table in front of Beanie with her wet dishcloth, then flicked it at him.

"You trying to put me back in the hospital?" Meatloaf said, mouth full of hamburger. "That guy is screwing things up."

"Cutting back the wife's shopping money, is he?" Shipyard said. "Everybody knows you was on to a good deal."

"The black guy is smarter than you give him credit for," Beanie said. "Smarter than all of yous put together."

"Anything new with the murder investigation?" Red asked.

Meatloaf choked suddenly, coughed, his face turning red. Beanie slapped him on the back. Meatloaf coughed a few more times and wiped his watering eyes.

Shipyard brayed. "Almost got you that time."

"What about the old lady who saw it all?" Red said. "Mrs. Trumbull, wasn't it? West Tisbury?"

"She has no idea what she saw or heard. She's in her nineties, for God's sake."

Meatloaf coughed a couple of times. "She doesn't know diddly-squat. Medeiros, the cop, not the plumber, talked to her." He chewed. "Whaddaya expect from an old bag?"

"She's a pretty damn smart old bag," Shipyard said. "Not much gets past her, from what I hear. She rides around with West Tisbury's police chief."

"So?" Meatloaf said.

"Writes the West Tisbury column for the paper, don't she?" Beanie said.

"Don't give me any more shit about Mingo or the old lady. Let me eat my lunch in peace, will you?" Meatloaf jabbed another hunk of hamburger with the fork and carried it to his mouth.

"Getting some pretty big boats in the harbor this year, ain't you?" Shipyard said. "I see that professor's boat is next to the fuel dock."

Dorothy brought a fistful of heavy white mugs of steaming coffee from the kitchen and chunked them down on the red-checked vinyl tablecloth in front of each of the men.

"Which one's his boat?" Red put his hands around his mug and turned to Shipyard. "That big motor sailer?"

"Yeah." Shipyard stirred a heaping

spoonful of sugar into his coffee. "His boat's the sixty-five-footer with the black hull, teak deck."

"*Dawn Chorus*," Meatloaf said through his hamburger.

Shipyard pulled a paper napkin out of the black dispenser in the middle of the table and wiped his own face vigorously. "Hey, Meatloaf! Can't you keep your food in your own mouth?"

"Professors make enough money to keep a boat like that?" Beanie asked.

"He's got plenty of money. You know which house he bought, don't you?" Shipyard looked at Beanie over his mug.

"That big house on the Sound, backing on Lake Tashmoo." Beanie dumped two spoonfuls of sugar into his mug.

"Yeah, five million dollars' worth," Red said. "Let me have the sugar when you're through, if you left any."

"That what he bought it for?" asked Beanie. "God Amighty! Real estate prices are outta sight."

"Definitely not a professor's salary." Red looked toward the kitchen. "Hey, Dotty, how about some cream?"

Dorothy returned with a small stainless-steel pitcher and plunked it in front of Red. "Sorry, boys, forgot all about it."

"Where does he get his money?" asked Beanie.

Red shrugged. "Someone said he developed some astrophysics software program."

"You mean there's enough call for astrophysics computer programs to make someone a millionaire?" Beanie said, looking at Red in astonishment.

"Astrophysics ain't what you think," replied Shipyard. "No one looks through telescopes anymore. It's stuff like *Star Wars*."

"That's old hat now." Beanie sipped from his mug.

"Yeah, well, it's other shit like that. Greenhouse effect. Ozone layer. Somebody told me he was working in Puerto Rico on a big radio telescope." Shipyard looked at Meatloaf, who sat there chewing. "Guess we finally shut him up."

"Where's he teach, Harvard?" Beanie stirred his coffee.

"MIT, I think," Red said.

"He used to," Shipyard said. "I heard he got fired."

"Professors don't get fired."

"Something about the guy ain't right," Shipyard said. "He's too good to be true."

"You're jealous," said Red.

Meatloaf wiped his mouth on a paper napkin, then reached for a second napkin and wiped his forehead. "Can't you guys think of anything else to talk about?" He balled up the napkins, dropped them on his plate, and pushed his plate away from him.

Dorothy bustled over to the table. "You done, Meatloaf? You left your cottage cheese."

"Yeah. I lost my appetite. Don't need a special diet when I'm around them." Meatloaf jerked his head at the others.

"Poor dear." Shipyard brayed his short laugh. Dorothy took Meatloaf's plate with its balled-up napkins, pool of blood, and dab of cottage cheese, then wiped the vinyl cloth in front of him. Meatloaf leaned his elbows on the table, small hands dangling in front of his gut.

"So what are you doing about the harbormaster?" Red said.

"You can't hardly fire the guy. He's doing a pretty good job, from everything I hear." Beanie moved his coffee mug in circles on the vinyl cloth.

"Don't you worry your sweet asses. We'll get rid of him," Meatloaf said, reaching for the cream pitcher. "And the old lady, too."

Shipyard leaned back on two legs of his

chair to talk to Dorothy. "Better bring two more pitchers of cream for Meatloaf. Another bowl of sugar, too."

"And two jelly doughnuts," Beanie said loudly.

"And a double slice of your banana cream pie," Red said.

"With two scoops of vanilla ice cream," Shipyard added.

"Holy smokes," Meatloaf said. "There are ways to get rid of you guys, too."

\\ Chapter 7 //

Louie, the green-haired dock attendant, sat back in the aluminum lawn chair in the harbormaster's shack.

"That computer guy musta put in some kind of code word," he mumbled to Allison, who was sitting on the desk, kicking her feet, her boating shoes dangling off the ends of her toes. "I can't get into the program."

Allison snapped her chewing gum. "So? Who cares?" She was sketching something in a stenography notebook.

"I want to see what Mr. D. is trying to hide. What's he got in there? Why does he need to keep anyone out of the program?"

"To keep you guys from, like, messing it up?" Allison swung her feet.

"While you're sitting there doing nothing, check the desk drawers, will you? See if they left any loose money in there, or any receipt books."

"They lock them up. Only Mr. D. and Elizabeth have keys." She swung her feet,

145

hands on the edge of the desk, and snapped her gum.

"Try the drawers. I want to see what's there." Louie typed a word into the computer and hit the enter key. The computer beeped.

"I'm not touching a thing. I don't want Mr. D. on my case again, you know?"

"What could he have used for a code word?" Louie said, half to himself, trying another combination. "You got nothing to worry about, Allie." He paused to look at her. "Your aunt is about to sue him, isn't she? Because he hassled you? He wouldn't dare touch you." He hit the enter key again. The computer beeped.

"I got plenty to worry about. He didn't harass me. He hollered at me is all." She swung her feet, and one of her boat shoes fell off. "I don't really blame him, you know? My father woulda smacked me if I gave him the lip I give Mr. D." She slipped off the desk, put her shoe back on, and lifted herself onto the desk again. "Mr. D. isn't so bad, you know?"

Louie tried another word, and when the computer beeped yet again, he said, "Shit. I'll never figure it out this way." He turned to Allison. "Your aunt was hoping for something to nail him with. Damn that guy.

There's no way to figure out what code word he used. I tried all the obvious things."

"Maybe he wrote it down somewhere."

"I doubt it." Louie looked up from the computer. "What're you drawing?"

"None of your, like, business," Allison said.

Louie looked toward the parking lot. "Here comes Howland now, with Mr. D."

Allison glanced over her shoulder and got off the desk in a hurry, gathered up her receipt book and a pencil, and scuttled out the door.

Domingo was ambling from the parking lot along the catwalk that led to the shack over the water, feet splayed out. Allison moved to one side to let him pass. He stopped.

"Did you clean up the mess in the shack?" His thumbs were hooked in his trouser pockets. He looked at her intently.

"No." She peered down at the wooden decking at her feet.

" 'No' what?"

"No, *sir*." She emphasized the last word.

"And why not?" Domingo looked at her.

"It's, like, already perfectly clean," she said. "Sir."

"Come back to the shack and we'll take a look."

Allison shrugged, tossed her long hair back from her face, turned, and retraced her steps to the shack.

Louie was standing as far from the computer as he could get, paging through his receipt book, apparently counting.

Domingo looked at him, and Louie avoided his eyes.

"Still haven't figured out the code word, eh?"

"Who gives shit about some code word?"

"Watch your language." Domingo stared at him. "Get out of the shack and patrol the harbor. Pick up the trash, empty the barrels into the Dumpster, and check boat lines."

Louie slapped his receipt book against his hand and avoided Domingo's eyes. "This isn't a job; it's slavery."

Domingo's eyes got brighter. "You don't know what slavery is, kid. Get out of here before I kick you someplace the bruises won't show, give your father something to complain about."

Louie hitched up his shorts and mouthed something.

"You say, 'Yes, sir,' understand?"

"Yeah."

Domingo grasped Louie's upper arm and looked at him. Domingo grinned, teeth white against his dark face.

"Yes, sir," Louie said hurriedly. Domingo released him, and the dock attendant scurried out of the shack and joined Allison on the catwalk. The two flew past Howland, who was giving directions to a tourist, pointing toward something on Circuit Avenue. Howland glanced at them as they passed.

"You abusing those poor children again, Domingo?"

Domingo stood in the middle of the floor, thumbs in his pockets, feet apart, toes facing out, looking at the computer, at the desk, at the window locks.

"So it would appear." Domingo reached into his shirt pocket for his cigarettes. "You sure the program is safe from them?"

Howland stood in front of the computer and entered a series of words. "They're not likely to hit on the code word. I'm more concerned that they'll accidentally erase something or hang up the hard drive. I don't suppose we can ban them from the shack?"

Domingo didn't reply immediately. He shook out a cigarette, then put it back in the pack. "My assistant's got me afraid to smoke in my own office." He put his hands in his pockets and paced the small shack.

"We can't lock them out, if that's what you're saying. They have to come in here with receipts, fill out time sheets, check the schedule. We can't keep them out."

"A pity." Howland sat in front of the computer and entered a string of words. "When did that motor sailer come in?"

"*Dawn Chorus.* This morning, early. Owned by T. R. Folger, old-time summer family. A couple years ago, he bought that big house on Tashmoo."

"That's an expensive boat," Howland said as he continued typing.

"He's got a live-aboard captain, too." Domingo paced the shack. "That's not cheap." He stepped outside and stood at the railing, looking out at the Harbor House.

"A yacht and a five-million-dollar house on a professor's salary?" Howland lifted his eyebrows.

"The money comes from something else." Domingo turned his back to the railing and put his elbows on it. "If I'm not mistaken," he said with a slight smile, his bright eyes on Howland, "*he* made his money developing a computer program."

Howland looked up at the harbormaster, and his mouth turned down. "Why didn't you ask him to develop the harbor-management program instead of me?"

"He's too busy."

"I suppose I'm not?"

Domingo continued to talk as if to himself. "In the couple of years he's lived here, he's become a pillar of the community. Volunteers at the hospital. Teaches in the literacy program." He glanced from the Harbor House to Howland. "You could be doing good works, if you'd only get going with that harbor program."

"Yeah, yeah." Howland went back to the keyboard.

The door of the shack was swinging slightly. Domingo leaned down and propped it open with a rounded beach rock. He turned and looked at Howland. "How are you coming with those receipts?"

"Between Elizabeth and me, everything's entered except the ones in this pile." Howland picked up an inch-thick stack of receipts. "Those, we couldn't read. Those kids can't write." He pointed to the top one. "Can you read this?"

Domingo fished in his pocket for his glasses and looked at the name written in the space designated "Boat owner." He shook his head and handed the stack of receipts back to Howland.

"Or this one." Howland handed the next receipt on the stack to Domingo. "What's that boat name?"

Domingo looked at it and shook his head again. "Looks like *Otter Creek*."

"Or is it *Sweet Life*, or *Other Wife*?" Howland slapped the pile of receipts. "Figuring out this program is difficult enough without having to deal with illiterate kids."

Domingo grinned. "Their aunts or fathers will probably cite me for abuse if I tell them to print clearly."

"In addition to the dock attendants' lousy writing," Howland continued, "boat owners give boats the most ridiculous names, spelled in improbable ways. We registered four boats named *Why Not*, spelled in four different ways. Puns, professions, pet names, naughty names. We registered three boats named *Wet Dream*."

Howland glanced up from his computer to look out at the parking lot. "Who's that?" He indicated a tall, extremely slender man with curly dark hair, white on the sides, and a large black mustache who was walking from the parking lot toward the catwalk. He was wearing tan chino slacks and a light blue knit collared shirt.

"That's the professor."

"*Dawn Chorus,* a five-million-dollar house on the beach." Howland looked closely at the man coming down the catwalk. "Inventor of a multimillion-dollar software program."

"Right."

The tall man approached the shack and grinned, perfect white teeth dazzling in his tanned face, as Domingo went outside to greet him. He thrust out his hand, Domingo thrust out his, and they shook.

"How're you doing, Professor?"

"Not bad. You having a good season?" Standing next to Domingo, he leaned his elbow on the railing, crossed his left foot over his right, and peered genially down at the small, dark harbormaster. The boat shoes on his sockless feet were new and polished.

"You heard about Bernie Marble's murder?" Domingo, leaning with his back against the railing, looked up at the professor.

"Not something you expect on the Island. Do they know who did it?" He raised his thick eyebrows in an upside-down V.

Domingo shook his head. "If they do, no one's saying."

"Probably don't want to make too much fuss with the president coming in a week or so. Wouldn't look good."

Howland, who had been listening from inside the shack, got up from his seat in front of the computer and joined Domingo and the professor on the deck. The professor was at least three inches taller and much slimmer than Howland.

The professor straightened up and extended his hand. "Name's Rocky," he said.

"Howland Atherton." Howland lifted his head so he could look down his nose at the taller man.

"Understand you're developing the computer program with my drinking buddy here."

Domingo turned to face the harbor, elbows on the railing, looking at the Harbor House.

"I believe you're the one who ought to be developing this program." Howland glanced at Domingo's back. "My experience is with the three-eight-six."

"That's what you need for this job. You don't want a high-tech program. Mind if I take a look at it?" the professor asked. "I don't want to intrude, of course. Believe me, I know what it's like to work out the bugs in one of these programs."

"Not at all." Howland bowed slightly

and held his hand out for the professor to lead the way. The professor ducked through the door, Howland following. He pulled the second aluminum lawn chair up to the computer and both sat.

Domingo lifted a hand. "I've got to check the dock attendants." He went down the catwalk and disappeared behind the tent with the butterfly display next to the snack bar.

"Good man," the professor said after Domingo had left.

"The selectmen don't seem to think so." Howland pressed a key and the screen demanded a code word. The professor averted his eyes politely while Howland typed in *"mujer."* Howland hit the enter key and the harbor-management program popped up on the screen.

"Nice. Straightforward, simple." The professor leaned forward in the lawn chair. "You must have had the deuce of a time setting that up. The simpler the application, in my experience, the more difficult the programming."

"It did take some thought."

"I can imagine. More than some. Would you mind showing me how you did that?" The professor sat back. "If you don't mind."

"No, no. I'm certainly delighted to show you."

The phone rang.

"Do you need to answer?"

"No," Howland said. "The machine will pick up on it. I don't work here."

The phone stopped after a few rings, and they could hear the answering machine whir.

"I'm interested in how you handled problems such as differing boat lengths and beams, varying slip sizes, where boats came from, and the length of stay."

Howland put a stack of clean paper into the printer. "I'll give you copies of forms we use for reservations. As I said, it's not original, I'm basing my work on existing software."

"All the more impressive. Domingo mentioned earlier that you've developed forms for the turnover reports. I take it those are the reports that accompany checks and cash you turn over to the town?" The professor moved his chair closer to the computer.

"Yes, that's right."

"Ingenious. Knowing Domingo, he probably doesn't appreciate what you've done."

"True, to some extent."

"He's not free with his compliments." The professor leaned back in the chair while Howland printed out copies of the forms he had designed. "He's pretty shrewd, Domingo is," the professor continued. "I wouldn't like to be on his wrong side."

The radio crackled on the wall behind them. A voice came on, saying, "Oak Bluffs harbormaster, Oak Bluffs harbormaster." The professor raised his eyebrows at Howland.

"Domingo has a handheld radio. He'll take care of it."

"You were saying about the program?"

"I think this management program will protect him to some extent." Howland turned to look at the other man. "We'll have all the information he needs to run the harbor — registration numbers, addresses, that sort of thing."

"Domingo seems to believe money is slipping through loopholes in the system," the professor said.

Howland paused before he answered. "Yes."

The professor showed concern. "You'd think the selectmen would support him more than they seem to be doing."

"Yeah," said Howland. "You would think so."

The shack swayed slightly on its pilings, and the professor looked up.

"Domingo's assistant, Elizabeth Trumbull," Howland said.

"Oh?" The professor raised his eyebrows.

"She's Victoria Trumbull's granddaughter, lives with her."

"Good place to be," the professor said.

Elizabeth reached the door and hesitated when she saw someone with Howland at the computer. She brushed her hair away from her face with the back of her hand. The freckles on her nose stood out against her tan.

"Come on in," Howland said. "Meet the owner of *Dawn Chorus*, Professor Folger. Elizabeth Trumbull." The professor got to his feet and extended his hand to Elizabeth, who shook it firmly.

"I don't often have to look up to anyone." Elizabeth tipped her head back.

The professor bowed slightly. "I understand there aren't many people you need to look up to," he said graciously. "So you're Victoria Trumbull's granddaughter?"

Elizabeth smiled and nodded.

"I'm a great admirer of her poetry. I believe I have all of her books. She must be along in years."

"She's ninety-two."

"And still writing, from what I read in the *Enquirer*."

"Please, sit down." Elizabeth stepped into the shack. "I'll sit on the desk and watch you work."

"It was your grandmother who witnessed Bernie Marble's murder, wasn't it?" the professor asked.

"I don't believe she actually witnessed it," Elizabeth said cautiously. "She heard a scream."

Howland said, "Victoria, Domingo, and Elizabeth found the body."

"That must have been a horrible experience."

Elizabeth nodded.

"The professor developed an astrophysics program," Howland said to Elizabeth. "I'm showing him our harbor application."

"Call me Rocky. My students do."

"Where do you teach?" Elizabeth sat on the edge of the desk.

"I was teaching at MIT," Rocky said. "However, I'm now an independent consultant."

Elizabeth looked out the window. "*Dawn Chorus* is beautiful."

"She's about thirty years old."

Elizabeth whistled. "She looks brand-new. What a lot of work to keep up that teak and all the brightwork."

"Would you care to come aboard?"

"I'm on duty today." Elizabeth looked at the sleek boat at the fuel dock. "How much longer will you be here in the harbor?"

"I'll be here for a while. It would be my pleasure to have you aboard for drinks. And you, Mr. Atherton?"

"Call me Howland."

The professor got to his feet. "Elizabeth, I'll send you an invitation, you and your grandmother, for drinks aboard." He went through the door, ducking his head.

Elizabeth sat on the edge of the desk and watched the professor stride along the bulkhead toward his boat. "Maybe my grandmother could practice her match-making on him." She turned back to Howland. "She's trying to pair me up with Ben Norton, who's at least thirty years older than me. This professor seems to have money, brains, and he's tall."

Howland gazed at her. "Too good to be true, right?"

"He's probably married." Elizabeth sighed. "Where did he get his money, from his computer program?"

Howland shrugged and turned back to the screen.

Elizabeth continued talking. "If you were to market your harbor program the way Domingo thinks you should, maybe you'd make your fortune, too."

"A million-dollar yacht with live-aboard captain?" Howland shook his head. "With the proceeds of a computer program?"

"You're just jealous." Elizabeth slid off the desk and sat next to him. "I guess we'd better try matching this pile of receipts with whatever we can that's in the computer."

"Who's guarding Victoria right now?" Howland paused in his data entry and glanced at Elizabeth.

"Chief O'Neill assigned the two West Tisbury patrolmen to watch her, and Ben Norton was going to stop by later. I don't believe there's anyone with her right now."

Howland finished the entry he was working on, stood up abruptly, picked up his green canvas briefcase, and put a sheaf of papers into it.

"I've got to go. Will you be okay, Elizabeth?"

"Of course. Why the sudden concern? I've been working here alone for more than two months now."

"Sorry. I don't mean to sound protective. See you later."

Victoria was opening a small can of cat food when Howland knocked. McCavity was on his hind legs, front paws up high, mewing. "Come in — the door's open." Victoria dished cat food into McCavity's bowl and set it on the floor. As the cat dodged under the table, his tail bumped the table leaf, which banged. By the time Howland entered, McCavity's head was in the bowl.

"Haven't seen you since this morning." Victoria looked up at Howland with a twinkle in her eyes. "Nice to be so popular."

"Can't stay away from you. Do you have any coffee left from this morning?" He lifted the pot off the burner.

"I've never seen anything like it. Everybody in town has dropped in for coffee. I've gone through three pots so far today. I haven't had a moment alone to write."

"Anyone you don't know?" Howland reached the cobalt blue mug down from the cupboard over the sink and poured himself a cup.

"Yes. The nicest man came by, left only a few minutes ago. He had copies of all of my books, and he asked me to autograph them." Victoria went into the cookroom and sat at the table.

"Oh? Who was it?" Howland poured milk into his coffee and sat across from Victoria at the table.

"T. R. something. I wrote it down to make sure I spelled it right in his books." She sorted through some papers on the telephone table. "It's here somewhere."

"T. R. Folger."

"Yes. That's right. Do you know him?"

"I met him today. About an hour ago, at the harbor."

"He must have come right here. Imagine that." She picked out a couple of wilted zinnias from the bowl of flowers in the center of the table and laid them next to her.

"What did he have to say?" Howland sipped his coffee.

"He's a great admirer of mine. He introduced himself, then asked if I would autograph my books he'd bought over the years. Oh, yes, something else." She got up stiffly from her chair.

"Can I get something for you?"

"No, I have to get it." Victoria opened the cabinet over the refrigerator. "It's where I keep my stash of sweets." She looked over her shoulder at Howland. "I don't want anyone to see how much I've hidden away here."

She returned with a small box of Chilmark Chocolates. "Rocky brought me this. Have a piece. Or two."

"Thank you." Howland watched her slip the golden elastic band off the box and put it on her wrist. She lifted the lid of the white box. "Have you eaten any yet?"

"Not yet." Victoria looked over the selection laid out in the box. "Such a treat. I don't often have them given to me." She poised her hand above one, then changed her mind. "Rocky must have known how much I like chocolate."

"You can hardly miss with those." Howland picked out a fat cream, turned it over, and looked at the bottom. He put it back in the box and picked out a second candy, turned it over, looked at the bottom. He did the same with a third piece.

"I wouldn't allow my children to do that, Howland," Victoria said tartly. " 'Look as long as you want,' I'd tell them, 'but once you put your fingers on a piece, it's yours.' "

"I'm sorry. That was rude of me. Let me take the box and I'll bring you a new one."

"That's not necessary." Victoria put the lid back on the box, slipped the golden elastic back around it, and pushed the box toward him. "It's yours if you want it. Take it."

"Thank you." Howland picked up the box, zipped open his briefcase, dropped the chocolates into it, got up from the table, and left.

"Did you notice the stars when you came in?" Victoria said to Elizabeth, who'd returned from her day at the harbor. The night was cool and clear, with a touch of fall in the air. "Orion is so brilliant, you can imagine the hunter striding across the sky with his starry belt and sword."

Elizabeth fetched the rum bottle and cranberry juice jug from the cupboard under the kitchen counter and mixed two drinks. She followed Victoria into the parlor, set the drinks on the coffee table, and knelt by the fireplace, where a fire was laid, ready to light. She put a match to the paper underneath and waited for the paper and kindling to catch before she got up.

"I'll bring in more wood," she said.

She had lifted the canvas log carrier out of the wood basket and was at the dining room door when Victoria said suddenly,

"Howland came by."

Elizabeth turned at the tone of her grandmother's voice. Victoria was sitting in the mouse-colored wing chair next to the sofa. "He did the strangest thing this afternoon."

"He can be pretty weird. What did he do this time?"

"He came over for a cup of coffee, and when I offered him a piece of chocolate from a box that nice man Rocky Folger brought me, he mauled several pieces, and when I told him sarcastically to take the whole box, he did." She held up her glass and looked thoughtfully at the firelight flickering through the ruby red cranberry juice. "That's not like Howland at all. He usually has such impeccable manners."

"I didn't realize the professor had come by." Elizabeth set the log carrier down on a chair.

"Yes. Shortly before Howland showed up."

"Mr. Folger was at the harbor today. He asked Howland to show him the harbor computer program."

"Yes, he told me," Victoria said. "He also told me about his own program, not that I understood what he was talking about."

166

"He seems like a nice man." Elizabeth looked through half-closed eyes at her grandmother. "He's closer to my age than Ben Norton is."

Victoria's face crinkled in amusement. "I can't start matchmaking until I know him better."

Elizabeth sighed. "I'm not interested anyway, Gram. I need to get my head back together before I look at another guy." She left the room with the log carrier and returned in a few minutes with a load of wood, which she stacked in the basket next to the hearth. Flames flared up briefly; a log shifted. She prodded the fire with tongs until it burned evenly, then sat on the couch next to her grandmother's chair.

"Rocky has invited us aboard his yacht," she said.

Victoria looked thoughtfully at her granddaughter. "I hardly know what to tell him about Howland and the chocolates."

"You don't need to say anything."

"I suppose not. I'll tell him, again, how pleased I was."

They sat quietly, looking into the flames for long minutes.

Victoria glanced up suddenly. "Is someone at the door?"

Elizabeth put her drink on the coffee

table and went to the kitchen. Howland stood in the dark entry with a white pasteboard box in his hand.

"Come on in," Elizabeth said. "Hear you've suddenly acquired a sweet tooth."

"Sorry about that." Howland strode into the parlor and presented Victoria with the box he was holding, a box of Chilmark Chocolates, twice the size of the one Rocky had given her. Victoria looked up, puzzled. "What is this all about?"

"It's my apology for being so rude this afternoon." Howland moved in front of the fireplace, put his elbow on the mantel, and looked down at the hearth.

"Will you join us for drinks?" Victoria asked him as she put the box of chocolates on the end table next to her.

Howland shook his head. "No thanks. I've got to go."

The fire sizzled and hummed. A log snapped and broke with a shower of sparks.

"I'll see you tomorrow," he said to Elizabeth. "You're on duty at the harbor, three to midnight, aren't you?"

"Yes."

Victoria lifted her glass to him. "Good night."

Howland nodded, then disappeared into the starry night.

"What is wrong with him? He's certainly acting odd." Victoria looked into the flickering fire. "I suppose it will sort itself out eventually."

\\ Chapter 8 //

Victoria almost canceled her trip to Boston when she saw Meatloaf Staples driving the medi-van. This was the first time she'd used the free van, and it hadn't occurred to her to question who the driver might be. However, Dr. Erickson had made an appointment with the foot specialist, Elizabeth had dropped her off at the ferry terminal, and she could hardly back out now. She hoped Meatloaf would not remember her from that brief encounter at the harbormaster's shack. Really, she had nothing against him, except his rudeness that time.

Victoria, who was sitting in the backseat, watched as a frail woman with a walker smiled up at Meatloaf, who helped her into the van. "You're so thoughtful, Mr. Staples." Meatloaf had set out a milk crate as a step, folded the woman's walker, and stowed it behind the front seat.

The woman patted his arm, and he pushed his sunglasses back on his nose. She settled into the middle seat, next to a man wearing a red plaid jacket and a yellow-and-green Hawaiian shirt.

The medi-van was the first vehicle in the ferry line. Mist drifted up from the harbor's glassy surface, which reflected sailboats moored between the breakwater and the ferry lane. Gulls circled and mewed; one dived and hooked a silvery fish in its bill, then soared into the air on strong wings. The harbor's mirror surface shattered into myriad sunrise colors where the bird had touched it.

Behind the rose-colored clouds over the shipyard to the east, the sun shot out bright rays. The masts of the topsail schooner *Shenandoah* etched black lines against the dawn sky.

The woman introduced herself to the man in the Hawaiian shirt, and they exchanged pleasantries about the sunrise. She shifted in her seat and peered at the people sitting behind her.

"George dear, what's taking you to Boston?" George was next to a black-haired woman, who was wedged between him and Victoria.

"Meatloaf's van." George gave a horse-toothed laugh. The frail woman tittered. "Actually, my stomach's acting up again." He adjusted himself between the women on either side of him. "I'm going for tests."

"It's terrible getting old, isn't it?" She turned with her arm across the back of the seat. "And Victoria! This is the first time I've ever seen you use the medi-van."

"Dr. Erickson wants someone to look at my toe."

The woman next to Victoria smiled at her. Victoria scowled back. The woman had plastered her face with makeup, as if she were an actress. It made her look spooky, clownlike. "One needs to take care of one's feet," the woman said brightly. Victoria's usually good-natured face wrinkled into a sour expression.

Meatloaf aimed his sunglasses through the open side door. "Everybody here?" He counted the passengers, pointing a thick forefinger at each one. When he came to Victoria, he paused. She saw him purse his soft lips. He remembers me, she thought.

"Let's see, five," Meatloaf continued. "One more's supposed to come." He looked at his watch. "They'd better hurry."

The sun broke above the clouds and the harbor brightened. Sunlight glinted off white hulls and sparkled on the quiet water. Tendrils of mist writhed up from the harbor's surface and vanished. The day was going to be warm.

A short elderly man, his face flushed,

darted toward them. "Medi-van?" he gasped, mopping his head with a handkerchief.

"None other." Meatloaf nodded. "Take your time, mister. You ride in front with me. I got laundry in back."

"Landry?" The man put his hand behind his ear, puzzled.

"Lawn-dree," Meatloaf said loudly. "When I do this medical run, I cart dirty lawn-dree from the Harbor House to the commercial laundry in Boston."

Victoria looked behind her and saw two folding metal carts with canvas sacks bulging with towels and sheets slung from them.

"Ah." The man regained his breath. "Killing two birds."

"You could say that." Meatloaf helped him into the front seat and slammed the door shut. An attendant beckoned the van toward the ferry. The line of cars and trucks followed up the gangplank, where they stopped to give the deckhand a ticket.

"Whaddaya say, Meatloaf?"

"Nothin' much, Beanie."

"See you at the diner this evening." Beanie tore off a portion of the ticket and handed the rest back to Meatloaf, who put the ticket under the visor and drove onto the vessel. The metal deck plates clanged under his wheels. He nodded to the deck-hand, who directed him into the left center lane, and stopped behind the chain strung across the bow.

Once he'd pulled on the parking brake and shut off the engine, Meatloaf reached into his shirt pocket and brought out a folded slip of paper. Victoria saw him take a pen out of his pocket and scribble what looked like numbers.

The vessel's diesel engines rumbled. The vehicle deck vibrated as a second line of trucks and cars formed in the right center lane, headed by two eighteen-wheelers. The ferry rocked as each truck drove on board.

"Anyone want to get out, go up to the snack bar?" Meatloaf turned to his passengers. "This van's not going anyplace else for forty-five minutes."

The woman in the middle seat and the woman next to Victoria raised their hands. Meatloaf set down the milk carton step and helped them out of the van. Victoria got out with them, taking Meatloaf's cold, moist hand reluctantly. "Watch your step, girls; the deck's slick." He peered into the van. "Anyone else?"

As she climbed the iron stairway that led

to the upper deck, Victoria felt someone watching her. Halfway up the stairs, she looked down and saw Meatloaf turn away quickly. He got back in the driver's seat, folded his hands over his stomach, and tilted his head back against the seat. His sunglasses covered his eyes.

At the top of the stairs, Victoria opened the watertight door that led into the lunchroom, then seated herself with the two other van passengers in a booth across from the lunch counter.

"How you doing, Mrs. Trumbull? Off to America?" Victoria looked up, to see Eddie Schultz, the electrician.

"Doctor's appointment. What about you?"

"I'm off to get some pipe sections myself. Christ, you'd think they was gold-plated." He tipped his dirty red baseball cap to the three women. "Have a good day. See you around."

He moved to the urn in front of the lunch counter and poured himself a large cup of coffee. "Keep the change," he said to the blonde behind the counter.

"Whaddaya say, Eddie?" A bulky, bearded man slapped him on the back. "Catch any blues lately?"

"They ain't running too good up to

Menemsha. How about you?"

"Running pretty good around Wasque, I hear. Give me one of them crullers." The man pointed to a sugary doughnut and the blonde lifted the plastic cover, picked one up with a piece of waxed paper, and handed it to him.

"Rough out there?" Eddie asked her.

She shrugged. "Slick calm."

The ferry whistled and pulled away from the slip. Victoria could see boats on moorings in the harbor, all pointing east. She nodded to a neighbor, who had come up the stairs into the lunchroom. Noting the clunky high heels of a young woman with two small children, Victoria marveled at how she managed to look so stylish with children hanging on her. She looked around at the other four booths, all of which were occupied, recognized a woman from church, who smiled at her. She turned back to the two women sitting across from her, and they talked about the children's posters displayed on the bulkhead above the table. The black-haired woman brought three cups of coffee to the table. They discussed summer crowds and how autumn was almost upon them. They continued chatting until the ferry turned into the channel between the barren-looking Elizabeth Islands and Woods Hole.

When the purser announced the vessel was docking, they returned to the van. The ferry's big doors opened, engines roared into reverse, and the vessel slid into the slip with a bump that rocked the vehicles on the car deck.

Meatloaf started up the van and led the procession of cars and trucks and motorcycles off the ferry.

As they left Woods Hole behind them, conversation died down, and the van's passengers dozed or read until they reached the outskirts of Boston.

"Medical Center, first stop." Meatloaf inclined his head toward the back of the van. "Tufts next, Beth Israel." He checked the side mirror and changed lanes, cutting in front of a bus.

"I've got to drop off the laundry. I may be late, so keep your shirts on, girls."

Victoria scowled.

When her appointment was over, Victoria strolled through the Commons until it was time for the van to arrive, then returned to the clinic entrance and sat on a bench under a tree. The shade felt good after the walk in the hot sun.

She took her pen and a pad of paper out of her pocketbook, intending to write. Before she put down the first word, she looked up and saw a stout man wearing sunglasses cross the street in front of her. At first, she thought it was Meatloaf, and for an instant she had a pang of fright. However, the man was no one she knew. Her heart was thumping. What was she afraid of?

Her poem vanished like the morning's mist. She thought about Meatloaf. He shouldn't be transporting a load of dirty hotel laundry in the same vehicle with elderly, possibly ailing, passengers. Surely, the health department would not approve. If he were engaged to drive the medi-van, it seemed unscrupulous to wring extra money out of the deal by combining it with a laundry run. Come to think of it, why drive the laundry off-Island, anyway? The commercial laundry had a regular Island route. She'd seen the truck in Vineyard Haven. She shook her head.

While she was musing, the van pulled to the curb next to her and Meatloaf opened the door. Victoria's was the last pickup. The three already in the backseat moved so she could take the same seat by the window that she'd had on the trip into town. Before she settled herself, she leaned over the backseat. The laundry carts now were loaded with cardboard boxes, taped shut. Clean laundry, she assumed. When she looked up, Meatloaf's sunglasses were reflected in the rearview mirror, lenses shining at her.

It must be the way the light reflects off his glasses, Victoria told herself.

During the trip to Woods Hole, she avoided looking toward the rearview mirror and Meatloaf's glassy stare. She wasn't one for chatter, especially about ailments, and after a few attempts, she gave up and looked out the window at the late-summer foliage. Whenever she glanced up, Meatloaf's bug-eyed sunglasses seemed to be aimed at her.

At the top of the hill approaching Woods Hole, where she could see the harbor and the islands beyond, she always felt a surge of pleasure. This time, she felt relief, as well.

The van continued down the hill, across the bridge, into the staging area for the ferry, and onto the waiting boat.

When they docked at Vineyard Haven, Victoria's head ached from tension, and she was glad to be out of the van. She went inside the terminal building to wait for

Elizabeth. While she waited, she had an eerie, prickly sensation that someone was staring at her. She looked around, expecting to see Meatloaf standing behind a column, but no one was there.

"Sorry I'm late."

Victoria started. She had been so preoccupied, she had not noticed her granddaughter come into the waiting room. When she looked up, she saw concern on Elizabeth's lean, freckled face.

"Are you okay, Gram? I didn't mean to frighten you." She put her hand on her grandmother's back. "How was the appointment?"

"A lot of nonsense over a toe. It doesn't hurt and I have no trouble walking, now that you cut that hole in my shoe."

"How did the day go otherwise?"

"I spent too much of it with Meatloaf."

At Elizabeth's frown, Victoria told her about the trip.

As they walked to the parked car, Elizabeth said, "Domingo wants us to stop by. He's acting mysterious, as usual."

"Maybe he's identified those slips in the checkbook we found washed up on the beach."

When they entered the living room, Domingo stood.

"Did you find out whose checkbook it was?" Victoria asked immediately, going over to him.

"I know whose deposit slip it was. And how much money was deposited on a certain date. Sit down." Domingo gestured to a chair, and when Victoria sat, he did, too. "Honey!" he shouted into the room off the kitchen. "Bring me the papers."

Noreen bustled into the kitchen and down the single step to the living room, placed both fists on her hips, and leaned toward Domingo, her face six inches from his. "You can't even say 'please,' can you?"

"Please, honey. Thank you. I'm sorry." His eyes opened innocently. "Please, if you would bring me those papers?"

"Asshole." She flounced out of the room and returned a few minutes later with the bank receipt and the deposit slip still enclosed in two pieces of glass. She set the glass on the tabletop with a clink.

Victoria, who was in the chair, and Elizabeth, who was still standing, leaned over it.

"The numbers on the account are clear." Domingo wiped the top piece of glass with a paper napkin. "The name is more difficult to read. We can't legally get the name that matches the account number without a court order."

"Merton something." Elizabeth narrowed her eyes at the glass-encased deposit slip. "The last name begins with 'St.'"

"Staples," Victoria said promptly. "Meatloaf Staples."

Domingo raised his eyebrows at her.

"It is Meatloaf, isn't it?" Victoria looked at him.

"It could be."

"Is Meatloaf's real name Merton?" Elizabeth asked.

Domingo shrugged. "I've never heard him called anything but Meatloaf."

"If it matters, we can look it up in the voter registration, I guess," Elizabeth said.

Domingo turned to Victoria. "Tell me, sweetheart, why do you think these bank papers are Meatloaf's?"

"When I was in the van today, he wrote something on a slip of paper." Victoria leaned closer to look at the papers under the glass. "It might have been checkbook entries."

"As if he'd misplaced his checkbook." Domingo extended his chunky hand to Victoria, who shook it gravely.

"How much did he deposit? And when?" Victoria leaned over the papers under glass.

"Look." Domingo pointed to the figures on the receipt.

Elizabeth put her hands flat on the table and leaned over. "Ten thousand dollars. Cash."

"The same day Bernie Marble was killed," Victoria said. "Did someone pay him to kill Bernie? Ten thousand down and the rest when he did the job?"

"I don't think so." Domingo smiled. "But you'd have made a good cop, sweetheart."

Victoria looked down at her skirt and smoothed it across her lap. She crossed her ankles, one shoe with the hole for her toe over the other shoe. Then she told him about the trip to Boston.

"Why do you suppose he's taking dirty laundry off-Island in the medi-van? There's no need to."

"Laundry." Domingo drummed his fingers on the table.

"He's hiding something in it, isn't he?" Victoria said. "And bringing something back in the clean laundry."

Domingo lit a cigarette.

"What would he be hiding?" Victoria gazed beyond the plants hanging in the window. "A body. Stolen goods. Something he wants to sell off-Island."

Domingo nodded as she ticked off each thought.

183

"Antiques. Books. Papers. Has to be something illegal. Stolen jewels." She looked over at Domingo suddenly. "Drugs. That's what it is, isn't it? Drugs."

Domingo looked at her with a slight smile. "Don't go jumping to conclusions."

"Of course that's what it is," she said. "It makes perfect sense. Something smallish and valuable."

"Sweetheart, drug smuggling is big trouble."

"Where do we go from here?" Victoria said.

Domingo stood at the window, his hands in his pockets, jingling coins. "Watch ourselves," Domingo said. "And wait."

\\ Chapter 9 //

The captain's white uniform was so sharply creased, it looked as if he had not moved after putting it on. Victoria looked with admiration at the black shoulder boards on his shirt, each with four glittering gold stripes. The shiny black visor of his cap was almost covered in gold thread with an intricate design of oak leaves and ivy. He stood at the foot of the wooden steps that led from the fuel dock to the deck of *Dawn Chorus.*

"Captain Harold Jones, ma'am." He touched his cap.

"How do you do. I'm Victoria Trumbull." She nodded regally, tilting her floppy-brimmed straw hat to him. They went up the wide steps together, Victoria holding the captain's arm with one hand, the railing with her other. When she reached the deck, Rocky was waiting. "Welcome aboard, Victoria Trumbull."

Victoria leaned her head back to look up at him. "Thank you so much." She took his extended hand and stepped over the low rail. She gazed at the scrubbed teak deck, varnished railings and brightwork, polished brass, the neat coils of white line on deck, and the pennants fluttering from the masthead above her.

"How beautiful!" She held her hand on the top of her hat as she looked up at the rigging.

"I'm glad it pleases you." Rocky was nautical in a blue blazer with gold buttons, white trousers, and white deck shoes. "It's such a fine day, I thought we might like to go for a sail." He smiled at Victoria's expression of joy. "I invited Howland and Selectman Tate. Let me show you around before they arrive."

He opened a varnished wooden door and held out his hand for Victoria to go first. She descended the five steps that led into a saloon as wide as the yacht.

The interior of the yacht looked like one of the great liners she and Jonathan, her husband, had taken to Europe years ago. At one end, there was a fireplace, at the other a grand piano, its legs held in metal braces bolted to the deck. Around the edges of the polished wood floor were dark wood inlays of diving whales and porpoises. The floor (Victoria found it difficult to think of it as a deck) was covered with an Oriental rug in red, black, and gray.

Victoria took it all in — the fireplace, piano, couch and armchairs, the large mahogany table secured to the deck, the oil paintings in gilt frames fastened to the bulkhead, the inlaid designs on the floor, the rug. The polished brass portholes were the only indication that this was a boat.

She pulled her hat off and patted her white hair into place. The creases of her face formed a sunburst of pleasure.

They walked across the carpet toward the bow, and Rocky opened a door into a spotless galley with stainless-steel refrigerator, sink, and stove. He showed her the captain's quarters forward of the galley, a stateroom large enough to hold a tightly made bunk bed, a built-in bureau, and a small desk with a lamp fastened to the bulkhead above it.

"How tidy it all is." Victoria ran her hand over the shiny fixtures and patted the neatly folded towels.

"Anyone living on a boat has to be tidy." Rocky led the way back through the galley, through the elegant saloon, into the master stateroom in the stern. A king-size bed strewn with a dozen soft pillows in shades of green and rose took up most of the space. A row of windows on the slanted bulkhead above the bed ran the entire width of the stern. Standing on tiptoe, Victoria could look through the windows onto the harbor below.

Rocky turned at the sound of footsteps above them. "I hear our other guests."

As they walked back across the dark green carpet into the saloon, Victoria asked, "Did you sail the boat here?"

"I sailed as far as Bermuda from Grand Turk, then flew from there. Captain Jones and the mate brought it the rest of the way." Rocky ducked his head to go through the door.

On deck, he greeted Howland. "Good to see you," he said genially.

Victoria noticed Howland's faintly superior expression.

"And our last guest, Selectperson Liz Tate." Rocky stood by the steps as the captain escorted her on board.

" 'Selectman' is fine." Liz Tate smiled. "There can be too much sensitivity."

Victoria had only seen Liz Tate from a distance. It was the first time she'd met her. Close-up, she was much younger than Victoria had thought, thirtyish, not much older than Elizabeth, and while her granddaughter usually dressed in jeans and T-shirts, Liz Tate could have been a *Vogue* model, thin, pale, with high cheekbones and a wide mouth with carmine lips. Her black hair glistened with blue highlights. Her sweater was the exact shade of her lipstick.

"Thrilled to meet you." She took Victoria's hand in both of hers, left hand on top of Victoria's right in what Victoria felt was a too-familiar gesture. "I've known of you, of course."

"Ready, sir?" the captain asked.

Rocky turned to his three guests. "If you sit on the deck chairs aft, you can see better."

The starters for the diesel engines turned, and the pressure alarms rang, then cut off as the engines kicked in, first one, then the other. Deep inside her, Victoria felt the excitement she had always felt when starting on an adventure.

The mate, a college-age boy, clambered aboard, undid the lines, and tossed them down to the green-haired dock attendant, who stood by. The yacht eased smoothly away from the dock and turned into the fairway between the moored boats in the center of the harbor and the slips along the bulkhead. They glided through the channel slowly into the Sound.

Rocky, who was standing next to the wheel, turned to Howland.

Victoria saw that Howland's sweater, a nondescript greenish thing, had a moth hole in the back. Next to Rocky, Howland looked like what Victoria's grandmother had called "an unfortunate."

"The channel has silted up," Rocky said. "*Dawn Chorus* is at her depth limit. A few inches more on her keel and we'd have to anchor outside the harbor."

Victoria stood by the rail as they passed the harbormaster's shack, and she waved when she saw her granddaughter on the deck.

From this angle, the shack looked especially small and rickety, projecting into the harbor on its slender pilings. She looked from the shack across the harbor to the East Chop dock, where they'd taken Bernie Marble's body the night they'd found it, less than a week ago. She noticed Rocky was watching her with an expression she couldn't decipher, a kind of wariness. He smiled suddenly when she looked at him. Such beautiful teeth, Victoria thought, set off so nicely by his dark, full mustache.

"I thought you might enjoy sailing across the Sound to Tarpaulin Cove. We can have lunch there, and be home by five."

Liz Tate sat next to Victoria and asked

her about her childhood. Victoria found herself telling the selectman how her grandfather had sailed to far places from the Vineyard.

"From Arctic waters to the Antarctic," she told Liz Tate, who listened intently, carmine-nailed hands folded in her lap.

They cleared the harbor entrance. To the right, Nantucket Sound stretched as far as they could see. Ahead of them, the mainland formed a thin line of white beach, with a thicker line of gray buildings and green trees. Victoria could make out a church spire and a water tower above the trees. To their left, low cliffs obscured their view to the west, but as they moved, the cliffs receded and Vineyard Sound opened before them.

The mate climbed onto the cabin roof and untied the white ribbons that held the neatly flaked mainsail onto the boom.

Victoria leaned back, her hand shading her eyes.

"Wonderful," she said to Liz Tate. "Just wonderful."

The mate uncleated the mainsheet and hauled the sail smartly up the mast.

Victoria watched every movement.

"You don't miss a thing, do you?" Liz Tate said.

"I try not to."

Liz Tate studied her. "I've known people half your age who are not as alert as you."

"Years of practice." Victoria tried to look modest.

The sail fluttered and snapped loudly, a giant sheet on a clothesline in the stiff breeze, rising smoothly to the top of the mast, until no wrinkles showed along its edge.

"I'm sure you must have to be a keen observer, to write the way you do."

"Thank you." Victoria straightened her lavender slacks over her knees. "There's so much to witness in the world today, to see and hear and feel."

"Speaking of witnessing, I understand you witnessed the murder last week."

Howland turned sharply and looked from Victoria to Liz Tate.

"Not exactly witnessed. I heard something on the other side of the harbor, that's all."

The yacht turned away from the wind, the sails filled, and the midmorning sun shone into Victoria's face. She put her straw hat on again and tied it under her chin.

The boat heeled with a gust of wind.

"Didn't that frighten you?" Liz Tate had her back to the sun. Even though her face was shaded, Victoria could see her wide eyes.

"Things like that don't frighten me." Victoria, who was on the high side of the yacht, leaned back as the deck tilted, as if her weight would counterbalance the wind in the sails. "Domingo — the harbormaster — and my granddaughter took me over to where I'd heard the commotion, and we found the body, floating."

"I suppose you heard voices?" Liz Tate said. "People talking or shouting? You must have heard a scream."

Howland, behind Liz Tate, was staring at the back of her head. Again, Victoria wondered what was wrong with him.

Victoria was aware, too, that Rocky was listening to their conversation, even though he seemed to be talking to the captain.

She went back in her mind over that evening. What exactly had she heard?

"It sounded like three men's voices. I suppose one was Bernie's. I could almost make out the words. I could tell they were disagreeing violently."

Liz Tate nodded sympathetically. "Must have been terrible."

"It must have been terrible for Bernie Marble."

"Yes, yes. Of course. Such an awful way

to die. Gutted like a fish." Liz Tate shook her head. Her silky blue-black hair swirled around her face, backlighted by the late-morning sun.

"You knew him, didn't you?" Victoria tugged the brim of her hat over her eyes so she could see Liz Tate's face better.

"Not well. He was the chair of the Harbor Advisory Committee," she answered. "I saw him often at meetings. He was not the sort I socialized with, of course."

"Of course," Victoria agreed.

They had almost reached the Elizabeth Islands, when there was a flurry of activity. The captain called out to the mate and swung the wheel rapidly to port. The yacht tacked into the wind, the sail swung to the opposite side, filled, and the yacht pointed toward the Vineyard's North Shore. When they were close to shore, they tacked again.

"Such a smooth operation," Victoria marveled.

"We'll turn into the cove in a few minutes," Rocky said. "We'll anchor without the engine. Ideal sailing weather."

Victoria's hooded eyes sparkled. She dabbed at a drip at the end of her great nose with a paper napkin. "I never dreamed we'd go out today."

The captain let out the sail, turned the boat away from the wind, and headed into the cove.

Victoria knew Tarpaulin Cove well from sailing with her grandfather as a girl. The cove was on the south shore of Naushon, one of the Elizabeth Islands. Elizabeth and she often drove to Gay Head, on the western end of the Vineyard, where they could see the islands, a sparsely populated chain that hung from the elbow of Cape Cod. She stood up to see better, holding the back of the deck chair. She could feel the same thrill she'd felt as a girl. She hadn't been here for more than a half century. Surely it wasn't three-quarters of a century? A century had once seemed an eternity. Now she'd almost lived through that eternity. How short a time it had been! She gazed shoreward. She held the brim of her hat to shade her eyes from the glare of sun on water, and held the back of the chair with her other hand. Nothing seemed to have changed. The cove was still cupped by low grassy bluffs, pale gold in the sun. Sheep grazed, as she remembered they had always grazed. She had the eerie feeling they were the same sheep, like the ones they put under the Christmas tree year after year after year. She could hear them bleat mournfully. She remembered standing next to her grandfather in this same spot, listening to that same sound, with the same breeze blowing over them. She remembered the big house with its gables and chimneys, half-hidden by a low hill. The house seemed to be in the same state of disrepair it had been in when she was a child. Her grandfather had said someone should reshingle the roof, or the weather would destroy the house. The roof seemed the same. She could see the tree line beyond the big house, stunted scrub oak and pine. It looked exactly like the tree line of her childhood. She recalled two large trees that rose above the other trees, their configuration looking like an elephant. She'd told her grandfather that. The elephant was still there, unchanged. The island was enchanted. Time had stopped for it, while she continued to pass through days and months and years.

The boat swung into the wind. Sails luffed, slapped loudly.

Victoria snapped back into the present. She turned, to see Howland staring at her with concern, Liz Tate watching her.

The anchor went over the bow, and the wind carried the boat back on the anchor line.

"Are you all right, Mrs. Trumbull?" Liz Tate asked.

"Yes. It's bringing back memories I didn't know I had."

"It's a beautiful spot." Rocky looked around at the sheep grazing and the tall grass rippling in the soft wind.

The sail slithered down the mast and was caught in the Lazy Jack, a net of lines. The mate lowered the jib, tucked it into a sail bag, and then tied everything with white ribbons.

"Well done," Rocky said. "I'll bring lunch out on deck, lobster rolls."

"I'll help." Liz Tate followed Rocky into the saloon. They returned with a platter of sandwiches garnished with nasturtium flowers, along with bottles of champagne and crystal champagne flutes.

Howland raised his eyebrows when he saw the champagne.

"There can't be too many bottles of Rothschild '57 around."

Rocky bowed slightly. "I can't think of a better occasion to share a bottle or two of this."

The sheep bleated softly, one to another. The boat rocked gently on anchor. The smell of sweet fern wafted from shore. Waves lapped on the beach.

During lunch, Victoria chatted politely with Liz Tate. She talked (and flirted) with Rocky, who complimented her on her pantoums. She was pleasantly surprised that he had recognized the unusual rhyme scheme of the Malay poetry form.

Liz brought up the subject of the murder again. They speculated on the effect of the president's visit on the investigation. Victoria was impressed with Liz's knowledge of politics, and she told her so, and Liz said that was because she lived in Oak Bluffs. She asked Victoria again about finding the body, then listened as Victoria repeated what she'd seen and heard. Rocky had come up quietly behind Victoria. She saw his shadow on the deck and could smell the faint scent of his cologne.

She was going to tell Liz about finding the broken bottle, but before she could, Howland clumsily knocked over one of the delicate champagne glasses.

"Damn it, you ox!" Rocky snapped. Victoria turned in astonishment and saw that Rocky's face was scarlet. He apologized immediately. "I beg your pardon, Victoria." He turned to the others, who were also staring at him in surprise. "I do beg your pardon, everyone. I was so interested in what Victoria was saying, I was startled."

The mate cleaned up the fine splinters of broken glass, amid Howland's profuse apologies and offers to replace it.

"No, no, please, Howland. I'm not in the least concerned about the glass," Rocky said.

Once the flap over the broken glass was over, Rocky said, "I was interested in what you were about to say, Victoria. Please continue."

As Victoria resumed her recollections, Howland suddenly pointed to a flurry of gulls on the water not far from them.

Victoria stopped talking and stood up. Everyone started to speculate on whether the flurry of gulls meant a school of bluefish or not.

Victoria saw Rocky stare at Howland with a faint smile.

"Looks as though you won't be able to tell us your adventures after all, Victoria." He turned to the others. "Would anyone like me to bring out the fishing tackle?" he asked.

Once they had finished lunch and Liz and the mate had made an unsuccessful attempt to hook a bluefish, Howland offered to help the mate carry the dishes back to the galley, but he was turned down with some civilized teasing about how clumsy he was.

Victoria reminisced about her childhood

with her whaling captain grandfather, and Rocky and Liz listened intently. All told, Victoria had had a marvelous day. The champagne, the lobster, the conversation, the warm sun, the soothing motion of the yacht, and the hay-scented breeze and bleating lamb sounds drifting out over the water had all combined to make her feel mellow.

"I'm afraid we have to start for home now if we want to get back before dark," Rocky said.

"I wouldn't mind staying here for an entire week." Victoria stood and gazed shoreward, taking in the sheep, the grasses moving like waves, the old house, everything bathed in the golden light.

As the sun settled over Gay Head, across the Sound from Tarpaulin Cove, they weighed anchor and headed home, the wind behind them.

Howland sat with her, leaving her only long enough to get a wool blanket from below, which he draped around her shoulders. By the time they rounded West Chop, Victoria had nodded off.

She awakened as they pulled up to the dock. The sun was disappearing behind the low bluffs of East Chop and the air had become chilly. Clouds had formed while she was dozing, and they promised a spectacular sunset.

She heard Allison — the dock attendant — and the mate call instructions back and forth as he tossed lines ashore; then she heard the scrape of the steps pushed across the dock to the side of the yacht. She listened as the throb of the engines slowed to a soft rumble.

She folded the blanket and got up stiffly from her deck chair. Several people stood at the foot of the steps, Elizabeth and Allison and the young man who pumped fuel. The other two took her by surprise, Police Chief Medeiros and Meatloaf.

Liz Tate's behavior surprised her, too. Victoria had walked over to the rail, expecting to be the first one off. Instead, Liz pushed by her, almost rudely, and leapt onto the steps before they had fully tied up. She scooted down the steps and confronted the police chief. She spoke to him in a low voice, so Victoria couldn't hear what she was saying, but Victoria could hear the selectman's icy tone and see her anger. The chief's face turned red. He looked up at Howland and Rocky and Victoria gathered at the rail, then at Meatloaf, then back at Liz Tate.

Victoria heard her say, "Don't ever let

me see . . ." and then the one-way conversation drifted off on the breeze coming off the harbor. The chief jerked his head at Meatloaf, who stood at the bottom of the steps, and the two men sauntered off the fuel dock. Victoria watched them get into a police cruiser, the chief on the driver's side, Meatloaf on the passenger's. The cruiser backed out of its space and turned, the sound of tires skidding on sand clearly audible. She glanced around the parking lot and saw a familiar gray van. She could see a hairy head with wild eyes staring through the grimy windshield at Meatloaf and the chief.

Liz Tate bustled up the steps and back on board. The lines had been secured while Victoria watched the small drama.

"Sorry about that," Liz Tate said to Victoria with an apologetic smile. "Chief Medeiros was supposed to be elsewhere, doing some business for the selectmen, not hanging around the dock like some boat-crazy kid."

Victoria looked thoughtfully at Liz Tate. "I don't suppose they see this kind of yacht in the harbor often."

Liz stared at Victoria for a moment before answering. "They see this one often enough."

\\ Chapter 10 //

"Why was Meatloaf waiting for us on the dock yesterday?" Victoria sat next to Domingo at the glass-topped table. "It was a perfect day until we tied up, and there he was, waiting."

Victoria and Elizabeth had stopped on their way into Oak Bluffs. Early-afternoon sunlight filtered through the plants hanging in the window, casting dappled shadows on the table. Domingo was wearing his blue plaid pajamas and was drinking coffee out of a mug marked I ♥ GRANDPA.

"I don't know, sweetheart. He's mixed up in this, but I don't know how."

"It was odd to see Chief Medeiros there, too."

"Chief Medeiros was there?" Domingo paused, his cigarette halfway to his lips. "That's interesting."

"Who's running the hotel now that Bernie is gone?" Elizabeth asked. Victoria toyed with the place mat in front of her.

"The chief, I would imagine. Bernie and he were partners."

"Maybe he wanted to invite us to take showers." Victoria's face wrinkled into a smile. "Five dollars each."

Noreen came through the sliding door into the living room with armloads of groceries. "Can't you get dressed, Domingo?" She brushed past him. "It's already afternoon."

"Why should I get dressed now? It's almost time for bed."

"What a slob," Noreen said from the kitchen. "Make some fresh coffee for Mrs. Trumbull, Domingo."

" 'Please, honey.' " He pushed himself away from the table and went up the step into the kitchen. Victoria saw him kiss Noreen on the side of the cheek, heard her say softly, "Go along with you." She heard the rattle of the aluminum measure against the coffee tin, the splash of water, the gurgle of the coffeemaker.

When he returned to the table, he asked Victoria, "Did those two seem surprised to see you? Meatloaf and the chief?"

"I don't think so. They wanted to talk with Liz Tate. She was upset when she saw them, sent them both away."

"Interesting."

"Howland was on the cruise, too." Victoria leaned back in the wicker chair. "He made a fool of himself, dropping one of those expensive Waterford glasses."

"Oh?"

"I was telling Liz Tate about finding the body. Just as I started to tell her about the broken bottle, Howland dropped his glass."

Domingo raised his eyebrows slightly.

"Then, as I was about to resume, he interrupted me, quite rudely, to point out a school of fish."

Noreen pulled up a chair between Victoria and Domingo.

"They're playing some kind of weird game," Noreen said. "Meatloaf and Liz Tate and Bernie Marble, God rest his soul," she said, crossing herself, "and the police chief and Rocky."

"And Howland," Victoria added. "He's certainly acting odd."

"No one knows about the broken bottle but us." Domingo scowled. "There's no need for anyone else to know, either. The broken bottle may have nothing to do with the murder."

"But we're sure it does," Victoria said.

Domingo shrugged, then scratched his chest under his pajama top. "Don't tell anyone any more than you have to. They don't need to know everything we know."

"I can give you a ride home, if you'd like, Mrs. Trumbull," Noreen said.

"Thanks, but I'm giving a reading at the Oak Bluffs Senior Center." Victoria looked at her watch. "One of the board members will drop me off at the harbor, and I'll go home with Elizabeth."

The ship's clock rang five bells. "We'd better get going," Elizabeth said, pushing her chair back and unfolding her long legs. "It's two-thirty now."

The late-night shift had been quiet. Elizabeth had caught up with much of the paperwork in the shack and was now sorting through the day's receipts. Outside, the night was clear and windless. The tidal current moved against the pilings of the shack and gurgled gently. Inside, the overhead lights made it bright.

"Hey, missy, I brought you two lobsters."

Elizabeth jolted to her feet, knocking over the chair.

"Scared you, didn't I?" Dojan stood at the harborside window. Again, she hadn't heard him or felt his footsteps on the rickety catwalk.

"Good heavens, yes." She went to the window.

"The sheik is bringing another vessel tonight," Dojan said, and then grinned. He wore the same outfit, black jeans, black mesh muscle shirt, black scarf imprinted with skulls, and his necklaces of bones and shells. "I hope you have a place for him this time."

"Yes," Elizabeth said. "Yes, I think we can find a place for the sheik. How big is his yacht this time?"

"Two hundred feet." Dojan's grin exposed the missing front tooth. "Where's Mrs. Trumbull?"

"She had a meeting this afternoon. Then one of the board members invited her to dinner. He's bringing her here afterward." Elizabeth looked at her watch. "She should be here any minute now. It's after ten."

"The sheik sends Mrs. Trumbull his regards." Dojan put his hands on the windowsill. Elizabeth noticed the grimy bitten nails and drew back involuntarily. He'd added a black crow feather to the osprey feather he'd worn before in his hair. It looked as if he had not changed his clothes since she had first seen him.

"Did she really know my great-grandmother?"

Elizabeth nodded.

Dojan shook his head; the feathers quivered, the bones rattled, and the scarf

swirled around his neck. "I got two lobsters in a bucket. Want me to put them inside the shack?"

"You can leave them out there," Elizabeth said. "I'll get them later."

"Scared of letting me in?" Dojan bared
his teeth. "*She's* not scared." He moved
back from the window. "I'll sit here until
she comes." Elizabeth heard the bucket
clank on the deck. The darkness closed
around the shack, and she heard a night
heron squawk, the current swish against
the pilings, carrying harbor water out to
sea. The silent Wampanoag waited outside.

After that, she gave up trying to do any
real work until Victoria came. She orga-
nized papers and straightened the shack.

In a few minutes, she heard Victoria's
deep, firm voice. "It's here somewhere.
Let's go into the shack, where there's
light."

"I brought you lobsters," Dojan said.

Elizabeth opened the door, and Dojan
stepped aside so Victoria could enter.

Victoria fumbled through her leather bag
and brought out a slim gray paperbound
book. "This is the long poem I wrote about
your great-grandmother. We kept in touch
through the years. Our lives were quite different." Victoria looked up at him. "I wrote

this before you were born."

"For me?" Dojan's eyes swam in their pools of white. "You're giving this to me?"

"I'll sign the book for you, if you'd like." Victoria found a pen in her pocketbook and looked up at him. "I'll say, 'To Dojan Minnowfish from his friend — and his great-grandmother's friend — Victoria Trumbull.' Does that sound all right?"

Dojan's mouth and eyes formed round circles in his hairy face, and he nodded.

"I'll put today's date on it." She wrote in the book.

Elizabeth looked from her grandmother to the Wampanoag.

"Miz Trumbull" — Dojan held his hand next to his ear, palm toward Victoria — "I'll watch out for you. Don't you worry. No one can get at you with me watching." He picked up the bucket of lobsters. "I'll put these in your car." He disappeared down the catwalk into the dark night.

Victoria and Elizabeth stared at each other.

"What was that all about?" Elizabeth asked her grandmother.

Victoria shook her head. "He's not as strange as he'd like people to think. I have no idea what's on his mind. Something, obviously."

The next couple of hours were quiet. Victoria wrote while Elizabeth worked on the computer. At midnight Elizabeth closed up the shack and deposited the bank bags in the night drop. Then they headed home. They had passed the head of the harbor, when Victoria looked in the side mirror.

"There's a car behind us."

"Dojan?"

"I can't tell. Its lights are on high."

Elizabeth looked in the rearview mirror. "A second car just turned out of the side road."

"You hardly expect to see so much traffic this time of night," Victoria said. "It's after midnight."

"Should we stop at Domingo's? It's creepy to have two cars following us."

"Let's go straight home," Victoria said.

Elizabeth turned past the hospital and crossed the bridge between the harbor and the lagoon. The car behind them followed. Shortly before Five Corners, the second car dropped back, and they no longer saw its lights.

At Five Corners, Elizabeth made a sudden left turn.

Victoria adjusted the side mirror so she could see better.

"They're still following us."

They passed the marine store on the left, passed the turnoff onto Skiff Avenue on the right, and continued straight ahead.

"This is a dead end." Victoria looked in the mirror. "We'll get trapped."

"There's a dirt road that leads into Weaver Lane and back onto the Edgartown Road," Elizabeth said. "I can't believe they'll follow us along that. It's only an old cow path."

"They're still there." Victoria turned to look out of the rear window, as if the mirror might have been mistaken.

"I don't like it." Elizabeth had slowed to twenty miles per hour on the narrow road. The trees on either side closed in. Branches slapped the side of the car. Their headlights picked out individual leaves on the huckleberry bushes on both sides. The sweet fern brushed against them, releasing its sweet, musky scent.

"I hope you're right about the side road." Victoria smoothed her green plaid skirt over her knees. "They're right behind us."

Elizabeth picked up speed, going twenty-two now, then twenty-three. The VW jounced on the ancient paved road.

"What are they thinking?" Victoria

peered into the mirror.

"I don't like this." Elizabeth pressed her foot on the accelerator, gripped the steering wheel. The car leapt over a bump and bottomed out on a pothole in the old macadam.

"Ouch!" Victoria winced as her elbow slammed into the door handle.

"Sorry."

The headlights picked out an open white gate and Elizabeth made an abrupt right turn onto a rutted dirt road with protruding tree roots and low brush in the middle. "Hold on!" she said.

The car skidded on a patch of sand, straightened out, and roared up the hill.

"We should have stopped at Domingo's," Victoria said, patting her hair. "I feel a bit out of my element."

The headlights behind them swerved and wobbled as the pursuing car hit roots and holes and bounced off rocks.

"Pray we don't get a flat tire," Elizabeth said.

The road rose steeply and turned, first to the left, then to the right. Small trees growing in the middle of the road scraped the underside of the VW. Their headlights revealed a pair of luminous eyes in the undergrowth. The pair of eyes became five pairs, and a skunk and four rat-size babies shambled out of the huckleberry bushes and into the road.

"Shit!" said Elizabeth, jamming on the brakes.

"How cute!" Victoria braced her hand on the dashboard. The VW stalled. "Look at that littlest one!"

"I should never have come this way." Elizabeth turned the starter grimly, and the VW coughed and the engine started.

Victoria looked in the side mirror. The headlights behind them swerved and jounced. They smelled the sudden pungent aroma of skunk.

"I hope it wasn't the mother," Victoria said.

"Didn't even slow them." Elizabeth's hands tightened.

Victoria peered into the night ahead of them. "Look out! There's a deer in the road."

"Damn!" Elizabeth leaned on the horn, and the deer bounded into the underbrush.

The cow track leveled off at the top of the hill.

Elizabeth sped up. "We're near the main road now."

The car behind closed in fast. Elizabeth

gunned the VW and it shot ahead, the speedometer climbing in increments.

Victoria wiped the steamed-up inside of the windshield with a paper napkin. "Do we have enough gas?"

"It reads empty, but there's always another half gallon or so," Elizabeth said, looking straight ahead.

A house appeared in the headlights, then another. A light shone in an upstairs window. A side road joined theirs, and Elizabeth pushed down on the accelerator, straightened her back, and gripped the wheel higher up.

"I hope you have your seat belt on," she said. "They're closing on us."

Victoria cranked the window all the way down and put her head out, holding her fuzzy tan hat with one hand. She gazed at the ground speeding under them.

"Hang on," Elizabeth shouted. "We're turning onto the main road."

"I'm right here," Victoria said. "You don't need to shout."

Suddenly, headlights flashed on behind the pursuing car. Victoria looked into the side mirror as the new car, a van, moved into the left lane, drew up next to the car behind them, and cut in front of it. Brakes squealed as the van wedged the other car off the road.

The van made a U-turn and sped off.

"What the devil was that all about?" Victoria said, settling her hat in place.

"Let's get on home and pour ourselves a stiff drink."

A few minutes later, they sat in the living room, sipping rum and cranberry juice. The cat settled himself on the rug in front of the fire, lifted one of his hind legs, and began the long cleaning process. They talked until the fire died down to coals. McCavity finished his bath, then sprawled on his back, paws up in the air, soft belly fur exposed.

Domingo listened solemnly as Victoria described the car chase. It was a bright, cool morning, smelling of autumn and leaves and damp earth. Elizabeth had parked in front of Domingo's garage, leaving room for Noreen, whose car was out.

"Could you tell what kind of vehicles they were?" he asked. "Was either of them the one that followed you the other night?"

"I couldn't tell what the one behind us was. The one that saved us was a van."

Domingo said, "I've been afraid of this. Someone's been watching your house since we found the body. Evidently, we need

215

someone watching you, wherever you go."

"No, thank you. I've seen what happens with the president. No privacy." Victoria sat down in the wicker chair by the table.

"You," Domingo said to Elizabeth. "Bring your grandmother some coffee." He turned back to Victoria. "Privacy is not the issue, sweetheart," he said with exaggerated patience. "The issue is, Who is trying to stop you, and why? I think I know why."

"Because someone thinks she saw something or heard something the night of the murder." Elizabeth stepped down from the kitchen and put a mug of coffee in front of her grandmother.

"Correct."

"And thinks she may be able to identify someone who doesn't want to be identified."

"And thinks she may put two and two together. Sweetheart, someone needs to be with you twenty-four hours a day until this is over."

"Elizabeth is with me all night."

"What would you have done if that car had forced you off the road last night? They'd find your bodies tomorrow or next week." Domingo placed his hand on the table. "No one uses that road."

216

"Domingo, you're being overly dramatic," Victoria said. A car door slammed and then Noreen came through the sliding door.

Elizabeth rose. "I'll help carry the rest in."

"Thanks, Domingo!" Noreen shouted over her shoulder as she and Elizabeth went to the car.

Domingo shrugged. "See what I have to put up with?"

Victoria straightened out the woven place mat in front of her on the table and smoothed its fringed edges.

"What do we know so far?" Domingo said.

"Someone killed Bernie Marble."

"Yas."

"With the broken rum bottle we found?"

Domingo sipped his coffee without answering.

"We found Meatloaf's checkbook cover with receipts showing he deposited ten thousand dollars in cash the day Bernie was killed."

"Correct."

"Does it fit together somehow?" Victoria stopped toying with the place mat and looked up at Domingo.

He shrugged and gazed out the window.

"Seems like too much of a coincidence, doesn't it?" Victoria, too, looked out the window, noticing the toys in the scuffed yard, the cars flicking by on the other side of the fence. A cardinal landed on the bird feeder, snatched a few seeds, and flew off in a flash of bright red.

Noreen and Elizabeth returned with armfuls of brown grocery bags.

"Coincidences happen." Domingo stood, went to the door, and slid it shut.

"Domingo, we're going right out again," Noreen said. "If you're not going to help, at least don't hinder us."

Domingo made a kissing sound and sat again.

"But you think a coincidence like that is unlikely," Victoria said.

"It's unlikely that Meatloaf dropped his checkbook close to where Bernie was killed and that the two aren't related."

"And the ten-thousand-dollar deposit?" Victoria insisted. "On the same date?" She sipped her coffee, eyes on Domingo.

"That, I can't tell you," Domingo said. "Maybe he deposited his Social Security check."

Victoria laughed. "He's not old enough."

They drank their coffee quietly. Victoria heard a jet plane overhead. A car door slammed. The cardinal called from the lilac bush. She heard Noreen and Elizabeth laugh, the rustle of more grocery bags as they came to the door.

Domingo broke their silence. "Everyone knows you were the one who heard something in the harbor that evening, is that correct?" His look was intense.

"Yes."

"Doesn't it seem reasonable that whoever was at the scene does not want you to recall what you heard? You know how things come back to you when you hear a sound or smell, remind you of something you didn't realize you knew."

Victoria stared at him. "When Chief Medeiros pulled out of the parking lot after Liz Tate scolded him, I had a feeling I'd heard that same sound of tires on sand before."

"Did you tell anyone that?"

"I thought of it just this minute."

"Honey!" he called to Noreen, who was talking with Elizabeth in the kitchen as they unloaded groceries.

"I hear you, Domingo." She started into the living room, when the telephone rang.

Domingo answered.

"No!" He stamped his cigarette out in the ashtray. "Not Joe!" He looked up at Noreen with a stricken expression. "How'd it happen?"

Elizabeth and Victoria turned to Noreen.

"Joe Palma," Noreen said, watching Domingo with concern. "Domingo's partner in New York."

Domingo listened, his head down, chunky hands cradling the phone. "Two months before retirement," he said into the phone. "He thought he'd beat the odds."

"Oh shit!" Noreen said. "Another cop killed."

Domingo took one hand away from the phone, picked up the pen lying on the table, and doodled on the paper in front of him.

"How's Gloria taking it?" he said.

Noreen put her hands up to her face. Victoria and Elizabeth watched Domingo.

"Wake tomorrow." He looked up at Noreen. "Funeral day after tomorrow. The cathedral?"

Noreen stood frozen, hands still up at her face.

Domingo listened. He wrote something on the paper.

"Thanks. We'd appreciate that. Any room is okay." He put the pen down and ran his hand over his face. "We'll be there. Noreen and me." His gaze went from Victoria to Elizabeth to Noreen, and stopped on Noreen's face. "You got enough to think about." He looked away again. "My condolences to Gloria."

He hung up the phone and gazed at Noreen with a look of desolation that made Victoria hurt.

"Joe Palma down," Noreen said. "That's what it was?"

Domingo nodded.

Noreen dropped to her knees. She threw her arms around Domingo and cradled him. Victoria looked away.

"He was helping with a drug bust," Domingo said. "He wasn't even with the drug force. Just like him, helping out."

"Can we do anything?" Victoria asked Noreen.

"You could do me a big favor, Mrs. Trumbull," Noreen said. "I told my daughter I'd sit with my grandson tomorrow morning."

"What time?" Victoria asked.

"I have the morning shift, Gram. I can drop you off around seven, pick you up whenever," Elizabeth said.

Victoria looked questioningly at Noreen.

"The school bus comes by around ten."

"Ten?" Elizabeth asked. "That's late, isn't it?"

"Kindergarten," Noreen said.

"I'll be here," Victoria replied.

"Do you need a ride to the airport?" Elizabeth asked.

"Ernesto will take us," Noreen said.

"Leave the dock attendants in charge of the harbor when you pick up your grandmother," Domingo said. "Take care until I get back." He patted Noreen's back. "Meatloaf is supposed to stop by tomorrow to pick up some papers that need to be signed. He can wait."

"Maybe I'll be here when he comes by?" Victoria's voice rose in a question.

Domingo gave a short laugh. "You can handle him if he does."

"Let me give you some phone numbers where you can reach us in an emergency." Noreen got up from the floor.

"Don't worry about us." Victoria accepted the paper with the phone numbers, and she and Elizabeth started for the door.

"Watch yourself while I'm gone," Domingo said. "I'll get back when I can." He stood and put his arm around Noreen; she put her arm around his waist, her blond head on his chest.

"Call Chief O'Neill in West Tisbury and tell her everything we know," Domingo said. "Everything. We have to trust her."

\\ Chapter 11 //

Victoria was on her hands and knees, picking up the toys Baby Mingo had strewn around his room before he'd dashed off to catch the school bus, when she heard a knock on the door. It took her a few moments to get to her feet. She braced herself against the small bed and chair next to it and slowly straightened her legs.

She heard the knock again, more impatient-sounding.

She tossed the dump truck she was holding into the toy box and walked stiffly into the kitchen, her knees not yet adjusted from kneeling to walking. When she reached the kitchen, she could see past the table in the living room through the sliding door.

Meatloaf was pacing the small patio between the house and garage, glaring at his watch. Even though Domingo had warned her, she still had a jolt of apprehension when she saw him.

"It's after ten-thirty, for God's sake," he muttered, loudly enough for Victoria to hear. He returned to the door, cupped his hands around his face, and peered in at the same moment Victoria slid the door open.

Meatloaf stepped back. "What the hell are you doing here, lady? Where's Mingo?"

"He went to a funeral." Victoria was reluctant to say more.

"He was to leave something for me to get signed." Meatloaf was wearing his sunglasses, and Victoria realized she had never seen his eyes.

"It's there on the table," Victoria said, not moving.

He lumbered over from the doorway, shuffled through some papers at Domingo's usual place, and picked up a pile with a note clipped to the top sheet. He read the note.

"I'm supposed to bring this back when Liz Tate signs it. You going to be here this evening?"

Victoria shook her head. "I'll leave the door unlocked."

Meatloaf straightened the papers by smacking the edges on the table, picked up the manila folder that had been under them, put the papers in the folder, and headed for the door. He stopped before he got there, then turned around. Victoria was still standing in the same place, glaring at him, eyes half-closed.

"Whose funeral?" he asked.

"His partner," Victoria answered. "A New York policeman."

"His partner," Meatloaf repeated. He shook his head. "That's tough on a man, partner and all." He paused. Victoria waited.

"Killed?" he asked finally.

Victoria nodded.

"I'm sorry." Meatloaf shook his head again, pushed his sunglasses back up on his nose, and slid the door open. "I'll be by this evening. I'll leave the signed papers on his table."

Victoria remained standing until she heard his van start up and pull away. She went back to Baby Mingo's room and picked up more toys and some clothing until Elizabeth came by to take her home.

"Where's Meatloaf?" Dotty asked the regulars at the ArtCliff corner table. "Haven't seen him for several days." She chunked mugs of steaming coffee in front of Beanie, Red, and Shipyard, then swiped the vinyl tablecloth with a damp rag.

"Who knows?" Beanie said. "Last time I seen him was here. After his medi-van run." He reached for the sugar bowl.

"Probably laid up with indigestion again," Shipyard said.

"Someone ought to call his wife, find out if he's okay." Dotty reached into a rack on the wall and brought out plastic-covered menus. "Want to see the specials?"

"His wife's visiting her mother in Scranton," Red said.

"Any excuse to get away from him," said Beanie.

"Maybe someone should call his house?" Dotty suggested. "He might be sick or something."

"He's sick all right," Beanie said.

Shipyard laughed. "Sick in the head."

"You guys lay off him. He's not so bad," Dotty said.

Shipyard brayed. "He's bad all right."

"Yeah, we want to see the menu," Red said. "Not that there's anything different on it."

"Take your time." Dotty slapped menus on the table and, before she bustled back into the kitchen, said over her shoulder, "One of you guys, *his friends,* ought to check up on him, make sure he's okay."

"It's good to be home again." Noreen kicked off her high heels. "Funerals depress me."

"He was a good cop, a good partner." Domingo stood next to the table and stared blankly at his harpoons. "I'll miss him."

"New York does cop funerals the way they ought to be done," Noreen said.

"He was going to visit this fall," Domingo said. "Kept promising me."

"I'll invite Gloria to come. Once she's had a little time," Noreen said. "She'll need to get away."

Domingo stared at the wall.

"You still look pretty good in your uniform, Domingo," Noreen said softly. "It still fits you and everything. You still got the ladies making eyes at you."

"A harpoon is missing." Domingo focused on the display.

"Cops were lined up from the station house to the cathedral. Must of been three blocks. Solid blue."

"It was there when we left three days ago."

"Maybe Ernesto took it." Noreen shrugged out of her rumpled linen jacket.

Domingo, standing in the middle of the living room floor, examined the harpoons, the couch, the floor, the table.

"Something's not right," he said.

"Because of the harpoon?" Noreen

picked up her shoes.

"Yes, among other things."

"You never told Meatloaf you couldn't meet with him, did you?" said Noreen. "Maybe he came by."

"He came by all right," Domingo said. "He got the papers signed and returned them. They're on the table."

"Maybe he took your harpoon." Noreen pulled off her panty hose and twisted them around her hand. "I gotta change."

When she returned, in jeans and a blue sweatshirt emblazoned with MARTHA'S VINEYARD, PRESIDENTIAL RETREAT across the front, Domingo was on the phone talking to Victoria.

"You're saying, sweetheart, all he did was take the papers and leave, is that correct?" Domingo said. "You weren't here when he returned them, were you?" He paced the length of the living room with the cordless phone held against his ear. "Did he say anything out of the ordinary to you?" Domingo laughed and repeated, "Polite!" He laughed again, then got serious. "Did he say anything about a harpoon?" While he talked, he faced the wall. "One's missing. Was it there when you came by in the morning, sweetheart? Did you notice?" Victoria responded, and he grinned suddenly. "You'd have made a good cop, sweetheart."

After he hung up, Domingo stood, feet apart, his thumbs hooked in the pockets of his good trousers, his blazer open, his tie askew, his eyes studying the harpoons, the couch, the floor.

Noreen looked closely at her husband. "What's bothering you, Domingo? Is it more than the harpoon?"

"Somebody wrenched the harpoon out of the display. See how the edge of the wooden bracket is chipped?" He pointed with two fingers of his right hand, an unlighted cigarette between them.

Noreen leaned over the couch and found the broken-off piece. "You can fix it, can't you?"

Domingo continued as if he hadn't heard. "There was another person here. See the marks on the rug? The rug nap is twisted."

"Not Victoria wrestling with Baby Mingo, was it?"

Domingo grinned. "I don't think so, honey."

"Want to call Meatloaf? Find out if he took it?"

"Not particularly. I'll ask him when I see him at the next selectmen's meeting. I'm in

229

no hurry to talk to him."

The whale-watch boat left Vineyard Haven at 7:00 a.m., heading southeast on Nantucket Sound toward Georges Bank. Some twenty people were on board, including several families with small children. The morning sun shone on puffy clouds, the sky was a brilliant blue, and a brisk wind kicked up whitecaps on the Sound.

"We've seen quite a few pods of whales during the last week," the marine mammals student observer announced over the loudspeaker. "We're still too close to the Island, but within the next hour, we should begin to see them. While we cruise out to the whale grounds, there are sodas and hot dogs for sale in the galley. You'll find displays on marine mammals there, too." The loudspeaker gave out a shriek of static. "The first person to spot a whale gets a free cup of coffee. Or, if you're under twelve, a free soda."

There was a general movement of people toward the galley.

The boat headed toward Cape Poge, a recurved spit at the tip of Chappaquiddick, an island connected to the Vineyard by a narrow sandbar with a lighthouse on the point. The boat's engine thrummed; the wake curled behind them. A trail of seagulls followed, diving after small fish stirred up by the boat's passing, arguing raucously over their catch.

A cluster of children in orange life vests stood on tiptoe on the anchor in the bow so they could look over the railing.

The bow dipped into a wave and sent a spray of salt water high into the air, and a bright rainbow sparkled, then faded.

"Mama! I see a whale!" a small girl with a baseball cap on backward called out.

"A whale, a whale!" The children pointed and looked around for their parents.

The skipper had already slowed the boat. Ahead and off to port, barely visible to the naked eye, was a large floating object. It dipped beneath the surface for several seconds and rose again, turning slowly in the current.

"Ladies and gentlemen, there is something to the port, or left side, of the boat," the announcer said over the loudspeaker. "It's unusual to see a whale this close to the Island, but maybe today's our lucky day."

The boat eased closer and whitecaps slapped against the bow.

"That's no whale," a man in a purple-

and-green windbreaker growled. "Looks more like a dead cow."

The children stood on tiptoe on the anchor, holding the flat varnished railing to lift themselves higher.

The bow rose toward the sky, then slapped a wave, and the boat shuddered.

The cowlike object sank beneath the surface again, and the skipper slowed the boat to bare headway as they neared the place they had last seen it. Suddenly, it popped to the surface again, close by, and revolved slowly.

A woman screamed.

"Holy shit!" A man leaned over the rail. "A corpse!"

"Get back, kids. Get away from the bow." The mate scrambled down from the pilothouse and herded the children into the galley. "Come on, kids, free soda, on the house."

The floating corpse turned slowly in the current. Protruding from its swollen belly was the shaft of a harpoon. The corpse was bloated and green, barely recognizable as once human. Fishes, gulls, and crabs had eaten away at its flesh. An almost-intact windbreaker drifted around it like a translucent caul. As the waves washed over it, the windbreaker wafted gently, making the hideous corpse seem to have a vestige of life.

The captain's voice came over the loud-speaker.

"Ladies and gentlemen. My apologies for the delay. The Coast Guard is on its way, and we will resume the whale watch as soon as they get here."

"I wanna go home!" a little girl in pink-and-lavender jeans and matching T-shirt wailed.

The whale-watch boat, idling broadside near the floating corpse, pitched and heaved with an oily circular roll.

"I feel sick, Mommy!" a small boy with his jeans hiked up almost to his chest cried.

In a short time, the flashing blue strobe lights of a Coast Guard cutter appeared in the distance from the direction of Woods Hole, and within minutes, it pulled alongside.

The radio in the pilothouse crackled with instructions. The blue light on the Coast Guard cutter rotated. One vessel rose on the crest of a wave; the other dropped into a trough. The sky was the only stable fix, and that seemed to move in a crazy circle.

"Do we have a consensus in favor of returning to Vineyard Haven?" the student observer announced.

Passengers lined up at the rail to watch the Coast Guard crew, in orange life vests, bring the corpse next to the cutter.

"Complimentary passes for another day's trip will be available at the office when you disembark," the voice on the loudspeaker said.

The boat rolled from side to side. Its bow dipped toward the whitecaps and cycled toward the sky.

"I'm gonna throw up, Daddy!" cried a boy in tan shorts and green T-shirt printed with LLAMAS ARE LLOVELY.

The port side rolled into a wave trough, lifted, rolled toward the sky. A deck chair skidded to one side, then back to the other with a metallic scrape.

"I don't feel so good, Mommy!" a boy with greenish freckles on an even greener face said.

"Get over to the other side of the boat, quick!"

The railing lifted toward the sky, dropped toward the water. The boat rolled; its bow corkscrewed.

"Jesus, I just had these pants cleaned."

When the whale-watch boat returned to

the harbor, earlier than scheduled, Victoria was walking along the beach near the harbor entrance, flicking over mats of seaweed with her walking stick, looking for shells and lucky stones. She glanced up in surprise. It was too nice a day for the trip to have been canceled because of weather. None of the passengers seemed to be smiling. Instead of laughter, or at least the sound of voices over the engine noise, there was an uneasy silence.

Victoria hustled back to the harbormaster's shack as fast as she could move, along the beach, up the steep wooden steps that led to the top of the low bluff, holding the railing tightly. She walked through the parking lot, lifting her feet so she wouldn't trip, and stepped onto the catwalk that led to the shack.

By the time she reached the shack, the whale-watch boat was tied up to the bulkhead where the passenger ferry usually docked.

Elizabeth was standing on the deck outside the shack, looking toward the boat, her hands in the pockets of her shorts, her feet slightly apart.

She greeted Victoria. "Did you hear what happened?"

Passengers were walking slowly down the

gangplank, not looking around the way debarking passengers usually did.

"Something serious, from the look of it," Victoria said.

"They found a body."

Victoria sat down on the bench to catch her breath. "In the Sound?" she asked. "Anybody local?"

"Nobody knows yet. The body has been in the water a couple of days. They know it was a man, but that's about all."

"Was it a fisherman?"

"I don't think they can tell, Gram."

"I suppose he wasn't wearing a life jacket." Victoria shook her head. "Accidents happen so quickly on a boat."

"This wasn't an accident." Elizabeth looked down at her feet and thrust her hands more deeply into her pockets. "Somebody killed him."

"How could they tell?" Victoria continued to shade her eyes with her hand as she studied Elizabeth.

"The weapon was still in the body," Elizabeth said.

"Weapon?" Victoria said blankly.

"A harpoon," Elizabeth replied finally. "He was harpooned."

Victoria stood up abruptly, and the bench fell against the side of the shack.

"Harpooned? Are you sure?"

"I listened to the whole thing on the marine radio. The whale-watch boat found the body and called the Coast Guard. I heard the whole thing in detail."

"I've got to call Domingo." Victoria stepped over the high sill into the shack and reached for the wall phone. "I've got to let him know immediately."

"He probably knows already," Elizabeth said, following her grandmother into the shack. "He and Noreen have a scanner."

"Not a marine radio, though," Victoria said as she dialed. "I don't believe they can pick up ship-to-ship transmissions."

It took several rings before Domingo answered sleepily. "Yas," he said.

"You were napping," Victoria said.

Domingo yawned. "What is it, sweetheart?"

"They found your harpoon," Victoria said.

"What are you talking about?" Domingo's voice was instantly alert. "Where? Who's 'they'?"

Victoria told him what Elizabeth had said.

"I'll be right there. No idea whose body it is?"

"Elizabeth said it had been in the water several days."

By the time Domingo arrived at the harbor in Ernesto's truck, the passengers from the whale-watch boat had left. Elizabeth repeated what she'd heard on the marine VHF radio. Domingo paced back and forth on the deck in front of the shack.

"The Coast Guard will take the body to Falmouth," he said almost to himself. "I'll find out from the state police whose body it is, when they identify it. Two killings in two weeks."

"You think they're related?" Victoria was sitting on the bench again, her back to the shingled wall, wearing her straw hat. The yellow ribbons drifted around her. She pulled down the brim to shade her eyes, then rubbed her neck.

Domingo paced back and forth before he answered. "I don't like to speculate," he said.

\\ Chapter 12 //

"Mingo. You don't mind if I come in." A statement, not a question. Police Chief Medeiros, creased motorcycle pants tucked into polished leather boots, a shiny Sam Browne belt across his slightly bulging uniform shirt, slid the door open and strode in, a uniformed patrolman behind him. The visor of the chief's garrison cap was pulled low on his brow, touching the rims of his reflective sunglasses, its flat top bent sharply up in front. His glance stopped at the display rack.

"I see you're missing one of your harpoons." The chief set his knuckles on his hips near the gun on his belt, arms akimbo.

"Yas." Domingo had come from the kitchen when the chief entered. He stood at the top of the step and waited.

The patrolman slid the door shut behind him.

"Hate to do this, Mingo, but I'm taking you in."

"May I ask why?"

"You know why." The chief moved his

feet apart with a thump.

"Why don't you tell me."

"We found your harpoon, Mingo."

"Mind telling me where you found it?" Domingo said.

"Don't play dumb with me." The chief stepped closer to Domingo, hands still on his hips.

Domingo stared at the reflective lenses of the chief's sunglasses and saw himself.

"Funny guy, aren't you, Mingo," the chief said. "The Coast Guard found it. Rather, a bunch of whale watchers found it."

"Oh?"

"Real pleasant thing for kids to find. Real pleasant." The chief lowered his arms, held them slightly away from his sides. "Come along, Mingo."

"You're not taking me anywhere until you tell me what you're talking about."

"They found the body, Mingo. The body. With your harpoon stuck in its gut."

Domingo stared at his reflection in the chief's glasses. "Whose body was it?"

"You know goddamned well who it was, Mingo." The chief rocked onto his toes and loomed over the short, dark man.

"Tell me anyway."

"Your good friend, Mingo. That's who it

was." The chief rocked from his toes to his heels and back to his toes. "Meatloaf."

"Meatloaf," Domingo said. "You think I had something to do with it."

"Riiight. We think you had something to do with it."

"And you're taking me to the Dukes County House of Corrections on suspicion, right?"

"Riiight again, Mingo," the chief said. "You coming along of your own volition? Or do we take you in?"

"Let me tell my wife."

"Go with him, Bobby." The chief nodded to the patrolman, his sunglasses fixed on Domingo. "Don't try anything funny, Mingo."

"Yeah, sure." Domingo turned his back on the chief and went through the kitchen to find Noreen.

Elizabeth and Howland were working in the harbormaster's shack when the news came over the scanner that Chief Medeiros was taking Domingo into custody for Meatloaf's murder.

"So!" Howland looked up from the computer. "The whale-watch corpse was Meatloaf's. That figures."

"What do you mean by that?" Elizabeth

turned in her chair to stare at Howland. "Domingo couldn't have killed Meatloaf. He and Noreen were off-Island for Joe's funeral."

"Joe?" Howland questioned.

"His partner when he was a New York cop."

By now, everyone on the Island knew about the whale-watch discovery, and everyone knew about the harpoon. Before long, everyone would know whose body it was, and everyone would know Domingo had been arrested on suspicion of murder.

"They'll have him out soon enough." Howland moved a pile of receipts next to him and began to enter data into the computer. "As soon as he can verify where he's been the past few days, they'll release him."

The catwalk swayed, and Elizabeth looked up, to see the skipper of one of the fishing boats docked in the harbor. She went to the window, tugging down her shorts as she did.

"Here's my monthly dockage check." The fisherman opened an atlas-size checkbook, signed a check with a flourish, tore it out of the book, and handed it to Elizabeth. "What's happening with the boss? Hear he harpooned Meatloaf."

Elizabeth shook her head. "No way."

"If he needs defense money, legal fees, you know, there are a bunch of us ready to contribute."

"Thanks. I'll tell him." Elizabeth stamped the back of the check and put it in the drawer.

"Tell him he's done the Island a service." The fisherman gave her a kind of salute, fingertips touching the visor of his cap.

Elizabeth slapped the windowsill. "He didn't do it!"

The fisherman grinned at her. "Whatever you say, lady."

She slammed the window shut and went back to the desk. "Ghoul," she muttered.

"Who had access to the harpoons?" Howland asked her.

"Everyone. They don't lock their doors unless Domingo's taking a siesta." She put away the receipt book. "By the way, do you know anything about the broken railing?"

"What broken railing?"

"On the far side of the shack. It's broken off, splintered."

"Let's take a look."

They stepped onto the deck and around to the side facing the Sound, where the railing was hidden by the shack.

"Someone could get hurt on those

jagged ends." Elizabeth braced her hands on either side of the gap in the railing and examined the fresh break.

"Looks as if someone's already been hurt." Howland knelt on the deck and examined it. "Looks like blood on the broken end. As if someone grabbed at it and got a fistful of splinters."

"I'll bet it was those dock attendants. They're like animals, always throwing punches and wrestling."

"Strange. Very strange." Howland leaned out over the water, holding the unbroken part of the railing for support as he examined the back side.

"What are you thinking?" Elizabeth stood up straight, her hands braced on the flat top rail, and watched Howland.

"I'm not sure what I'm thinking. An idea came to me, and I lost it again."

"Something to do with this broken section?" Elizabeth moved away from the gap and leaned against the side of the shack.

Howland nodded. "It couldn't have been the kids."

"Why not?"

"They're not heavy enough, any of them."

"Even if one gave a good shove?"

Howland shook his head. "Something

244

heavy went through this."

"Like what?" Elizabeth tilted her head. "A Harley-Davidson? I mean, you don't get something heavy down the catwalk unless it's on wheels, or walks." She stopped. "Or walks," she repeated.

"Yeah," said Howland.

"Someone big and heavy." She pushed herself away from the side of the shack. "Like Meatloaf."

"Yeah." Howland got to his feet and faced her.

Elizabeth looked down and saw a school of small fish swimming around the pilings, nibbling microscopic food that washed past. She could see the bottom through the clear water.

"The whale-watch boat found his body somewhere around Cape Poge." Howland indicated the water eddying around the pilings. A long streamer of seaweed wafted toward the channel that led into the Sound. "If he'd been killed here before the tide turned, the current would have carried his body out."

Elizabeth started toward the shack door, then stopped abruptly and turned to Howland. "You know, the night we found Bernie Marble's corpse, Domingo remarked that the tide was about to change."

She gazed across the harbor, past the channel, past the osprey pole, to the dock on the far side.

Howland, one hand on the unbroken section, waited.

Elizabeth continued after a pause. A breeze lifted her hair, flicked the collar on her shirt. "The chief said something that seemed odd at the time." She jammed both hands in her pockets.

"What did he say?" Howland asked sharply.

"Something like, 'What bad timing.' Words to that effect."

"Possibly referring to finding Bernie's body before the tide carried it out of the harbor?" Howland said almost to himself. "Two murders, almost the same. Kill the guy, dump the body in the harbor on an outgoing tide."

"The railing seems like such blatant evidence," Elizabeth said. "Whatever happened must have been on the spur of the moment."

"Whoever did it would hardly be likely to fix it," Howland said. "Of course, it took several days for us to notice it."

"Domingo would have seen it right away. This is where he comes to pee when no one's looking."

Howland ignored her and looked again at the underside of the railing. "What possible connection did Meatloaf have to Domingo's harpoon?" He peered into the water.

"Meatloaf was supposed to stop by Domingo's with some papers the day after the call about Joe."

"That would give Meatloaf access to it. But how did it end up in him?" Howland rubbed his chin. "It throws suspicion on Domingo, whether we like it or not. Do we know he was off-Island?"

"Of course we do," Elizabeth said hotly. "If Domingo is going to murder someone, it won't be with his own harpoon."

Howland changed the subject. "We need to make some kind of temporary repair to the railing."

"I've got some yellow tape." Elizabeth stepped inside and opened one of the desk drawers. "Until Domingo gets out of jail, I guess I'm in charge. I'll call the town maintenance guy."

Once they had strung the fluorescent yellow tape across the gap in the railing, Howland returned to the computer, and Elizabeth made her phone call.

"They'll have someone here first thing tomorrow." She picked up the stack of receipts and dealt them into separate piles.

After a few minutes, Howland said, "Meatloaf had plenty of enemies, but he also had some allies."

"Victoria thinks Meatloaf killed Bernie. Do you suppose the same person killed them both?" Elizabeth paused to look over her shoulder at Howland.

"Could be. Same modus. Violent death by a nasty weapon. Both bodies in the harbor. Meatloaf worked with Bernie at the hotel. There may be some connection we don't know about." Howland continued to enter data while he talked.

"At least we won't have to worry about my grandmother anymore. She was convinced Meatloaf was following her." Elizabeth went back to the receipts, dealing them onto piles on the desk.

"He probably was." Howland was quiet for a few minutes. The computer keys clicked softly. Finally, he said, "We have all the more reason to worry about Victoria. Meatloaf was probably trying to frighten her. He didn't try to harm her."

"My grandmother isn't about to be frightened by some bully."

"They know that now. Next, they're likely to try to stop her from talking, period." Howland shifted the monitor slightly to shade it from the glare coming off the water.

"Who is 'they'?" Elizabeth asked. "Victoria thinks Meatloaf and the chief were in cahoots."

"Quite possibly." Howland tilted his head at the screen.

"She likes Rocky and Liz Tate."

He shook his head without looking at her. "Bad choice."

"She has her doubts about you. Your chocolate caper really threw her."

"I know." Howland leaned back in his chair.

"Don't lean in that chair. It can't take it."

He set the front two legs back on the floor with a thunk.

"What is your problem, anyway?" Elizabeth said. "You think Domingo is faking the funeral trip. That Domingo killed Meatloaf with his own harpoon. You suspect Rocky of poisoning Victoria. Did you test the chocolates? Feed them to your white mice?"

"Very funny."

"So what did you do with the poisoned chocolates?"

"There was nothing wrong with them." He looked over at her, hands still held above the keyboard.

"What a surprise. How did you determine that?" Elizabeth had turned in her chair to face him.

"I sent them to the lab for tests." He continued to stare at the computer screen, hands above the keys.

"Lab?" Elizabeth said. "What lab?"

"The FBI lab in Washington."

"What?" Elizabeth gathered up the unsorted receipts and stood up. "The FBI lab?" She stared at him. "Not just anybody can get the FBI lab to test a box of chocolates on a whim."

Howland said nothing. He stared at the screen.

"I've known you since I was a little kid and you were a big wheel in college. But I have no idea what you've been up to since then. I used to watch you play softball in Doane's pasture. I had such a crush on you. I must have been six."

Howland smiled. "You were a cute kid. I remember you with bare feet and a dirty freckled face. You still look the same."

"I haven't seen much of you for the past twenty years. Almost thirty years?" Elizabeth wrinkled her nose. "I don't even know what you do for a living."

Howland said nothing.

"I figured you retired early. On invest-
ments or something," Elizabeth said. "I
mean, you don't spend valuable time designing a computer program for free out of
the goodness of your heart. If you have to
earn a living, that is."

Howland smiled. "Domingo thinks it
will earn me a million dollars."

"But you don't. So how do you make
your living?" Elizabeth continued to stare
at him, one hand holding the receipts, the
other hand clenched in a fist on her hip.
"What are you, anyway?"

Howland pushed his chair back, and the
metal legs grated against the sandy floor.
Elizabeth winced at the sound.

He reached into his back pocket,
brought out a black leather folder, and
flipped it open. On one side was a gold
badge, on the other an ID photo. Elizabeth
took the folder and studied it.

"DEA." She looked from the badge to
Howland and back at the badge. "Drug
Enforcement Administration? What does
this mean? What are you doing here? Does
Domingo know about this?"

"No." Howland stood with his hands at
his sides.

"Why not? He's a cop. A retired cop."
She handed the folder back to Howland,

who put it in his pocket.

Howland said nothing.

"Why not?" Elizabeth insisted. "Why tell me and not him?"

"I wasn't sure I could trust him, that's why."

"Why trust me and not him?" Elizabeth glared at him.

Howland averted his eyes. "You don't fit the profile."

"Profile!" Elizabeth sputtered. "Profile! Domingo's a mouthy black guy who puts on a dumb act, so he fits your profile?" Her face reddened, her freckles stood out on her nose. "I'm not a suspected drug pusher, but Domingo is, because of your profile?"

"Hey." Howland put up both hands as if to ward her off. "Profiles are a valid place to start. Otherwise, the list of persons suspected of drug trafficking would be unwieldy."

"My God! You sound like a bureaucrat. 'Unwieldy' indeed. You're talking about human beings."

"Exactly," Howland said. "Traffickers destroy human beings, fry their brains, impoverish them." He thrust his hands into his pants pockets. "And you're in a dither because we narrow down a list of suspects by using a profile? You think we're trespassing on people's rights? Get real, Elizabeth."

" 'Get real'?" Elizabeth flung the pack of receipts she had been holding at Howland. "Get real yourself, you fascist!" Receipts flew onto the counter, splayed out on the floor. One landed on Howland's shoe. He wriggled his toe, and the receipt slid off. Elizabeth wrenched the door open. A gust of wind coming through it tossed the papers into the air, spiraled them down onto the floor in a blizzard of receipts.

She turned. "Fascist!" she said again, and slammed the door behind her. She pounded down the catwalk.

Allison was coming up the catwalk toward her, and Elizabeth brushed past her, spinning her around. Allison was wearing a knit orange halter that exposed her navel, the pierced flesh sporting a gold ring. Her ragged cutoff jeans exposed as much bare skin as a bikini bottom. Elizabeth didn't see her.

"Hey!" Allison said. "What do you think you're doing?"

"Get lost," Elizabeth snapped.

Allison watched, wide-eyed, as Elizabeth got into her car, started it, and skidded out of the lot. Allison flipped her long curls out of her face with one hand and opened the shack door.

"What's with her?" she said to Howland, who was standing in the middle of the floor.

Howland focused on her suddenly. He pointed to the receipts strewn around the shack. "Pick those up," he ordered.

"Hey!" Allison said.

"Pick them up," Howland said again.

"You're not my —"

Howland turned on her. "Do it."

"But it's not my —"

He glared at her.

"Okay, okay. I'll pick them up." Allison knelt on the floor and gathered up the loose receipts, scooped them off the counter, and evened them on the desktop.

"Get busy," Howland growled. "Sort."

"But —"

"Sort!"

She sat at the desk, her back to Howland, and fiddled with the receipts. He worked furiously at the computer. The only sounds were the soft clicking of his keyboard, the gurgling of the water around the pilings, the cry of the osprey returning to its nest, and the hum of a boat engine in the distance.

After some minutes, Allison turned and

said, "I just stopped by to see how Mr. D. is doing. I heard about him being picked up, you know?"

"What do you care about Mr. D.?" Howland said curtly. "As I recall, you have a suit pending against him."

"Mr. D. didn't do anything funny. He just yelled at me."

"Tell it to the judge."

"My aunt Liz filed it. I told her it wasn't nothing." She bent her head over the piles on the desk. "She made me sign it."

"Yeah, yeah," Howland said. "Sort the receipts."

"Am I getting paid for doing this? I'm not supposed to work today, you know?"

"No," Howland said. "Tell that to your auntie."

"Her and me don't get along too good," Allison said. "I don't tell her much." She worked quietly for a few minutes. "Who's in charge of the harbor today? Mr. D. is in jail, and Elizabeth looks as if she just quit. You in charge?"

"Ask your auntie," Howland said grimly.

\\ Chapter 13 //

Victoria stopped in front of the Harbor House, perspiring and out of breath. She could see Domingo across the water, leaning over the rail of the shack, smoking. By the time she reached the end of the catwalk, he was waiting for her.

"I don't know when I've been so hot." Victoria flapped the sides of her light jacket to air herself. "Where's Elizabeth?"

"She's not here yet." Domingo flicked his cigarette into the water and offered her his arm, which she took.

"I really came to hear about your prison experience."

"That's the first time I have ever been locked up. It's not something I want to do again, sweetheart."

"It's such a nice jail." Victoria stopped to catch her breath. "Whew! It's muggy. How do you manage to look so cool?"

Domingo raised his eyebrows quizzically. His shirt was rumpled. Sweaty dark patches stuck to his back and under his arms. "Cool?" He pulled his shirt away from his stomach.

Across the Sound, thunderheads were building over the mainland, their tops towering into the sky, flattened by winds aloft. The heavy cloud bottoms were dark and ominous.

"Not many jails are white clapboard like ours," Victoria continued. "Black shutters, pink roses growing on a wrought-iron fence. It's really quite a lovely jail."

"It's a place of incarceration." Domingo stood aside at the door to let her enter first. "A long time ago, I had a career choice: Be a crook and get rich or —"

"You'd have made a good crook."

"Or become a cop. Cops usually don't get locked up. I didn't want to get locked up, ever."

"Does the chief think you murdered Meatloaf?" Victoria sat in one of the aluminum chairs and fanned herself with a "Say No to Drugs!" pamphlet that was lying on the desk.

"The chief suspects I used my own harpoon because no one would think I could be that stupid. He's convinced I conjured up an alibi. Joe, my partner, shot and killed." Domingo crossed himself, looked skyward, and changed the subject abruptly.

"Your buddy shared the holding cell with me."

"My buddy?" Victoria stopped fanning herself.

"Dojan."

"What was he doing in jail?"

"They picked him up for creating a disturbance. Dojan was doing a war dance in the middle of Circuit Avenue. Traffic couldn't get around him."

"Instead of tossing him into jail, why didn't they simply escort him to the sidewalk? He's such a gentle person."

A muggy breeze eddied through the open door. Victoria ran her hand around the back of her neck. "Think what it must be like on the mainland. I hope we get a thunderstorm soon."

"They're calling for heavy showers later this evening." Domingo studied the clouds building over the mainland. "The police tried, unsuccessfully, to escort Dojan out of the middle of the street. In fact, several officers were on the scene. Dojan took exception to their escorting him. He blackened a few eyes and noses, loosened a few teeth, broke a couple of ribs, and, in general, left a trail of other people's blood behind him."

"Something must have upset him."

"I believe he'd stopped at the Sand Bar."

Domingo stepped to the door, his thumbs hooked in his pockets. The surface of the harbor was an oily calm; the air felt heavy. Cicadas shrilled on the shore and the osprey soared high over the nesting pole.

"I didn't think he drank."

Domingo turned to her. "He doesn't." He shrugged, walked to the end of the deck, and turned. His glance stopped at the broken railing festooned with yellow tape. "What happened here?"

"Elizabeth said they were supposed to have fixed it. She was going to ask if you knew."

Domingo leaned down and inspected the splintered ends. "I have a good idea about what happened." He checked his watch. "Where is she?"

"What time is it?"

"Three-thirty. She was scheduled for three." He paced the small deck. "She's a half hour late."

"I wonder if she had car trouble."

"She can always get to a phone." Domingo paced. "Did she say anything about a meeting? Or errands? Getting her car fixed? That VW of hers is a piece of junk."

"She didn't say anything to me about being late."

"Call home, sweetheart. See if she's left." He handed the telephone to Victoria, who dialed and let it ring several times. The answering machine picked up.

"No answer." Victoria handed the phone back to him.

"Was she coming directly from home?"

Victoria shook her head. "I have no idea."

"What route does she usually take to get here?"

"It varies," Victoria said. "Usually, she goes past the airport."

Domingo tugged the visor of his cap down over his brows. "I'm calling Chief O'Neill. Have her check your house." He took down the telephone book that was hanging on a string under the phone, wet his finger, and paged through the *W* listings.

"West Tisbury Police Department," he mumbled to himself. He held the phone book at arm's length, grunted, then tugged his glasses out of his pocket and set them on his nose. "I'll ask her to see if they spot your granddaughter on the road."

"This isn't like her at all." Victoria stood to get a better view of the road and the cars on it. "She hates being late."

Domingo dialed.

"Wait, Domingo, I think I see her car now." Victoria stepped out onto the deck.

Domingo slammed the phone back on the wall. "She'd better have a good excuse." He looked at his watch.

When Elizabeth came up the catwalk, her face was flushed. Her usually crisp shirt was rumpled and soiled. Domingo met her at the door of the shack, his thumbs hooked on his pockets.

"Well?"

"Am I glad to be here."

"What happened?" Victoria said. "We were worried."

Elizabeth pushed past Domingo, went into the shack, and flopped into a chair. "I've had a horrible afternoon, so far. It can't get any worse."

"This had better be good." Domingo leaned his elbows on the railing. He pushed his cap back on his forehead and glared through the door at Elizabeth.

"I got held up by a bunch of small accidents. First, there was a big branch down in the drive that I had to move. Then I skidded on a patch of oil on Barnes Road, turned a hundred and eighty degrees. Fortunately, there was no traffic coming the other way."

"How frightening," Victoria said.

"Then the road was blocked by a pickup with two flat tires."

"You might have called," Domingo said.

Victoria was aware of the sound of water below them, swishing past the pilings of the shack.

"I thought I'd better get here as soon as I could. The nearest public phone is almost at the harbor, anyway."

Domingo looked steadily at Elizabeth. "Interesting." He glanced from Victoria to Elizabeth. "I'm calling in an extra dock attendant to be on duty tonight. I don't like what's going on."

"I don't have any problem handling the evening shift," Elizabeth said defensively.

"I'm sure you don't. But until this is over, I don't want you working alone at night." Domingo stepped over the sill and checked the list of phone numbers posted on the wall.

Elizabeth snorted. "Thanks a whole lot."

"Where is Howland?" Victoria asked Domingo. "Couldn't he come in tonight?"

Domingo dialed a number, and while it was ringing he muttered to Victoria, "Howland went on a business trip." He turned back to the phone and spoke to someone.

"Allison is coming in shortly." He hung up the phone.

"Liz Tate's niece?" Victoria had been fanning herself with the pamphlet again, but now she stopped.

Domingo nodded.

"She's the last person I want working with me on the night shift." Elizabeth went inside and flipped through some papers on the desk, her back to Domingo. Her shoulders were stiff and straight. "I don't like her. I don't trust her."

"Tough." Domingo's jaw was set. "She'll be here in a half hour. Your grandmother and I are going to the jail."

Victoria got to her feet. "To visit Dojan," she said.

When Elizabeth looked up in surprise, Domingo explained about the war dance.

She laughed. "It's not funny, I know. But I can just see him with his hair and eyes and skull scarf and feathers."

"I'd like to take something to him," Victoria said to Domingo. "Maybe candy."

Domingo nodded and turned to Elizabeth. "I'll be by later."

After he and Victoria settled into the leather seats of the white Corniche, hot from baking in the closed car, he turned on the air conditioner and a blast of hot air blew around them.

"Let's put the top down. I'd much prefer hot fresh air to that hot recycled stuff." Victoria fastened the yellow ribbon of her hat under her chin as Domingo obliged. Hazy sunlight poured into the open car.

They stopped at the store, and Domingo returned with a bag of candy. "That should hold him." He handed the paper sack to Victoria, who opened it, looked in, and smiled.

They turned right onto the shore road and followed the curve of low bluffs facing Nantucket Sound. The water was bright turquoise in the eerie light of building storm clouds. Sailboats, all headed for shelter, dotted the Sound, moving slowly in the light breeze. Victoria saw an occasional flicker of lightning in the roiling tops of clouds that billowed upward and outward, and she could hear a distant grumble of thunder. A fishing smack, its net spreaders high in the air, chugged toward Georges Bank, trailed by a flock of seagulls.

Most of the large shingled summer houses that faced the water had been converted to inns and B and Bs. On the large porches, wooden rocking chairs sat empty. As they passed, Victoria could see flickering television screens inside the houses.

"Why on earth do they spend their vacation watching TV?"

Domingo shrugged. "There's a game on."

"You'd think they could stay home in their New York apartments for that."

"They wouldn't be on Martha's Vineyard if they stayed home. They're vacationing with the president."

A car came toward them in the opposite lane; the driver lifted his hand from the wheel, and Domingo did the same. Victoria held the top of her straw hat and waved, too, ribbons fluttering as Domingo accelerated and the Rolls made its own breeze.

"Who was that?" Victoria asked.

"I have no idea." Domingo grinned.

They passed the golf club where the president would play. A car was parked by the side of the road, and a man sat next to it in a beach chair, earphones shutting him off from the sounds around him.

"Secret Service." Domingo lifted his hand from the wheel as they drove past, and the man raised his hand in return. "Aren't you going to wave to him?" he said.

The road ran along the slender barrier

bar that separated Sengekontacket Pond from the Sound and formed the bathing beach Islanders called "the Bend," a smooth arc of white sand that sloped gently into the sheltered waters of the Sound. Usually, the water shaded from transparent yellow, to green, then to deep blue. Today, though, the water was an almost tropical aqua, contrasted against the blackening sky over the mainland.

As they passed, bathers were gathering up towels and children and hurrying up paths that cut through patches of thorny wild roses to cars that were parked in an almost-solid line along the road. Even this late in the season, the roses were in bloom, some white, some red. The darkening sky accentuated the bright colors of roses and water and beach umbrellas, which bathers were rapidly taking down as the building clouds covered more and more of the northern sky.

They crossed Anthiers Bridge, which spanned one of the tidal outlets from Sengekontacket Pond. The bridge had been a setting for the movie *Jaws* more than twenty-five years earlier. Victoria and Jonathan had been extras in the movie, as had most of their friends and neighbors. Their scene had been filmed on a chilly, bright June day, and, Victoria recalled, Jonathan had gotten a painful sunburn on his insteps. She thought of Jonathan and the filming of *Jaws* every time she crossed Anthiers.

As they approached Edgartown, the slender beach widened, and the waters of Sengekontacket on their right shoaled into a broad salt marsh. Scrub oak and pine closed in on the left. They reached the outskirts of town, went past the A&P and Cannonball Park.

The jail was on Main Street, near the end of the West Tisbury-Edgartown Road, in the block before the house in which Victoria had been born. The white clapboard jail building blended in with the town's tidy architecture. Domingo parked behind it.

They went up the brick walk to the jail entrance.

Inside, the jail looked much more the way Victoria thought it should, dark and barred, with locked doors and a uniformed jailer with a gun.

"How ya doing, Mingo?" The jailer greeted him as if he were an old friend. "Long time no see." He laughed heartily and slapped Domingo on the back.

"Yo, Elmo." Domingo put his hand on

the larger man's shoulder. Elmo gave Victoria a fistful of papers. She seated herself in an institutional metal armchair and signed where Elmo told her to.

Domingo gave Elmo the paper bag. "For Dojan," he said.

"Mars bars. Milky Ways. Snickers." Elmo pawed through the assortment. "Not bad. Three Musketeers. No file?" He laughed at his joke. "I thought you already gave the Injun a box of candy. Some sweet tooth that guy must have."

Victoria, puzzled, looked from Elmo to Domingo, who was standing next to him.

"A box of candy from me? Who brought it?"

"The kid with green hair." Elmo moved some papers onto a high shelf behind him.

"Louie," Domingo said. "One of the dock attendants. Did he say who the candy came from?"

Elmo jerked his thumb toward Victoria. "Her. A box of homemade fudge. The card's here somewheres." He shuffled through a heap of papers on his desk. "Yeah. 'From Victoria Trumbull,' it says." He handed the card to Domingo.

"I didn't send him candy." Victoria stretched her neck to look at the card in

Domingo's hand. "And that's not my writing."

"When did he bring the candy?" Domingo handed the card back to Elmo.

"A couple of hours ago. I took it up to him. He didn't want none. Feeling squeamish, he said." Elmo retrieved the forms and the logbook from Victoria, who'd finished writing the required information. "Heavy-duty hangover, if you ask me. He really tied one on."

"Where is the fudge now?" Domingo asked.

"In the rec room. He told the other guys they could have it." Elmo moved behind the high counter again and put the logbook on a shelf next to the barred window.

"Can we get the box back?"

Elmo came out from behind the counter. "Indian giver, huh?" He nudged Domingo. "Get it?" He winked at Victoria. "It ain't evidence, that's for sure. I'll send someone up for it." He called up to the second floor and turned back to Domingo. "Don't want those jailbirds rotting their pretty teeth because of too much sweets here at the country club." A couple of minutes later, a young sandy-haired, acne-faced officer came down to the front desk with the open box. Four pieces of fudge were missing.

"Who ate the candy?" Domingo looked from the box to Elmo.

"What's with you, Mingo?" Elmo said. "There's plenty left for you. He'p yourself."

"Find out who ate the four missing pieces — right away," Domingo said sharply.

"Howie!" Elmo shouted, and the sandy-haired kid clattered down the stairs. "Find out who ate the fudge."

"Sir!" Howie saluted, then turned on his heel. He returned a few seconds later. "Fatso ate three, Jernegan one. If you ask me, those two guys are acting weird, high on something."

"Get the medics here — right away," Domingo barked as if he were still a New York cop. "Call nine-one-one. Call the hospital. Tell Dr. Erickson we have a case of suspected poisoning."

"Come on, Mingo, what in hell's your problem?"

"Do it. Get Fatso and Jernegan ready to go."

"Okay, okay. Druggies, both of them. If she," Elmo said, jerking his head at Victoria, "poisoned them, she should get a medal."

"Call the sheriff. Tell him to treat this box of candy as evidence. It needs to go to the forensics lab." As Elmo stood motion-less, Domingo said, "Move!"

When Elmo got off the phone, Domingo said, "I need to speak with Dojan."

He and Victoria followed Howie up the narrow wooden stairs to a long, high-ceilinged room, almost completely taken up by a scarred wooden conference table. Dojan sat at the table, hands in front of him, shaggy head bowed. He looked up when Victoria entered the room, and his bleak expression brightened.

"My friend! You came to see me!"

"How are you?" Victoria put out her hand, and Dojan took it in his grimy paws.

Howie, who had settled into a chair in the hall, scraped the chair back and stood up.

"No contact with the prisoner." He sat down again.

"I don't feel so good," Dojan said.

"I brought you some candy."

Dojan paled and shook his head. "Let the guys have it."

"I need to warn you, Dojan," Domingo said. "Don't eat anything until we get you out of here, not even jail food."

"I'm not hungry."

"And don't tell anyone what you told me this morning."

Victoria looked at Domingo in surprise. "What . . ." she started to say. Domingo put his hand on top of hers.

"The spirits got to me." Dojan's eyes were rimmed with red.

"Spirits is right," Domingo said. "Stay away from booze."

"I had to talk with the spirits. . . ."

"Don't talk to anyone, especially spirits!"

Victoria looked quizzically from one to the other. Howie sat at the doorway, within hearing. He leaned back in the chair, the front legs off the floor, the back against the banister. He began to clean his fingernails with his penknife.

"No one's pressing any charges against you," Domingo said.

"I . . . I . . ." Dojan looked around, wild-eyed.

"We'll get you out this afternoon, you understand? Don't say anything to anybody. Understand me?"

"Yes." Dojan looked down at his hands. "Yes," he said again.

Victoria put her gnarled hands on top of Dojan's. Howie tipped his chair back onto all four legs with a thump.

Victoria pulled her hands away. "When you get out, will you bring me more lobsters? I want to pay."

"Yes, ma'am." Dojan looked at her bleakly. "I'll bring you lobsters. You don't owe me nothing."

Howie stood, pulling up his uniform trousers by his gun belt, which was dragging them down around his slim hips.

"Time's up."

"Take care, Dojan." Domingo rose to his feet.

Dojan's eyes wobbled from Domingo's face to Victoria's.

"Maybe sometime you'll show me your boat," Victoria said.

Dojan cracked a small smile. "I can take you out in my boat. I can take you lobstering. You can help me pull my lobster pots."

Domingo's eyes went from Dojan to Victoria. He started to say something, then seemed to think better of it.

"Yes," Victoria said. "I'd like that."

When they were out on the brick walk that led away from the jail, Domingo took her elbow. "You don't want to go out in that leaky bucket of his."

"I don't know why not," Victoria said tartly, her mouth a firm line. "I'm perfectly capable of hauling lobster pots."

"I guess you are," Domingo said. "Yes. I guess you are."

273

★ ★ ★

When they arrived at the hospital, the ambulance had already pulled up in the emergency room bay. Domingo glanced at the sky and put the top back up on his Rolls. Victoria watched as the EMTs unloaded Fatso and Jernegan from the ambulance, and she and Domingo followed them through the wide doors. Both men were strapped onto wheeled stretchers. A uniformed man stood to one side of the stretchers, and Victoria recognized Howie, the freckle-faced jail attendant.

As they entered the emergency room, Victoria heard an orderly say, "They're both on something, that's for sure."

Fatso was straining to get to a sitting position. His eyes were wide open, and the irises were so huge, Victoria couldn't tell what color they were.

"Let me outta this fucking straitjacket before I beat the shit out of all of yous." Fatso gasped for air, and the straps creaked.

"Chill it, man," the orderly said.

"Jesus Christ, get them fucking spiders offa me!" Fatso screamed and strained against the straps. The stretcher flexed and creaked with his movements.

On the other stretcher, Jernegan, whose

eyes were shut, kept gasping in a weak voice, "Water! Water!"

Victoria watched in awe from a safe distance.

Domingo took her arm and led her to the row of seats in the waiting section. "Sit here, sweetheart, until we know what this is all about."

It seemed a long time before Dr. Erickson came out of the examining room. He was shaking his head.

"Domingo, we got to contact their families. They're sick puppies, both of them."

Victoria left the *Vogue* magazine she had been thumbing through on the table next to her seat.

"Are they going to be all right?" She joined Dr. Erickson and Domingo by the examining room's door.

"One probably will. The other" — Dr. Erickson waggled his hand, palm down — "I'm not so sure about." He took off his glasses and slipped them into the pocket of his white lab coat. "We've pumped both stomachs. Flushing them with a weak solution of tannic acid now. Found remains of chocolate in both."

"Any idea what poison?" Domingo reached unconsciously for his cigarettes, and patted his shirt pocket instead.

"We're analyzing stomach contents now, as we speak," Dr. Erickson said. "Don't know yet."

"You got a best guess?" Domingo put his hands in his trouser pockets and paced a couple of steps from the doctor and back again.

"Well . . ." Dr. Erickson said, drawing the word out. "Dilated eyes. Rapid pulse. Aggressive behavior. Hallucinations. Thirst. Flushed skin. Could be several things." He unbuttoned his lab coat and put his hands in the pockets of his tan slacks, flipping his coat behind him. "You think it might have been administered in the fudge, eh? Not something they had for lunch that might already be digested?"

"Fudge," Domingo said.

"How long ago?"

"Couple of hours at most."

"Well . . ." Dr. Erickson drew the word out again. "An easy poison to acquire, the right symptoms, same time frame from time of administration to appearance of symptoms would be atropine." He stuck his jaw out and nibbled at his pale mustache with slightly crooked ivory-colored lower teeth.

"Atropine?" Domingo said thoughtfully. "Belladonna. Deadly nightshade."

Victoria made a choking sound and put her hand to her mouth. Domingo stopped his pacing, scowled at her, then turned back to the doctor.

"Easy to acquire?"

"Deadly nightshade grows everywhere on this Island. Every part of it is poisonous — roots, leaves, flowers, berries." Dr. Erickson glanced at Victoria, who seemed to be about to say something. He continued. "Easy to make an infusion and doctor whatever you want to doctor. Inject it into mashed potatoes. Chop up the berries and mix them into fudge. Add it to someone's drink. Doesn't take much. One berry can be fatal to a child. Surprising it isn't used more."

"They use atropine to dilate eyes for examinations, don't they?" Victoria asked.

"They used to. In minuscule quantities." Dr. Erickson turned to an orderly who'd come out of the examining room. "Yes?"

The orderly looked at Victoria, at Domingo, then back at the doctor.

Outside, the sky had turned a greenish black. Newly planted trees in the small garden outside the waiting room windows whipped back and forth against their supports. The trickle of water in the fountain blew to one side. Leaves and small branches whirled across the grass and pelted the large windows.

"Speak up," Dr. Erickson said. "Problems?"

"The larger man" — the orderly consulted his clipboard — "Medeiros, has lapsed into coma. Vital signs are weak and getting weaker. His heartbeat is loud, but erratic."

"Still flushing his stomach?"

"Yes. It's clear solution."

"Discontinue it. Get their families here immediately."

Rain suddenly began to hammer against the windows. Lightning illuminated the small garden in the courtyard outside. Thunder rattled the windows.

"Medeiros?" Domingo said. "What's his first name?"

The orderly consulted the clipboard again. "Manuel."

Domingo patted his shirt pocket and paced. Victoria stood there, feet slightly apart, her arched-up toe protruding through the hole in her shoe, hands hanging quietly at her sides. Domingo stopped pacing abruptly.

"How old is Medeiros?"

Dr. Erickson consulted the clipboard the orderly held. "Twenty-two."

"Which Medeiros is he?"

"I don't know," Dr. Erickson said. "A hell of a lot of Medeiros on this Island." He turned to the orderly, who was standing beside him. "The jail will have the number for his folks. Get them here right away."

The lightning flashed. Rain beat against the windows. Thunder crashed. A nurse walked past with a sheaf of green forms in her hand, her shoes squeaking on the linoleum. In the waiting room around the corner, a baby cried. Victoria sat down again and picked up the copy of *Vogue* she'd been looking through. A soft voice came over the speaker, "Dr. Montrowl to Obstetrics. Dr. Montrowl to Obstetrics." The rain slashed outside the windows.

The wide emergency room doors were flung open, and Chief Medeiros strode into the room, yellow foul-weather jacket glistening and dripping rainwater. His boots left wet puddles on the linoleum floor. He threw back the hood of his jacket. His garrison cap was in place, visor straight on his brow, flat top curved sharply up in front. He pulled open his jacket with the ripping sound of Velcro disconnecting.

"What's this all about, Doc?"

Dr. Erickson looked up at the much taller man. "You have a son, Manny?"

"I got a son Manny," the chief said. "In jail at the moment. What's the kid done now?"

Victoria's eyes widened.

Domingo stopped pacing and stared from the chief to Dr. Erickson and back at the chief.

"Bad news," Dr. Erickson said. "Your son is here, and it doesn't look good."

"What happened? He was in jail, safe."

"Suspected poisoning." Dr. Erickson looked down at the floor and rocked onto his toes. "Administered in jail."

"How in hell did he get hold of poison?"

"You'd better see him right away. What about his mother?"

The chief winced. "She's on the West Coast somewhere. She has nothing to do with the kid. Where's he at?"

Dr. Erickson led the chief into the curtained-off examining room. Medeiros's boots squished on the floor. He came out almost immediately.

"He doesn't know me." The chief whirled on Dr. Erickson. "Don't stand there! You, Mingo. Who slipped drugs to him? Who?"

Domingo turned and gazed out the

280

window at the storm pelting the little garden.

The chief glared at Domingo's back. "My kid's a pothead. This isn't pot." He marched back and forth, his boots squishing. "What did you have to do with this, Mingo?"

Domingo said nothing.

The chief turned to Dr. Erickson. "Save that kid of mine, whatever it takes." He poked his forefinger into Dr. Erickson's madras-clad chest.

"We're doing everything we can." Dr. Erickson hunched his shoulders, hands back in the pockets of his chino slacks, lab coat behind him. "We can't do much at this point."

The chief marched back into the examining room and out again.

"Helicopter him to Boston. Get the Coast Guard here. If anything happens to that kid of mine, you'll never practice medicine again. Anywhere. You get me?"

A jagged fork of lightning slammed into the fountain in the patio garden outside the window, turning it for an instant into a fluorescent yellow-green torch. Thunder exploded, rattling windows. A woman in the waiting room screamed and put her hands over her ears. The hospital lights dimmed and went out, then came back on almost instantaneously with the sound of a generator kicking on. Rain beat against the building, slammed the roof, poured down the windows, flowed in wide lakes of water, mud, and gravel across the concrete walkway on the other side of the garden.

A few minutes later, an orderly reported to Dr. Erickson. Victoria heard him say quietly, "The medevac helicopter can't get to the Island. They'd route it through Providence, but the wind is too strong."

"Shit!" The chief slammed his hand onto the admitting desk.

"If the substance he ingested is what I think it is, atropine," Dr. Erickson told the police chief, who was pacing again, "everything that can possibly be done has been done." The chief glowered as he continued. "There's no known antidote. Boston can't save him."

The chief flung off his yellow slicker, threw it onto a chair. It slid onto the floor. Victoria picked it up and put it over the back of the chair. Domingo gazed past the sheet of water that poured off the roof.

Manuel Medeiros had a series of convulsions, one after another, in the emergency treatment room, then straightened out his body, arched his back, gasped, and lay still.

Chief Medeiros was with his son at the end. He laid his hand on his dead son's chest, put his head down, and wept.

\\ Chapter 14 //

Neither Victoria nor Domingo had much to say on the way back to West Tisbury. The death of Chief Medeiros's son was too appalling to discuss. The storm had moved on to the southwest and was now only a distant flicker and rumble in the evening sky. Domingo drove by way of Vineyard Haven. The power was still off and houses and shops were dark; the few streetlights that marked intersections were out. They passed white ComElectric trucks parked by the side of the road. Workers in hard hats conferred with one another, looked up at transformers, pointed to lines.

"I must say, it's pleasant with the electricity off," Victoria said. "I wouldn't mind if they didn't get it back for a few days. There's too much light pollution."

As they drove up the hill by Tisbury Meadow, branches and leaves littered the road. They crossed a wash of sand and gravel, dodging football-size rocks. Near the Chicama Vineyards road, they moved over into the oncoming lane because a

284

downed tree blocked their way.

The sun settled behind the receding storm clouds, and brilliant rays shot high into the clear sky. Scarlet and crimson edged the clouds. As Domingo negotiated Victoria's rutted driveway, the sun set over Doane's pasture, and while they watched, the vivid colors changed to muted rose and purple.

When Domingo opened the door for Victoria, McCavity flipped himself over on his back in the driveway and rolled back and forth, soft belly and paws in the air, eyes closed.

They walked to the kitchen door. In the entry, tucked under a shingle next to the WELCOME FRIENDS sign, was a yellow paper.

"What's that?" Domingo nodded at the paper.

"The fuel bill." She tugged the yellow slip out from under the shingle. A second folded paper fell onto the brick floor. Victoria picked it up. "Here's a note from someone."

"From Packer's Oil?" Domingo leaned over her shoulder.

Victoria unfolded the paper. "No. It's not signed." She turned it over. "I don't recognize the writing. Let's go inside. I'll turn the light on so we can read it."

"You got a generator?"

Victoria laughed. "I wasn't thinking." She set her pocketbook on the ancient captain's chair inside the door. "I suppose there are advantages to electricity. I'll get candles."

"Where is everybody?" Domingo walked into the living room and back into the kitchen. "The guy in the shack out back?"

"It's not a shack; it's a cottage. He works late."

"What about the artist in the attic. Angelo?"

"He went to Boston this morning to see the exhibit at the Fine Arts Museum." Victoria felt her way through the darkening rooms, reached the front hall, and returned to the kitchen holding two brass candlesticks with stumpy half-burned green candles. "He planned to be back on the afternoon boat, but I'm sure the ferries weren't running in that storm."

Domingo lighted the candles with his Zippo and picked up the paper that Victoria had dropped on the kitchen table.

"Lined paper. From a stenography notebook. Why don't you see what it says before I leave." Domingo walked into the cookroom, opened the door into the bathroom, looked in, and shut it again.

Victoria held the note so the candlelight illuminated it. She read to herself, then read again.

"What does it say, sweetheart? Read it out loud."

"I can't." She handed the paper to him.

Domingo held the paper in one hand, took his glasses out of his pocket, shook them open, and put them on his nose.

" 'You like what happened to your granddaughter today?' it says. 'Better not recall too much more.' " He glanced up from the paper over his glasses and his dark eyes met Victoria's. He continued to read. " 'She could be number three.' "

" 'Number three'?" Victoria moved her pocketbook to the floor and sat down in the captain's chair.

"I suppose that's a reference to Bernie Marble and Meatloaf." He studied Victoria's solemn face before he continued. "I'm taking this note, if you don't mind." Victoria shook her head. "I want to talk to your police chief." He reached into his pocket for an envelope and examined it briefly. Victoria saw it was from the IRS. He put the note into it, then put the envelope back into his pocket.

"Those accidents that happened to Elizabeth today weren't really accidents, were

287

they?" Victoria leaned against the back of the chair. It had grown dark outside, and the candles made an island of light in the kitchen. Her strong features were accented by light and shadow, her large nose, her deep-set eyes. She stared into the candlelight.

"Not likely," Domingo said. "Someone thinks you're getting too close, afraid you'll recall too much and put it together."

"It's true." Victoria clasped her hands around one knee of her threadbare corduroy trousers. "Things do keep coming back to me." She stared into the flickering candle flames. "I heard a boat that night, too, I'm sure."

"It's more than your good memory, sweetheart. Someone thinks you're onto something."

"But I have no idea what that something is," Victoria said.

"Let me say the same thing to you that I said to Dojan. Don't tell anyone what you remember. They tried to scare you, didn't they, spooky looks and car chases? But they didn't." On the other side of the table, Domingo's dark face blended into the shadows. Only his eyes showed, gleaming in the soft light. "Now they're attempting to hush you up by going after your granddaughter." Domingo walked over to the east door and peered out into the blackness. "They tried to kill Dojan today, and it backfired." Lights from cars passing on the road flashed across the wall, lighting the room briefly before they moved on.

Victoria picked absently at a rough spot on the back of her hand. "Why would anyone want to harm Dojan? He's not a threat to anyone. What do they have against him?"

Domingo turned away from the east door, where he'd been staring out into the darkness. "They have a good reason to get him out of the way. He talked too freely at the jail when I was in the holding tank with him."

Victoria waited for him to explain.

"I'll tell you eventually. It's as well you don't know now."

"For heaven's sake. I'm not a child."

Domingo grinned and his white teeth reflected the candlelight. "No, I guess not." He became serious again. "I'm worried about you and your granddaughter. Whether you like it or not, I want you to stay with me and the wife for a couple of days."

"We don't need to do that." Victoria's jaw was set stubbornly. "Winthrop should be home shortly. And if the boats start running again, Angelo will be home soon, too."

She pushed herself out of the captain's chair and faced Domingo across the candles. "I'm worried about Elizabeth. She wasn't happy about working with Allison tonight."

"No one will try anything as long as Allison stays there."

"Allison is hardly an ally." Victoria stood straight so she could look into Domingo's eyes. "What about her lawsuit?"

"Don't blame her for the lawsuit. It's her aunt's. But I'm more concerned about you right now. I have to talk to your police chief. I also need to check on things at the harbor." He looked out of the east door again. "I hope they get the electricity back, and soon. This is not good."

Victoria watched him for a few moments. "Can they actually carry out a threat against Elizabeth?"

"Sweetheart, we won't let them," Domingo said. "Wonder why they left that note? Stupid of them."

He picked up the phone, held it to his ear, and hung it back up. "Dead. I should have known. Come with me now. I don't want you alone in the house."

"I'll be quite all right," Victoria said testily. "It won't be the first time I've been alone in this house."

"I don't want it to be the last time, either. Get your nightie and toothbrush. And Elizabeth's. You're staying with the wife and me tonight and tomorrow."

"This is a lot of foolishness."

"Three people are dead. Someone is sending you threatening notes. No, this is not foolishness. You're coming with me."

Victoria thought a moment, then shook her head and wrote a note to Angelo or Winthrop, instructions on feeding McCavity.

She carried a lighted candle with her up to the dark bedrooms on the second floor. Domingo waited at the foot of the stairs.

Victoria remembered how, as a child, she used to watch the shadow of the railing progress along the wall when her aunt went downstairs with a candle after she'd tucked Victoria into bed.

She found her small blue Samsonite suitcase in the attic, and then packed her underwear and nightgown and Elizabeth's pajamas.

She set the suitcase down by the kitchen door and Domingo took it out to the car.

When they pulled into the two-car

parking lot at the West Tisbury police station, the ducks and geese had hunkered down on the crushed oyster shells, settled for the night, their heads tucked underneath their wings. When Domingo's car lights flashed on them, they untucked their heads, got to their feet, stretched their necks, hissed, honked, and quacked.

The racket brought Chief O'Neill to the door of the police station. She was silhouetted by the light of two small emergency lamps. Behind the station, the generator throbbed. The chief escorted them inside and Victoria sat in the chair in front of her desk. Domingo took off his cap and looked around the small station house, at the two desks, the potbellied stove, the computers, a calendar on the wall that showed fluffy kittens playing with a ball of yarn. He laughed out loud.

Victoria looked questioningly at him.

"I was thinking what my partner, Joe, would've said if Chief Kelly had hung a kitty-cat calendar in our station house."

The windows that overlooked the Mill Pond were so dark, Victoria could see only her own reflection and Domingo's and Casey's in the glass. After a moment, Domingo said, "You heard about Chief Medeiros's son?"

"I heard something on the scanner. What happened?"

"He died at the hospital this afternoon. During the storm."

"No!" Casey said.

"He was in jail. Suspected poisoning."

"What was he doing in jail?"

"DUI and possession of a controlled substance." Domingo leaned forward in the chair and laced his fingers together between his knees.

"He was poisoned by fudge I was supposed to have given to Dojan, who was also in jail," Victoria said.

Casey thumped the end of her pen on the desk. The point of the pen went in and out, in and out as she tapped.

"Is this related to that Oak Bluffs murder?" Casey asked.

"It's gotten more complicated." Domingo took Victoria's note out of his shirt pocket and handed it to the chief.

Casey read the note, frowning.

"It was stuck under a shingle in the entry," Victoria said.

"And you don't think it's some crank?"

Domingo shook his head. "Victoria and her granddaughter are staying with the wife and me for a couple of days. Can you keep an eye on her house? Something should break soon."

"As soon as the phones are back, I'll talk with Ben," Casey said. "He misses police work."

Domingo stood and saluted the chief. "I know all about it."

The afternoon shift had been busier than Elizabeth expected. A fleet of powerboats had come over from the Padanarum Yacht Club, and the boaters had a hundred requests — liquor store, bar, action, best restaurant, girls, car rentals, hotels. Elizabeth was fed up with powerboats and potbellied men and their doll-women. She didn't want to admit, even to herself, that she resented all the tips Allison was amassing. Twenty dollars, ten, fifty, even a hundred-dollar bill. Allison had made, in one sultry afternoon, more than Elizabeth, her boss, earned in a week. On top of it all, Allison was a sullen brat, and Elizabeth had not wanted to work with her on this shift. Damn Domingo!

She tucked her shirt into her shorts, leaned down and retied the leather laces of her boat shoes, and ran her fingers through her hair.

As the storm clouds billowed out of the north, Elizabeth looked up at the sky with concern. She strode down the ramp to the floating dock, then started up the motor on the harbormaster's launch that was tied to the dock.

"Get in," she ordered Allison, who stepped gingerly into the bow, brushed sand and dried seaweed off the seat, and sat.

Elizabeth steered the boat toward the sailboats moored in the center of the harbor. Allison trailed her hand in the water.

"Cut that out," Elizabeth snapped. Allison quickly withdrew her hand and put it in her lap, where it made a wet spot on the thighs of her tan shorts.

"When I get alongside this boat, get aboard and check the bow lines. Take this chafing gear with you." She handed Allison a bundle of thin canvas strips and waxed twine. "Do you have a knife?"

Allison nodded.

"What did you say?" Elizabeth snapped.

"Yes, ma'am."

"Hurry up," Elizabeth said sharply as Allison balanced herself in the launch. "We have a dozen boats to check."

Elizabeth wheeled the launch from one sailboat to another. Allison scrambled aboard each to check lines, double them up where necessary. She replaced the canvas strips that protected lines from the sawing motion of a boat riding on a mooring in wind. Allison worked faster and more surely as the storm clouds moved toward them and the wind picked up. Footing on the boats was treacherous. At one point, Allison caught her finger between the bow of a boat and its mooring line. Elizabeth saw her grab her hand and double up in pain, saw her reach into her pocket, take out a tissue, and wrap it around her bleeding finger. Allison, hair blowing back from her face in the steadily increasing wind, didn't even look at Elizabeth. She continued to knot waxed line around the canvas strip.

They finished checking the moored boats, not speaking to each other, and put the launch away in a slip beside the shack.

"Put extra lines on it," Elizabeth said. "Then let me see your finger."

"It's okay." Allison held her hand behind her back.

As soon as they were inside, Elizabeth opened the first-aid cabinet that hung on the wall next to the radio.

"Let's see it." Allison held out her finger reluctantly. The paper she had wrapped around it was blood-soaked. Elizabeth clipped it off and examined the crushed finger. "It doesn't look too bad. I'll soak it with peroxide and bandage it. You might want to check it with Doc Erickson."

Allison shook her head, then bit her lip as Elizabeth poured the peroxide over her finger.

Elizabeth looked down at her. "The town has medical coverage. If it still hurts tomorrow, you'd better go."

The wind picked up, whirling sand and seaweed and kicking up whitecaps in the sheltered harbor. Elizabeth and Allison went out again, heads down in the wind, and walked rapidly along the bulkhead, moving from one boat to another, checking lines, warning skippers, fending off flirtations. By the time the storm hit, the boats were secure and they were back in the shack.

Lightning, thunder, and pelting rain assaulted the small building. The usually calm harbor was a furious mass of breaking waves that crashed against the pilings and shook everything. Sailboats on the moorings bucked like terrified horses. The electricity went out, and with it the computers, the lights, and the telephone. Elizabeth picked up the radio mike, but it was dead.

"Shit," she said.

"I brought a flashlight," Allison said. "There's a battery lantern in one of the cabinets."

"Great," Elizabeth said sourly.

"There's a deck of cards. We could play gin," Allison said. "Or hearts."

"How about Go Fish?"

"I know how to play that, too."

"Gin, then," Elizabeth said. "For play money, we can use twenty-dollar bills from the bank bags."

By the time the storm passed, Allison owed Elizabeth more than she'd made in tips that afternoon.

The storm rumbled in the distance and the sun came out. Water dripped from the eaves of the shack and off the deck into the now-calm harbor. The yachters from Padanarum emerged and wiped off the brightwork and stainless-steel trim of their yachts and laughed and shouted to one another. Elizabeth smelled cigar smoke, heard men talk. The sun dipped behind the storm clouds beyond the osprey pole.

Allison stood up and took her tip money out of her pocket, counting out the bills she owed Elizabeth.

"Forget it," Elizabeth said, waving the money aside. "That was a learning experience. Pick up the mail in town and we'll call it even."

During the storm, the two had reached a sort of truce.

"Okay. I'll be back in ten minutes. Fifteen."

"Get us a pizza, if the place is open. I think they cook with gas. Here's some money." Elizabeth opened her wallet.

"It's on me this time," Allison said. "I, like, owe you guys, you know?"

Elizabeth looked at her doubtfully.

"I'm sorry about that lawsuit, you know? I didn't want to file it. Mr. D. is okay."

"Yeah?" Elizabeth took a couple of bills out of her pocket. "Pick up the mail. Take this money, not yours. Anything but anchovies for me. We'll talk about it later."

Allison tossed her hair back from her face, left the shack, and disappeared around one of the gingerbread buildings that lined the harbor. Elizabeth wiped off the bench outside the shack and sat down. She watched the brilliant sunset fade. She thought about Domingo being taken to jail, about Dojan's war dance on Circuit Avenue, about her grandmother's hearing Bernie's scream, and their finding his body, about the whale-watch boat finding Meatloaf's body.

She watched the first stars come out in the evening sky. Then she stood, stretched her arms above her head, leaned over and touched her toes, yawned, and went into the shack. She set the battery lantern on the counter and was opening a drawer to see if she could find something she could work on until the electricity came back on, when someone knocked on the window frame, startling her. She turned abruptly, stumbled against one of the chairs in the dim lantern light, tripped, recovered herself, and opened the door.

No one was there.

She looked down the length of the catwalk, but it was so dark, she couldn't see anything. She stepped out onto the deck and looked. No one was there, either.

"Hello?" she called out into the night.

No answer.

She went back inside and locked the door. The window had been opened a crack for air during the storm. She started to slide it wide open, when she saw a folded paper wedged into the frame. She tugged it out. The corner, soaked from rainwater accumulated in the frame, ripped off as she worked the paper out.

She unfolded it under the lantern light. She could barely read the writing in the dim light, pencil on lined paper torn from a stenography notebook. Part of the message was on the corner that had torn off in the window. She unfolded it carefully, pieced it together, and smoothed it on the desktop.

"Tell your grandmother she better lay off," the message said. "Or she knows what will happen."

Elizabeth sat down abruptly. That sneaky Allison, she said to herself, just as I was beginning to think I'd misjudged her. What does she think she's doing? Why drag my grandmother into this? She put her elbows on the desk, her chin on her hands, and stared at the paper. It figures, she thought. A kid who wants the attention she'll get from the lawsuit will do anything.

She was so angered by what she figured was Allison's sick joke that she had to work off steam. She found another flashlight in one of the desk drawers, tested it to make sure it worked, slammed the door behind her, locked it, and went out into the night. There wasn't much she could do inside anyway. In the meantime, she could make her rounds of the harbor to see if the storm had caused any major damage.

She walked along the bulkhead and

shone her light on the lines tied off on cleats. Candles and kerosene lamps flickered in the cabins of the boats. The Padanarum yachters, whose boats were tied up next to one another, bows out, squared-off sterns facing the bulkhead, were partying on one of the larger cruisers, and as she approached, the noise level grew. She heard drunken male banter, the words indistinct. She heard a woman laugh, and a man's response. Hope they don't decide to go for a ride, she thought. I need Domingo to deal with this.

A large sloop, *Clotho*, its home port Saint Croix, Virgin Islands, had tied up alongside the fuel dock. She could see a kerosene lamp through the porthole. A dock line had frayed, and she reached over the rail and rapped on the side of the cabin.

"Anyone aboard?"

"Righto!" The cabin door opened and a stocky man stepped out into the cockpit, dark against the light from below.

"I'm the assistant harbormaster. You need to replace one of your lines." Elizabeth directed her flashlight at it. Several strands had chafed through.

The man swung his legs over the rail and leapt lightly onto the dock. He was several inches shorter than Elizabeth. She noticed he was barefoot and was wearing cutoff jeans and no shirt. She turned her light onto his face. He had sun-bleached hair and a full blond beard. He was in his early thirties, younger than she had first thought, about her age.

"Thanks, mate." He pronounced the word *mite*. He took the light and examined the line. "She'll hold tonight. I'll take care of it in the morning. Is there a ship's store around?"

"There's a small one behind the butterfly exhibit," Elizabeth said, waving the flashlight toward that side of the harbor. "It doesn't have everything. I'll run you down to the shipyard in Vineyard Haven tomorrow, if you'd like."

"That's kind of you." He handed the flashlight back to her and leaned his hand against the glossy white side of his boat. "Horace Chadwick's my name." He pronounced it *nime*.

"I'm Elizabeth Trumbull."

He stood up straight and held out a massive hand, twice the size of hers, and they shook.

"Trumbull," Horace mused. "Good name."

"Where are you from?"

"I'm a Kiwi. From New Zealand."

"You're here for about a week, aren't you?"

"At least a week." Horace nodded. "I have personal business to attend to. I've been searching for someone. I won't leave until I've found him."

"Shouldn't be too difficult if he's on the Island," Elizabeth said. "It's a pretty small place, actually."

"He's here all right."

Above them, the rigging of *Clotho* stood out against the Milky Way. The storm had washed the sky, and the night was clear and bright.

"Did you sail alone from New Zealand?"

"I've been batting around the world for a couple of years. With someone at first." He paused. "Bought this in the Virgin Islands." He gestured behind him at *Clotho*. "Came into a spot of money there. I single-handed it from there."

"As long as you're staying, perhaps you'd like to come to my grandmother's for beans on Saturday night?" Elizabeth asked.

"Beans?" Horace said blankly.

"Boston baked beans for supper on Saturday night. A New England tradition. My grandmother likes to invite all sorts of interesting people."

"That's kind of you."

"She'll feel as if you're practically related. Her grandmother came from Australia."

Horace nodded. "Same hemisphere as New Zealand."

Elizabeth heard footsteps on the dock and turned. "Nice evening," a man said. "Right," said Horace. "Yes, beautiful," said Elizabeth.

"I'd be delighted to come for beans on Saturday," Horace said when the man had passed. "Shall I bring anything?"

"Bring wine, and I'll pick you up around six."

Before she left to return to the shack, Elizabeth arranged to go with him to the shipyard the next day.

She walked lightly back to the shack, her anger washed away. She'd forgotten about Allison and the letter.

When she returned to the shack, Allison was sitting on the bench outside, a flat pizza box in her hand.

Allison looked up at her. "It's gotten cold. Where were you?"

Elizabeth returned to reality with a nasty thud. "Your note was not amusing." She unlocked the door.

"What note?" Allison got to her feet and went inside, where she laid the box on the table.

"Don't play dumb. It wasn't funny."

"I didn't leave a note, honest." Allison sounded perplexed.

"Here. Let me switch on the lantern." The note lay flat on the desk in a circle of weak light.

"That's not mine," Allison said when she saw it. "It's not even my writing. It's not my paper. It's not mine, honest!"

"You didn't stick this in the window right after you left? You didn't knock on the side of the shack and then run?"

"No. Honest!"

Allison sounded genuinely baffled.

"Here, read it," Elizabeth said.

" 'Tell your grandmother she better lay off. Or she knows what will happen.' What's that all about?" Allison looked up at Elizabeth, whose cheekbones were highlighted by the lantern light below her.

"You have no idea what this is?"

"No. I don't know nothing about it."

"Anything," Elizabeth said, correcting her automatically. She lifted the phone off the wall. "Damn. I forgot the phones are out. I've got to talk to Domingo. Go ahead and eat the pizza before it gets any colder. I'm not hungry."

"I bought us Cokes, too."

"Thanks anyway."

"There wasn't much mail in the harbor box," Allison said. "Stuff for Mr. D., catalogs, ads, memos from the selectmen."

"Put it on the counter. We can look at it later. Don't get pizza on it."

When Domingo and Victoria came up the catwalk, Allison was eating pepperoni pizza, sipping a Coke, and selecting toys from a catalog to match the dock attendants' personalities, and Elizabeth was pacing back and forth inside the shack.

Allison opened the door for them.

"How's it going?" Domingo stepped into the shack behind Victoria.

"She got a note," Allison said, nodding at Elizabeth.

"Note?" Domingo said. "What kind of note?"

Elizabeth moved to the desk. "Under the lantern." She adjusted the light so the writing showed up better.

Domingo put on his glasses and leaned over it. He grunted.

"The same note?" Victoria asked.

"Same notebook paper. Same pencil writing. Says about the same thing," Domingo said. "Slightly different wording." He took off his glasses and looked at Elizabeth. "How did you get it?"

She told him.

"She thought I left it," Allison said.

"Allison didn't write it," Domingo said. "But I don't know who did." He spotted the mail on the counter. "Anything in today's mail?" He shuffled through the envelopes.

"Memo from the chief about parking. Dated yesterday."

"Before his son died," Victoria said quietly.

"Died?" Allison said. "Fatso died? Are you kidding?"

"No." Domingo folded his glasses and put them in his pocket.

"When? What happened?" Allison sat suddenly in the empty chair. "I just seen him day before yesterday."

" 'Saw,' " Elizabeth said.

"Died this afternoon in jail," Domingo said. "Friend of yours?"

"Nothing like that," Allison said sullenly. "There wasn't nothing wrong with him two days ago."

Allison glanced up at the three people in the shack, Victoria, who was seated on the edge of the table, and Domingo and Elizabeth, who were standing next to the lantern on the desk.

"He told me he was doing some security stuff he couldn't talk about. I thought he

308

was just, you know, bullshittin'."

Domingo studied her. "He was poisoned."

Allison's face was hidden in the shadows. She put her hand up to her throat. "He runs — he used to run — messages for my aunt. He tried to make out with me couple of times, you know? Only he's not my type."

"He was in jail for possession. Where did he get drugs?"

Allison shrugged.

"Do you know?"

"I don't know, honest. He tried to give me some stuff one time, but I don't, you know, touch dope."

"What kind of messages did he deliver for your aunt?"

"Like he picked up packages from the Harbor House, delivered stuff there. You know." She shrugged again.

"Do you know about a package Louie delivered to jail today?" Domingo stood as still as a post. Victoria watched silently.

"Yeah. Louie told me some old guy gave him a package to take to that crazy Indian in the jail. Gave him twenty bucks."

"Do you have any idea who the old guy was?" Domingo said.

"No. Louie seen him around, but he

didn't know him, neither."

"Would Louie recognize him if he saw him again?"

"He said he was an old guy, you know, with greasy long gray hair and earrings and really, really filthy clothes."

"Sounds like the guy who's always going through the Dumpsters to collect bottles," Elizabeth said to Domingo.

"Leo Wolfe," Domingo said. "Louie say anything else?"

"I don't think so," Allison said.

"When does Louie come on duty next?" Domingo asked.

Elizabeth took a flashlight and shone it on the schedule posted on the wall. "First thing tomorrow morning."

"We'll have to wait, then. We can't call until the phones are back in service."

"Okay if I go now?"

Domingo nodded.

Allison went off into the night, past the darkened buildings, her flashlight making a cone of light in front of her.

\\ Chapter 15 //

Victoria awoke to the smell of coffee and to sunshine streaming through the skylights in Noreen's sewing room. It took her a moment to recall where she was. She got out of bed, dressed quickly, and found Domingo cooking bacon and scrambled eggs.

"Good morning, sweetheart."

"I don't usually sleep so late. Any news?"

"I've seen the lab report. It's a miracle both men didn't die. Coffee?"

"Yes, thank you. Did they find out what was in the fudge?"

"Atropine — nasty stuff. As Doc Erickson said, there's no known antidote." Domingo lifted bacon slices out of the pan and laid them on a paper towel on the counter.

"Atropine in the fudge I was supposed to have given Dojan." She watched Domingo pour bacon fat into a glass dish.

"Easy to get hold of," Domingo said. "Deadly nightshade grows all over the place. I'm willing to bet I can find some

311

plants in my backyard now." He held out the coffeepot. "Refill?"

"Thank you." Victoria pulled a stool up to the kitchen counter. "Deadly nightshade," she murmured. "Elizabeth and I were weeding it out of the garden a few days ago."

Domingo stirred the eggs as he spoke. "All of it is poisonous, especially the berries. A couple can be fatal."

Victoria thought about her aunt warning her, years ago, against eating nightshade berries, even against touching the plant without washing her hands afterward.

"The berries are supposed to be sweet," she said. "You wonder how anybody discovered that. Manny and the other boy probably didn't realize anything was wrong."

"Manny must have ingested seven or eight berries in those three pieces of fudge." Domingo lowered the heat under the eggs and continued to stir.

Victoria sipped her coffee, squinting her eyes against the steam. "Why would anyone want to harm Dojan?"

"You don't want to know, sweetheart."

"Of course I want to know. Stop sheltering me. Why is someone after Dojan?"

Noreen came into the kitchen, brushing

312

her blond hair. "Sleep okay, Mrs. Trumbull?"

"Wonderfully, thank you. Where's Elizabeth?"

"Still getting her beauty sleep." Noreen patted Domingo on the shoulder and kissed his cheek. "Thanks, honey."

"For what? I'm doing my usual morning routine."

"Usual! You haven't touched that stove since we bought it seven years ago. I'm surprised you know how it works."

Victoria laughed.

Domingo turned to her. "You see how much my woman appreciates me?"

"Domingo." Victoria returned to their conversation. "I want to know what is going on."

Domingo brushed eggshells into his hand from the countertop and dropped them into a plastic basket in the sink.

"She's right, you know," Noreen said. "You and your macho shit, protecting us little women. You think Mrs. Trumbull is stupid or something?"

"No, honey. The fact is, someone is trying to silence her because she knows too much. Somebody thinks she's meddling. I don't want her to have any more knowledge than is necessary."

Noreen laughed. "Come off it, Domingo. You think you're God or something? You think you have the right to decide what Mrs. Trumbull needs to know?"

"I'm thinking about her safety." Domingo spooned salsa from a jar labeled VOLCANO! into the eggs and stirred.

"Domingo! At least ask her if she likes that hot stuff in her eggs."

"Who's cooking, you or me?"

"I want to know what's going on." Victoria slapped her hand on the table. The saltshaker fell over, and she righted it.

"Morning, Gram. Morning, Noreen, Domingo." Elizabeth appeared in the kitchen door, hair tousled, eyes puffy. She sat next to her grandmother at the counter. Noreen poured coffee.

Victoria curbed her irritation with Domingo long enough to greet Elizabeth, who looked, at the moment, like the sleepy six-year-old Victoria remembered from a quarter century ago.

She turned again to Domingo and slapped her gnarled hand on the countertop with each word. "What is going on, Domingo?"

"It's too early in the morning for this, Grammy." Elizabeth reached for a paper towel and mopped up spilled coffee.

Domingo dished out eggs and placed rashers of bacon on the side without answering, then set the plates on the kitchen table.

"You witnessed Bernie's murder, you heard a vehicle leave the scene, and you heard a boat. But we don't know why Bernie was killed. It's possible it was connected with drug trafficking; we don't know for certain." Domingo reached across the table for a piece of toast. "Pass the marmalade," he said to Noreen.

"Say 'please,' " Noreen said.

"Please, honey."

"Maybe some woman's father decided to get even with him," Elizabeth said.

Domingo turned to Elizabeth. "Someone is concerned about how much your grandmother knows." Domingo's heavy brows were drawn together in a frown. "They are also concerned with how much your grandmother is involved."

"I'm not involved at all," Victoria said hotly. "I don't know any more than what I've already told the police." She sloshed orange juice into her empty glass.

"Don't forget," said Domingo, pushing eggs onto his fork with his toast while he spoke, "you found that broken bottle and the checkbook cover. You haven't told the police that." He shoveled eggs into his mouth and swallowed. "Of course, we have no reason to think those may be evidence. Also, you recognized the police chief's car as the one you heard the night Bernie was killed."

"I don't know that I recognized it. All cars sound alike skidding on sand."

"Next, someone followed you, quite possibly Meatloaf, at least twice, maybe more, possibly only trying to frighten you."

"Well, he didn't." Victoria scraped up the hot salsa from the edge of her plate, heaped it on top of her eggs, took a bite, and wiped her watering eyes.

"Someone else followed us," Elizabeth said. "Dojan?"

"Most likely. Dojan is feeling protective of your grandmother." Domingo bared his white teeth in a wolfish grin.

"I feel like the president," Victoria said.

Domingo got serious again. "At first, I assumed that Meatloaf killed Bernie. Meatloaf would have done it that way — crude."

"That's what I think, too." Victoria toyed with her glass.

"Not so, sweetheart. Meatloaf was trying to hush you, but not because he was the killer. He was trying to protect someone else. He was trying to protect his boss, the one who paid him."

"Then who killed Meatloaf?" Elizabeth put her toast back onto her plate. "And who was the boss he was trying to protect? Who tried to kill Dojan?"

Victoria interrupted with her own questions. "Who hoped to stop Elizabeth with the fallen tree limb and the oil slick? And who wrote those threatening notes to both of us?"

"One thing at a time." Domingo pushed his chair back. "I don't know everything. However, when I was in the cell with Dojan, he told me things he should have kept to himself."

"What did he tell you?" Victoria folded her napkin and set it beside her plate.

"The day Bernie was killed, Dojan told me, he'd gone out in his boat to pull his lobster traps on the Sound. When he came back into the harbor, he had engine trouble, so he pulled his boat up onto the beach near the osprey pole, in that small bay. He landed, fixed his motor, and watched the sunset."

"I remember how spectacular it was that night," Victoria said.

"Dojan sat on the beach in the shelter of a wild rosebush. He could see the dock, but unless someone knew he was there, they wouldn't have seen him. He saw the police car pull up and Bernie and Chief Medeiros get out. He watched them walk to the end of the dock. They argued, loudly enough so he could hear what they were saying. While they were arguing, Dojan saw Meatloaf scull a dinghy over from the dock by the liquor store, so quietly, Dojan didn't see him at first."

Noreen got up and brought a fresh pot of coffee to the table.

Victoria watched Domingo through hooded eyes. "Then what?"

"Meatloaf tied up at the foot of the dock and waited. The argument got louder. Bernie grabbed a liquor bottle out of the chief's hand, broke it against the metal ring on the piling, and started after the chief, who whisked out that razor-sharp bayonet he wears in his boot. At that point, Meatloaf climbed the ladder. Dojan saw him twist Bernie's arms behind him. He couldn't see what the chief was doing, but he saw him jab the knife into Bernie, heard Bernie scream, saw Meatloaf cover his mouth. Dojan witnessed the whole thing."

Elizabeth grunted.

"So Chief Medeiros killed Bernie," Victoria whispered, her hand at her throat.

"That's what Dojan said. Meatloaf started up the motor on the dinghy and landed on the beach where you found the bottle and the checkbook cover. Then he returned to the liquor store dock."

"That must have been the motor I heard," Victoria said.

"Dojan told me other things he saw. He hung around for some time before he left. In fact, he saw Victoria and me go out in the launch. . . ."

"Hey, I was there too," Elizabeth said.

"Yas. He told me he saw Ms. Elizabeth, Victoria, and me searching; then he heard me call in. And after that, he saw the chief's car return to the scene."

"Why didn't Dojan say anything?" Victoria frowned.

"Who would he report the killing to, Chief Medeiros?"

Victoria gave Domingo a tight smile. "You said there was something else Dojan talked about."

"Yas."

Victoria said, "What else?"

Domingo set his elbows on the table and looked intently from Elizabeth to Victoria to Noreen.

"What else?" Victoria said again.

"Dojan claimed he killed Meatloaf."

"What!" Elizabeth stared at him.

Noreen shook her head.

"Everything is backward and upside down." Elizabeth stood suddenly.

"Why?" Victoria asked, puzzled.

"Dojan had been tailing Meatloaf in an attempt to protect you, sweetheart. When the wife and I were in New York, Meatloaf came by to pick up the papers."

"That was while I was watching Baby Mingo," Victoria said.

"Later, that same evening, around eleven, eleven-thirty, Meatloaf returned with the signed papers. Dojan was following him and told me what happened."

The room was quiet. Victoria heard the coffeepot burble, a car pass on the road.

"Dojan saw him open the sliding door into the living room; Meatloaf was carrying a folder. He picked up a paper from the table and read it, then put the folder down and set a coffee mug on top. Dojan followed him into the house, here." Domingo pointed down at the floor. "He must have been quiet, because Meatloaf apparently didn't see him at first. When he finally looked up, he was startled. He called Dojan a 'crazy Indian,' and asked him what the hell he was doing here."

"What did Dojan say?" Elizabeth asked.

"Nothing. He said he stared at Meatloaf."

"I can just see him, with those wobbly eyes like boiled eggs, only black, and those feathers quivering in his hair, and his dark clothes blending into the night," Elizabeth said. "He'd spook anybody."

"Go on, Domingo," said Victoria.

"Meatloaf went over to the couch, sat down, and put his sunglasses on."

"At midnight?" Elizabeth said.

Domingo shrugged. "That's what Dojan said. He said he walked toward the couch, where Meatloaf was sitting. The telephone rang, and Dojan didn't know whether he should answer it or not. He didn't, and it finally stopped ringing. He told Meatloaf he'd been watching him, and he asked him why he'd been following you." He nodded at Victoria.

"Then what?" Victoria said.

"Meatloaf said, 'Get outta here, you crazy Indian.' Dojan stepped closer and told him to stay away from his friend. Meatloaf half-rose from the couch and twisted one of my harpoons out of the rack and threatened Dojan with it. Dojan backed away, and Meatloaf went out of the door, still holding the harpoon. When

Meatloaf got into his van, Dojan went after him, followed him to the harbor. Apparently, Meatloaf expected to see someone on duty at the shack, but it was midnight by then, and no one was there."

"I wasn't on duty that night," Elizabeth said.

"Go on, Domingo," said Victoria.

"Meatloaf was carrying the harpoon in one hand, banging on the door of the shack with the other. He turned when Dojan came up next to him, and he pointed the harpoon at Dojan. Dojan grabbed it and twisted it out of his hands. Meatloaf then pulled a switchblade on him, tried to slash his hands. Meatloaf yelled at him to keep away, but Dojan shoved him against the railing with the shaft of the harpoon. Meatloaf kept trying to slash him with the knife. Dojan could see the sweat pouring down his face. Suddenly, the railing gave way and Meatloaf dropped his knife, which skidded off the deck and fell into the water. He tried to grab the harpoon as he lost his balance, then tried to grab the broken railing, but his hands slid off. He tumbled, arms flailing to the sides, his feet bicycling in the air, and hit with a splash that sent water up the sides of the shack. He surfaced, blowing water out of his mouth in a spume, his cap and dark glasses gone, his hair plastered on his scalp, his windbreaker translucent and filled with water. He paddled frantically with both hands. Dojan stood above him with the harpoon in his hand and flung it."

"My God!" said Noreen.

Victoria looked down at her plate. "And after that, Dojan went to the Sand Bar and had a drink or two."

"More like five or six," Domingo replied. "But not right away. He built himself a sweat lodge on top of the Gay Head cliffs and tried to sweat out the evil."

"It's not Gay Head anymore," Elizabeth said. "The name's Aquinnah now."

"He's attempting to get back to his roots," Victoria said, toying with her fork. "I suppose when that didn't work, he went on his binge."

All of them were silent.

Finally, Victoria pushed her chair away from the table. "This is awful. Shouldn't we notify the police?"

"Chief Medeiros?" Domingo said, raising his eyebrows. "I don't think so."

"If he hadn't been so hungover, he'd probably have eaten the fudge," Elizabeth said.

Domingo nodded.

"Why did he tell you? Was he afraid they were going to charge you with Meatloaf's murder?" Victoria asked.

"He needed to get it off his chest, sweetheart."

"Did anyone overhear him?" Victoria asked.

"While we were talking, I saw Howie tiptoe past the cell. I don't know how long he'd been listening. When I went to the door and rattled the bars and shouted obscenities at him, he left."

"You think Howie reported what he heard to someone? To Chief Medeiros, maybe?" Victoria asked. "Surely the chief would want to silence anyone who knew what had happened."

"Before I became aware that Howie was listening, Dojan told me that he was on the beach fixing his motor the night of the killing."

"Whom would Howie have reported the conversation to?" Victoria said.

"Probably Elmo, the jailer, who undoubtedly told the sheriff, who told the chief over coffee at Linda Jean's."

Victoria took an envelope and pen out of her pocket. "What do we know so far?" She held the end of the pen to her mouth. "We suspect a drug ring might be operating out of the Oak Bluffs Harbor."

"But we don't *know* that."

"Has Howland said anything to you lately, Domingo?" Elizabeth said abruptly.

Victoria was startled by the change of subject. She noticed Domingo dart a quick look at Elizabeth and shake his head very slightly. She looked from her granddaughter to Domingo. Elizabeth studiously avoided her eyes.

Noreen didn't seem to have noticed the small exchange. "It fits with everything that's happened," she said. "A drug ring."

Victoria smoothed her trousers over her knees with the hand holding the pen. She thought about Domingo's oddly secret shake of the head. "It would explain everything if we assume Bernie Marble's murder was a drug deal gone wrong," Victoria said finally. "We thought Meatloaf killed him, when it was actually Chief Medeiros who did. Over drugs."

"Let me caution you." Domingo stood and hiked up his trousers by his belt. "We have no evidence that drugs are involved. As yet."

"We'll get that evidence," Victoria said with assurance. "Chief Medeiros is obviously the ringleader of a drug-smuggling operation."

"We don't *know* that, either," Domingo said. "In fact, I don't believe he is the ring-leader."

"So who tried to kill Dojan?" Victoria put her envelope and pen next to her plate. "And who is sending the notes?"

"It would appear to be two different people," Domingo said. "A killer and a blackmailer. The killer thinks Dojan knows something. I don't know what the black-mailer is after."

"What about Liz Tate?" Victoria asked. "She certainly was acting strange that day we came back to the dock on Rocky's yacht, bawling out the chief for being there."

"I wouldn't put it past the bitch," said Noreen.

\\ Chapter 16 //

Chief Medeiros was standing on the steps of the Town Hall, staring off into space, unread mail in his hand, when Domingo, Victoria, and Howland pulled up in the white Rolls-Royce.

The bright, clear morning, crisp and rare, was what Victoria called "typical Vineyard weather." The sultry heat had moved off-Island leaving everything clean and new.

The chief was in uniform: navy blue motorcycle pants with a light blue stripe on the sides, polished black boots with a knife hilt showing at the top, navy shirt with leather belt, a strap across his chest, his gun, radio, club, keys slung from the belt. His dark glasses touched the brim of his garrison cap. He shifted his gaze to the car and his mouth pursed.

Domingo stepped out of the car, slammed the door shut, and stood on the sidewalk, looking up at the chief, who was at the top of the steps. Victoria waited in the front seat, Howland in back. Domingo hitched his pants up and walked toward the steps.

"You got some nerve showing up here, Mingo," the chief said.

"My condolences on the passing of your son," Domingo said, and took his cap off. "I'm very sorry."

"Yeah. I bet you are." The chief shifted his gaze to the mail in his hand.

"I know this is a bad time for you, but we need to talk."

"You can talk to me right here." Without looking up, the chief shuffled envelopes, top onto bottom, the next, the next.

"In private." Domingo stood still, hands in his pockets.

"I got nothing to say to you, public or private."

"We have something to say to *you*. I think you're going to want a more private place," Domingo said.

"What the hell do you have to say to me in private? I don't want to talk to you, period."

"Have it your way." Domingo shrugged. He put his cap back on and turned to the car. "Atherton?"

Howland unfolded himself from the backseat of the Corniche and walked deliberately up the brick steps. The chief inclined his head to look up at him. Howland reached into his back pocket, brought out his black leather folder, and flipped it open. Victoria saw a flash of reflected sunlight on a gold shield.

The chief took the folder from Howland and studied it.

Howland started to say something, but before he could, the chief said, "Where do you want to talk?"

"We can go to your office, if you'd like." Howland waited.

The chief stared across the street. "No, not there."

"The Harbor House?" Howland said. "Perhaps you have a private room, a small conference room there?"

"I don't think so." The chief returned Howland's leather folder to him.

"This is unofficial, at least at this stage." Howland put the folder with his shield and ID in his back pocket and crossed his arms over his chest.

"Mingo's place?" The chief turned to Domingo, who was facing away from them. A young man in splotched painter's overalls was walking toward him with an athlete's springy step.

"How ya doing, Mitch?" Domingo greeted him.

"Pretty good, Mr. D. And you?"

"Can't complain. How's the wife and baby? A boy, was it?"

"Yessir, Mr. D., both fine. Mitch junior, nine pounds two ounces."

"All right!" Domingo jabbed an emphatic fist at the ground.

Mitch went up the steps of the Town Hall two at a time, brushed past Howland and the police chief. "Pardon me." He pushed open the screen door, which slapped a couple of times before it shut.

"Your place, Domingo?" Howland said.

"Fine." Domingo swung around to face them.

"We can talk over a cup of coffee," Howland said to the chief, who gathered up a lot of something in his cheek and spit it into the privet hedge that surrounded the Town Hall.

"We'll see you there." Domingo got back into the driver's seat. Howland seated himself again in back.

The chief flexed his legs one at a time, as though his muscles had stiffened, and clumped down the steps of the Town Hall. Victoria could hear his boots squeak.

Domingo parked in front of his house and left a space for the police cruiser. The chief pulled into it.

Once inside, Victoria lowered herself onto the couch, Domingo sat at the glass-topped table, and Howland and the chief stood.

"She sitting in on this?" The chief jerked his head at her.

"Yas." Domingo lighted a cigarette, snapped his Zippo shut, and laid it on the table with a small clink.

"As I said, this is unofficial." Howland indicated one of the wicker chairs around the table. "Won't you have a seat?"

The chief hesitated before he sat. "Where's the wife?"

"My wife has taken my grandson to see the fire station."

Howland stepped up into the kitchen, and Victoria heard him open the cupboard where Noreen kept the coffee, heard him fill the pot with water, heard the clatter of mugs as Howland took them from the rack next to the stove.

While the coffee brewed, Howland returned to his seat at the table. Victoria attempted to break the awkward silence with small talk, but she gave up after a few tries. Chief Medeiros sat with his arms folded, staring sullenly at the tabletop in front of him. Domingo looked out the window. Howland toyed with the place mat. Victoria watched all three from her seat on the couch.

When the coffee had finished brewing, Howland went up into the kitchen and poured. "How does everyone take it?" he asked.

"Black, thank you," Victoria said.

"Cream, milk. Double sugar," the chief muttered.

Once Howland was seated again, Domingo spoke first, turning to the chief with an unsettling, calm stare. "We suggest you admit to the murder," he said quietly, gazing at the chief.

The chief started, his eyes twitched. He stared back at Domingo, his mouth seeming to form words that never emerged.

"Murder," he said in a choked voice. He brought the coffee mug to his mouth.

Domingo watched the chief steadily. After a pause, he said, "Of Meatloaf Staples."

The chief, who had that moment taken a sip of coffee, spewed it across the table with a convulsive movement and got to his feet. Domingo blotted the tabletop with the paper napkin Howland had given him with his coffee.

"What in hell! You're crazy." The chief

rose out of his seat, grabbed his cap, which he had placed on the table, jammed it on his head, plucked his sunglasses out of his pocket, and strode toward the door. He turned. "You know goddamned well I had nothing to do with killing Meatloaf." He slammed the door open, and it bounced on the track. "Trying to cover your own ass, are you? You're more of a fool than I thought, Mingo."

Domingo sat serenely, his hands folded over his stomach, cigarette smoldering in the ashtray. "We know for a fact you didn't kill Meatloaf."

Howland said nothing. He'd put his elbows on the table and had both hands around his coffee mug. He gazed absently through the hanging plants into the bright, sunny garden outside, where Baby Mingo's plastic toys lay where he'd left them. Victoria leaned back and watched through half-shut eyes.

"You're out of your minds." The chief paused in the doorway. "I have nothing to say to you."

"However," Domingo said, "we know the person you did kill. And how you killed him."

"Whaaat!"

"We have a witness to Bernie Marble's

death." Domingo said it softly. "An eye-witness."

The chief froze and glanced at Victoria.

"Not her," Howland said.

The chief moved back into the room.

"Shut the door, please." Victoria looked over her shoulder. "You're letting in flies."

The chief lifted the door back onto its track and slid it shut. He took off his sun-glasses and glanced quickly at Victoria, then from Domingo to Howland and back again at Domingo.

"What in hell? Come out with it."

Howland continued to stare out at the garden. "Why don't you sit," he said. "You might want to hear what we have to say."

The chief sat, took his cap off, and, after a few moments' silence, put it under the chair. He took his glasses off and put them back in his pocket, leaned forward, hands clasped on the table, and looked around.

"There's no one else here," Domingo said.

"Yeah?" the chief said.

"We are not recording this," Howland said. "Victoria Trumbull is here as an observer."

"What's on your mind, Mingo?"

"We'll talk, if you don't mind," Howland said politely.

The chief glared at him.

Victoria sneezed three times in a row.

"God bless you." The chief glanced at her.

"Domingo?" Howland said. "Care to continue?"

"As I said, we think you might want to admit to killing Meatloaf Staples."

"Jee-sus," the chief said.

"Or, if you prefer, we can produce the individual who actually witnessed what happened to Bernie Marble."

"What in hell is this?" The chief was beginning to sweat. Howland handed him a paper napkin, and the chief mopped his forehead with it.

"You'll say you killed Meatloaf in self-defense, of course," Domingo continued. "Better than a charge of first-degree murder."

The chief wiped his forehead again, crumpled up the napkin, and tossed it onto the table. "You're crazy, both of you."

"I don't think so," Howland said.

"What do you expect to get out of this?" The chief pushed his coffee mug away from him and stared at Domingo.

Domingo nodded his head at Howland. "Atherton, take over."

"Once upon a time," Howland said,

"there was an elder son of a wealthy New England family, blue-blood stock. A difficult kid, brilliant, charming, and shifty. Summers on Martha's Vineyard, winters in the Caribbean, private boarding schools. Father was a great philanthropist, mother a patron of the arts, that sort of thing. The son dabbled in drugs during his preteen Caribbean winters, not as a user — he was too smart for that — but as a courier. By the time he entered college, he had built up his own network of sources, distributors, and dealers."

From where Victoria sat, she could see the chief's profile. He sat motionless, his face expressionless.

"Are you still with me?" Howland asked.

The chief said nothing.

Victoria saw Domingo's dark eyes through a blue haze of cigarette smoke.

"To continue," Howland said. "Daddy, who never did trust his son, got suspicious, hired a private investigator, found out what the son was up to, and disowned him. The son finished college on an academic scholarship, went on to graduate school on a fellowship, got a Ph.D. in astrophysics, and won a professorship at MIT. A professor's salary being what it is, he maintained his drug contacts at a low-key level, enough to support his lifestyle without arousing undue suspicion."

The chief shifted in his seat. Domingo stubbed out his cigarette. Victoria saw a vein or artery pulsing in the chief's temple, a muscle twitching in his jaw.

"Our professor," Howland went on, "developed a computer program under a university grant from the Defense Department to track electromagnetic pulses. He did much of his research in Puerto Rico, on the giant radio telescope. He believed, however, that the university was not giving him his share of the royalties for the very successful program. He felt he had a right to appropriate a portion of the grant money for his own purposes. When the university found out about what they considered his misuse of the grant money, they ousted him. Since much of his research had been in the Caribbean, he had, quite naturally, maintained his contacts there.

"To make up for his lost income, he switched into high gear with his drug business. Importing high-profit goods from South America by way of the Caribbean. Are you with me?"

Victoria sneezed again.

"God bless you," the chief said. "Go on."

337

Domingo watched the chief.

The chief stared at Howland, the throbbing in his temple the only sign that he was listening.

"He learned that vessels putting in at the Vineyard after a long sea voyage seldom go through U.S. Customs." Howland took a sip of coffee, his eyes on the chief. "He knew he could enlist yachting adventurers heading north from the Caribbean, delighted to carry goods for him for a small fee. The Oak Bluffs Harbor was ideal for his purposes."

"Where are you going with this?" the chief said finally. "What does this have to do with my 'killing' Meatloaf?"

Victoria blew her nose.

The chief glared at Howland.

"He decided he could easily explain his high living by capitalizing, so to speak, on his software invention. Few people understand university policies, few people would question his involvement with the university, and few people are going to wonder how lucrative an astrophysics software program can be."

He glanced at Domingo, who was playing with his Zippo, snapping it open and shut.

Victoria shifted on the couch, crossed

one ankle over the other, put her handkerchief back in her pocket.

"You're not catching cold, are you,
sweetheart?" Domingo looked over at her
with concern.

She shook her head.

"To continue," Howland said. "Our professor needed three things: a depository,
where he could keep his goods temporarily
until he could move them to their point of
sale; a means of transporting them safely
off-Island; and, most important, a team he
could trust." He looked up at the chief.
"Are you still with me?"

The chief lowered his head and looked at
his clasped hands.

A cardinal flashed by in the garden outside. Victoria heard the melodic call of a
Carolina wren. A car passed on the road,
and her view of it was chopped up by
Domingo's tall wooden fence.

Howland continued. "Our professor
needed to bring his goods into a place
where the record keeping was haphazard,
and where no one asked questions." He
looked from the chief to Domingo. "Oak
Bluffs was ideal. The harbor takes in half a
million dollars over a three-month period.
A lot of boaters pay cash. The former
harbormaster had a little cash slush fund

he used to supplement his salary, pay for favors, that sort of thing."

Domingo cranked the window open slightly.

"Our professor did his homework," Howland continued. "He found, to his delight, that one of the town's selectmen and the two owners of the major hotel — one owner a convicted criminal on probation, the other the town's police chief — were benefitting from the sloppy management of the harbor.

"Now our professor hoped, ideally, to distance himself as much as possible from day-to-day operations of his business. So he enlisted this particular selectman to act as his right-hand person, to keep records and deal with subordinates." He stopped talking. "You still with me?"

"Go on," the chief growled.

"Our story's hotel was situated at the head of the harbor, and it was the only place where showers were available for boaters. What could be better, our professor must have said to himself. The imported goods came in small packages, one kilo each, something the size of two pounds of butter. What could be simpler than asking his Caribbean adventurers, sailors who were about to take their first hot freshwater showers in some time, to carry a small parcel into the shower room and 'accidentally' leave it behind when they were through. The parcels were small enough to be unnoticed among towels, soap, and clean and dirty clothes. Later, a trusted minion could retrieve the parcels when he — or she — cleaned the shower room. The minion took the parcels to the hotel's lost and found, conveniently near the shower rooms. This way, the minion was absolved of any responsibility for taking part in the business transactions. From the lost and found, the parcels found their way to the hotel's hamper for soiled laundry. Probably a specially marked hamper, wouldn't you say, Chief?"

The chief said nothing. He picked at a loose flap of skin on his finger.

Howland went on. "The goods were indeed laundered. The soiled linen would then go to Boston, taken by a trustworthy, low-echelon member of the team, and be returned to the hotel as clean towels, sheets, and, voilà! laundered money."

Victoria laid her right arm along the back of the couch.

The chief continued to pick at his finger.

"In addition," Howland went on, "the selectmen had hired what they thought was a dumb black guy who would take orders from them without question." He turned to look at Domingo and his mouth turned down in a smile. "To go on: In our story, the imaginary selectman takes her — or his — orders from our professor. How can our professor guarantee her — or his — loyalty? That's critical, don't you think?" He paused and looked at the chief, who said nothing. "I myself can think of several ways. One, or a combination, would do the trick. Affection, greed, and fear come to mind. Or a certain sense of adventure. I'm sure you can think of others."

The chief unfolded his hands and looked at his watch.

Howland smiled. "We're taking your valuable time, aren't we? Shall I stop?"

"Jesus Christ," the chief said. "Go on."

"Why kill Bernie Marble?" Howland continued. "We can only guess that Marble began to realize how much money was involved. He may have felt he was being shortchanged. Perhaps Bernie got greedy. Maybe he threatened to divulge this elegant scheme. Bernie was already on probation for his behavior to a female employee of the hotel. Had that gotten out of hand?"

Chief Medeiros shifted in his chair. "What do you expect me to do about all this garbage you're feeding me?"

"Ah!" Howland said. "As with much fiction, this is grounded in reality. Now let me tell you about Bernie's death. Tell me if I'm mistaken on some fine point. This was — let's see — about two weeks ago now."

He turned suddenly to face Chief Medeiros and his voice no longer had its polite edge.

"Okay, Medeiros. You summoned Meatloaf to your office at the Harbor House, told him you couldn't talk on the phone, 'Get your ass in here,' you said."

The chief stared at Howland.

"Meatloaf lumbered into that office of yours that looks out over the parking lot in back of the hotel, right?"

The chief said nothing.

"Meatloaf was probably breathing heavily and sweating, although, as I recall, it was not a hot afternoon. He plopped himself into that wooden armchair in front of your desk where the light from your window must have shone in his face. A cop technique, right?"

The chief stared at Howland.

"I can imagine the conversation," Howland continued. "You probably made him cool his heels for a long time. Then you leaned forward across the desk. 'I'm having a slight problem with Bernie,' you may have said. I suppose Meatloaf, who was sure you'd found out something he didn't want you to know, was relieved. Just as you intended. Maybe you said something like 'He seems to have forgotten who's boss. He's getting greedy. Wants a bigger cut.' I can hear you now, playing the good-cop/bad-cop routine all by yourself, and Meatloaf, who was not the brightest, fell for it, didn't he?"

The chief looked down at his hands. Domingo sat motionless. Victoria shifted slightly on the couch.

"Meatloaf couldn't see your face, backlighted the way it undoubtedly was. He had to guess how he was supposed to react, probably squinting into the light, trying to see your expression. 'I'd say he's had a pretty generous cut,' you may have said.

" 'Damn right. Want me to talk to him?' Is that what Meatloaf said? Did he make a fist of his right hand and smack it into the palm of his left? I've seen him do that. He probably glared like a thug for your benefit.

"Then I can imagine you saying, 'He thinks he can cut a couple of middlemen out of the operation, delusions of grandeur.'

"I'll bet Meatloaf agreed with you, 'Not good,' or something like that.

"To really hit home, you might have said, 'Bernie's letting his prick do his thinking for him. Not smart in this business.' "

The chief glanced nervously at Victoria, who was studying the backs of her hands.

"You undoubtedly reminded Meatloaf of the way Bernie bought off one woman who threatened to file charges against him. Followed her all the way to Ireland, right? You said to Meatloaf, 'We don't need this kind of publicity.'

"Were Meatloaf's eyes watering from the bright light? Probably. You planned it that way, didn't you? I know that gesture he had, reaching into his pocket for that blue bandanna, lifting his glasses, and wiping his eyes."

The room was still except for a fly buzzing at the sliding door. Sounds filtered in from outdoors. Two boys rode past the house on bicycles, calling to each other and laughing. The chief sat motionless.

" 'He thinks we need him more than he needs us,' I suppose you said. 'Plenty of other places to store stuff. They don't have to use this hotel.' The way I imagine it," Howland continued, "you stood up, stuck your hands into your pockets, and probably jingled change, the way you do. Did you look out the window at the parking lot? From your office, you can see the Camp Meeting Ground, can't you? Quite a contrast, those quaint gingerbread houses painted in pastel colors, the oak leaves rustling in the breeze.

"You probably stood at the window for some time, letting Meatloaf wonder. Did you rock back and forth on those squeaky leather boots of yours? Good way to make someone nervous, isn't it? I can hear you saying, once you decided Meatloaf was softened up, 'He needs to be taught a lesson. We need to take care of him — permanently.' Did you say that?"

The chief swallowed. His neck quivered.

"I suppose you told Meatloaf that you were meeting Bernie at the East Chop dock around dark. Did you check the tide table? Figure out that dead high tide was around seven-thirty? I'm sure you did."

Victoria noticed that the chief had crossed his feet and was rubbing one against the other. Except for that, the muscle in his jaw, and the pulse in his temple, he was motionless. Domingo, too, was absolutely still.

"I suppose you told him to scull a dinghy from the dock by the liquor store to

346

the East Chop dock, and to get there before seven-thirty. You didn't want any noise, did you? Maybe you told him he could use the exercise." Howland smiled. "Did you tell him to wait at the foot of the ladder until you needed him?"

The chief said nothing. The fly buzzed and bumped against the glass door.

"I suppose Meatloaf was wearing those pointed Italian shoes he was so vain about. You probably gave him that steely cop look and asked him if he could get his fat self up the ladder in a hurry, right?"

The chief said nothing.

"Then you must have jerked your head at him. 'Okay,' I imagine you said, 'get outta here. We never had this discussion.' "

Howland stopped. Domingo's clock rang six bells. Victoria checked her watch.

"Eleven o'clock, sweetheart," Domingo said.

"Have you heard enough?" Howland asked the chief.

"Shit," said the chief, then turned to Victoria. "Excuse me, ma'am."

"Go on, Howland," Victoria said.

"I imagine when Meatloaf left, you got on the phone to Bernie. 'Bernie,' you probably said, 'how's it going?' And while Bernie talked, I'll bet you doodled those square boxes on your desk calendar, right?"

The chief stared without expression at Howland.

"How did you get him to agree to meet you, Medeiros? You tell him one of the couriers was getting too big for his britches? Tell him you were not sure who? That you figured he was taping goods to the underside of the dock to come back for them in his own sweet time? I can see you now, doodling, probably connecting those boxes you'd drawn with lines so they looked three-dimensional."

The chief blinked.

"I've seen your calendar, Medeiros. Boxes with arrows shooting into them. You probably suggested that the courier would be at the dock at high tide so he could reach the underside of the dock, didn't you? Seven-thirty, you said. Then, to allay suspicion — Bernie was a suspicious guy, right? — you probably said you weren't sure it would be that night. 'We may have to wait a day or two,' I'm sure you said. Then, to make it seem like a good-time junket, you told him you'd bring a bottle, didn't you? Said you'd pick him up in the cruiser.

"I can see you now. You slammed the

phone down and turned your chair to the window. Were those two kids riding their pink-and-lavendar bicycles down in the parking lot? Or did you even see them? You didn't want to be reminded of *normal*, did you?"

The chief shook his head and looked at his hands, which were still clasped in front of him on the table.

"Everything went according to plan, didn't it? At least until you learned that Victoria Trumbull had heard you and Meatloaf, had heard Bernie's screams, and found his body before the tide took it out to sea." Howland stopped and waited for the chief to say something.

Medeiros continued to look down at his hands.

"Back to my story. You and Bernie went together in the police cruiser to the dock. You took along a bottle of Caribbean rum one of your couriers gave you."

The chief looked up in surprise.

"You didn't know we found the bottle, did you?"

The chief was silent.

"I suppose he put up a fight, didn't he?" Howland said. "Kicked out at you. But you've been trained to kill. Vietnam, the Marines. Or did you learn at police school?"

The chief stood up and slapped his hand on the table.

"I don't want to hear any more of this shit." He reached under his chair and snatched his cap. "I don't know where you're getting it from. Straight out of some TV show."

"First-degree murder carries life," Domingo said quietly.

"No one can pin anything on me." The chief turned to the door. "Your eyewitness is another figment of your imagination. There was nobody around. Nobody." He started to open the door.

"The witness saw Bernie break the bottle against the piling," Domingo said. "Saw you pull the knife on him. Saw Meatloaf hold him. Saw what you did next."

"Meatloaf did it, not me."

"The witness heard you order Meatloaf to drop Bernie's pants. Saw Meatloaf cover Bernie's mouth with his arm when he started to scream."

"Oh yeah?" The chief paused in the half-opened doorway.

"The witness saw what you did." Domingo stopped and looked uncomfortably at Victoria, who was regarding the chief with disgust.

350

"I know what he did to that man," Victoria said. "You can stop trying to shelter me." She pushed herself off the couch and pointed to the chief as if he were in fifth grade. "Come back in this minute. Shut the door. And sit down and listen."

She stood until the chief obeyed her.

"You'll listen to the rest of this nasty tale. You should be drawn and quartered. Instead, you're getting a chance you don't deserve." She sat down again. "I thoroughly disapprove of giving him that chance," she said to Howland.

Domingo avoided Victoria's bright eyes.

Howland tilted his chair against the wall and looked away.

"Don't lean back in your chair," Victoria said, and Howland set it back on its legs.

"You." She nodded her head at the chief. "You cut off his testicles and stuffed them into his mouth, didn't you?"

The chief looked from Domingo to Howland. Both men were staring out the window.

"The barbarian answer to rape," Victoria said. "You have a fourteen-year-old daughter, don't you?"

The chief looked blankly at his hands on the table.

"He raped your daughter, didn't he?

Melody, your only daughter."

"Stop!" The chief sagged over the table. "Yes. It wasn't money. Or drugs. I know what happens to rapists. Nothing." He looked out the window. A chickadee was picking at seed in the bird feeder that hung from a post in the garden.

"Bernie Marble." He spat out the name. "On probation for assault against a female employee. It wasn't assault. It was rape." He laid his arms on the table and put his head on his arms. "I've seen what happens to women who are raped." He lifted his head. "Girls. They're damaged for life by rape. When they go to court, what little they have left is ground into pieces by the defense lawyers and the courts. Ground up and spit out."

Victoria, Howland, and Domingo were silent.

"I wasn't going to put my daughter through that."

Birds chirped. Cars went by on the road beyond the tall board fence. The coffeemaker sputtered and stopped.

"And they say justice is done." The chief sat up straight. "My only daughter fouled by that beast, my only son killed, my wife gone."

The room was silent for several minutes.

Then the chief said, "What do you want from me?"

"We have been after Folger for years," Howland said. "He's smarter than most of us put together. For the first time, we have someone who can testify against him."

"Not me!" the chief choked.

"You," Howland said. "We want you to testify against him."

"Christ! Put me away for life for Bernie. If Rocky gets me, he'll kill me by inches."

"You testify, and Rocky will be put away forever," Howland said. "He's been destroying lives for years. For years, we've been hoping he would make a mistake. He's too smart to make a mistake. But with your testimony and Liz Tate's, we've finally got him."

"You'll never get Liz Tate to talk."

"I think we will," Domingo said.

"They're thick. What have you got on her?"

Domingo and Howland spoke at the same time. "She killed someone," they said.

"Killed?" the chief said. "Killed who?"

There was a moment's silence. Finally, Victoria spoke up. "Your son." She gazed at the chief with sympathy. "I'm sorry."

\\ Chapter 17 //

The chief leapt to his feet, slammed his cap on his head, patted his gun holster, stuck his reflective glasses on his nose, and, in two agile steps, was at the door.

"Where do you think you're going?" Domingo asked.

"None of your fucking business." The chief wrenched the handle of the sliding door, which jounced out of its track and bounced onto the patio pavement with a crash of breaking glass.

Howland was out of his chair and through the empty door frame before the glass shards settled, but the chief was already in the cruiser. The engine caught with a roar, the siren started with a howl, and the strobe lights began to rotate. The vehicle took off with a squeal of tires and a blast of swirling sand.

"Where's he going?" Victoria, too, had stood up.

"More to the point, what's he going to do?" Domingo said.

Howland strode back in the room.

"Hand me the phone book, Domingo. I need to call Liz Tate." He already had the phone in hand and had dialed the first three digits.

"I'll look it up for you." Victoria reached for the phone book as Domingo searched through his pockets for his glasses. She read the number to Howland.

"Seems to me it would solve the problem if we let things take their natural course," she said to Domingo as Howland waited for someone to answer the phone.

Howland put his hand over the mouthpiece. "We can't afford to lose her as a witness. We've finally got something on one of the biggest drug operations in the Northeast."

"I can't believe Rocky is involved in anything like this."

Domingo snorted.

"He seems so refined," Victoria said.

"Yeah," said Domingo. "Refined."

"No answer. Not even a machine." Howland slammed the cordless phone onto the glass-topped table.

Victoria winced. "Don't break anything else."

"Look up Allison Phipps's number." Domingo pointed to the phone book. "She has her own phone. Her aunt may be there."

Victoria paged back to the *P* listings and gave the number to Howland, who punched it in and handed the phone to Domingo.

"You talk to the kid," Howland growled.

Domingo looked from Howland to Victoria while he waited for an answer.

"Yas," he said into the phone after what seemed a long time. "This is the harbormaster. I need to speak to Ms. Tate."

Victoria could hear a woman's voice come on the line.

Domingo identified himself, and Victoria heard the woman talk at a higher and higher volume, until finally Domingo interrupted her.

"Chief Medeiros is looking for you in connection with his son's death."

He listened, looking from Howland to Victoria.

"I understand. However, the chief seems to believe you had something to do with it."

He waited.

"You knew Fatso was his son, didn't you? His only son?"

He listened.

"Correct." He nodded. "Yas."

He shrugged at Victoria. "That may be.

However, you had better stay out of his way for the time being."

He interrupted the flow of talk. "You have no time to go home. He left here less than five minutes ago with his siren on. He'll try your niece's place when he finds you are not at home."

Long pause.

"Go to Victoria Trumbull's. It's unlikely that he'll think of her house." He looked questioningly at Victoria, who nodded. "She has room. Drive the long way around, through Edgartown. You know where she lives. He's heading into Oak Bluffs on Barnes."

Domingo showed impatience. "For God's sake, get out, now." He pressed the off button and set the phone down.

"She has to argue over everything I say."

"Maybe she and the chief will have a shoot-out, and that will be that," Victoria said.

"I need both of them." Howland paced. "I can't afford to lose either one. Those two are the break we've needed."

Domingo looked at his watch.

Howland stepped carefully over the doorsill, then paused when Victoria began to speak.

"What about Dojan?" she said. "Should he get off scot-free?"

Howland came back slowly into the room and faced Victoria, who was standing by the couch, her hooded eyes on him.

"What about Dojan?" he said.

"Dojan killed someone." Victoria looked intently at him.

"The only reason we know is because he told Domingo. We can't hang him on his own word," Howland said.

"Will he go unpunished, then?" Victoria's knobby hands hung by her side.

Howland sat down again, and Victoria did, too.

"You know how much I care for Dojan," she said. "But he did kill Meatloaf, by his own admission. Shouldn't he be tried? I would be if I'd harpooned somebody."

Howland and Domingo were silent. Domingo looked out the window where his grandson's tricycle lay on its side in the trampled grass. Howland studied his fingernails.

Finally, Howland said, "The government has been after Rocky for a long, long time. He's been responsible for more than a dozen deaths. Indirectly, he has probably killed three times that through drug trafficking."

"What does that have to do with Dojan?" Victoria asked.

"We can get Rocky only if someone with credibility will testify against him. Chief Medeiros and Liz Tate have that credibility."

"So you're making deals, blaming the chief for Meatloaf's death, blaming Meatloaf for Bernie's murder, and letting Dojan off entirely?"

"It's not my decision, Victoria," Howland said.

"Blame your superiors," she said. "More buck passing. I'm ashamed of you, Howland."

Howland looked down at his hands. "Victoria, if I were running the world, Rocky would be put away forever. Chief Medeiros would be put away almost forever. There were some mitigating circumstances. Dojan would be . . . I don't know what I'd do with Dojan."

"But you're not running the world," Victoria said.

"You're right. My bosses tell me what to do. Presumably, they know more than I do about the Rocky Folger drug case. It's their judgment, right or wrong, to get Rocky, any way we can."

"No matter how you do it?" Victoria

said. "What's happened to the justice system?"

"Rocky has wriggled and squirmed through every loophole in the system. The killings, of Bernie, of Meatloaf, then of the chief's son, offer our only hope to nail him."

Victoria gazed at him steadily.

"Hear me, Victoria. Medeiros will be put away permanently. He'll have to start life all over again in the witness protection program. He's not rotten. He's weak."

"You're not listening to *me*," Victoria said. "You can't let Dojan off completely just because you have some bizarre plan to trap Rocky. You — or your superiors — have no right to judge Dojan. Maybe the courts will find him innocent by reason of self-defense or insanity, but in this country, you, some government employee, can't just let him go" — she gestured with a casual wave of her hand — "like that. That's not justice. You ought to know better. You're blaming the less horrible killing on Chief Medeiros so he'll testify against Rocky. Will you say Meatloaf killed Bernie? Meatloaf, who can't defend himself?"

"Wait one second, Victoria." Howland looked up. "We have to be concerned with the greater good here."

"None of it is good," Victoria said. "It's all rotten."

"Least bad, then," Howland responded. "We've been after Rocky for fifteen years. During that time, he has destroyed more lives than you and I can count. Kids on the street shooting up dope. Murder, prostitution, muggings, the whole panoply of crime. He's got to be stopped. For the first time, we have two people we can negotiate with in exchange for their testimony. Dojan's not a killer. His conscience will punish him."

Victoria shook her head vigorously. "Noreen said it to Domingo — neither of you is God. Nor are your superiors. What right do you have to judge Rocky and Meatloaf and Chief Medeiros and Liz Tate? And Dojan? Who gave you the right?"

"Can I say something, sweetheart?" Domingo said.

"I've heard enough." Victoria struggled to her feet.

Domingo held his hand up, palm facing her like a crossing guard. "Tell me, sweetheart, how would you make sure justice is done? What do you suggest?"

Victoria sighed and sat down again. She studied the two men, who gazed back at her intently. Domingo's clock ticked; a car went by on the road; a chickadee landed on the feeder, which swung on its hook.

Victoria hoisted herself up from the couch with dignity. She drew herself up to her full height; although she'd shrunk somewhat over the years, she was still stately. "Turn him over to the tribe," she said. "The Wampanoags will know what to do."

Domingo sat still. Without moving his head, he looked from Victoria to Howland, who was staring in astonishment at Victoria.

"He's a tribal member," Victoria said. "The tribe has jurisdiction over its members."

Domingo got up, too, and held out his hand to her. "You'd have made a great judge, sweetheart."

Victoria heard a car drive up, heard Baby Mingo's voice and then footsteps.

"Shit, Domingo. Now what have you done?" Noreen stopped and stared down at the shower of glass fragments on the patio.

"I can explain, honey," said Domingo.

"I'm leaving." Howland stepped through the open door frame and kicked at the paving of broken glass. "Let me drive you home, Victoria. If Liz Tate shows up, I want to deal with her."

They were parking beneath the Norway maple just when Liz Tate's white Mercedes pulled in beside them.

Liz stepped out of her car, slammed the door shut, and marched over to Howland's car.

"Would you mind telling me what this is about?" she said. "I gather you were at Domingo's and heard. I'm too busy for this."

Howland nodded. "You may have nothing to worry about. However, we thought you should play it safe, at least until the chief cools down."

"Come in," Victoria said. "I'll show you to your room."

"I have no intention of staying here." Liz marched back to her car and opened the door.

"At least come in for a cup of coffee. Won't take a minute to brew it," Victoria said.

After a few moments, Liz followed Victoria into the cookroom. Without a word, she sat in one of the caned chairs at the pine table and crossed her legs. McCavity followed her, looked up at her, turned, and left.

"I'm allergic to cats. If I decide to stay, it

will have to remain outdoors. I hope it hasn't been in my room."

Victoria's jaw set. She opened the refrigerator door to take out the half-and-half. McCavity rose up on his hind legs.

"You've had your food, Cavvy." Victoria looked at Liz Tate sitting stiffly in the chair that Victoria considered her own. Liz placed her elbows on the red-checked tablecloth.

Howland joined her at the table.

"Do you plan on letting me know what this is all about?" she asked. She shook her foot impatiently.

"I think you have a good idea. Chief Medeiros is prepared to testify against your boss."

"What are you talking about?" Liz stopped shaking her foot.

"You didn't realize the chief's son was in jail, did you? Did you even know he had a son?"

Victoria carried two cups of coffee to the table. Liz Tate put her hands in her lap. Victoria could see they were trembling.

"Thank you, Mrs. Trumbull," Liz Tate said dismissively. "You don't need to sit in on this."

"Yes, I think I do." Victoria pulled the chair that was usually Elizabeth's up to the table and sat across from Liz.

Howland turned back to Liz. "What did you have against Dojan? Did you think you had to get rid of him because he was onto your scheme? You botched that big-time. Dojan didn't have any idea of your involvement."

Liz Tate looked from Victoria to Howland. "I came here only because Domingo was so insistent. Not to be insulted."

Victoria lifted her mug to her lips and watched Liz Tate over the rim.

"I think you know what an angry Chief Medeiros can do," Howland said. "It's not pretty. You were wise to take Domingo's advice. Stay out of the chief's way until he cools off. Perhaps you can discuss things with him then."

"This conversation is too strange." Liz Tate pushed the chair back and stood.

"Let me tell you a story. It made things much clearer to the chief." Howland reached into his back pocket, withdrew his black leather folder, flipped it open, and held the DEA badge and ID out for Liz to see.

Liz Tate examined it and sat down again.

"Where's he going in such a hurry?"

Shipyard was at the corner table in the ArtCliff Diner. He stood up and went over to the window as the cruiser sped by on Beach Road.

"Who was it?" Beanie slurped his coffee. "That black cop who's been causing all the trouble?"

"The black cop didn't make the trouble. It was that jerk-off redneck patrolman." Red reached for the sugar bowl, dumped two spoonfuls of sugar into his coffee, and stirred vigorously.

Shipyard returned to the table. "It was the Oak Bluffs po-leece chief himself."

"What's he doing in this neck of the woods?" Red put the spoon on the table and took a sip.

"Who knows?" Beanie said.

"Tough about his kid. I hear he's taking it hard." Red set the mug back on the table.

"Can't blame him. The kid was a handful, but still in all . . ." Shipyard studied a puckered spot on the plastic tablecloth where someone had spilled something hot.

The three were respectfully silent for a moment.

"Anything happening with the investigation into Bernie's murder?" Beanie asked.

"And Meatloaf's? Haven't heard a word about that since they arrested that" — he looked up and saw Dotty, hands on her hips, glaring at him — "that Latino harbormaster."

"He wasn't even on the Island when Meatloaf got it," Shipyard said. "The cops released him."

Dotty brought menus and swiped the tablecloth with her damp rag. "Want to hear today's specials?"

"Might as well."

"Meat loaf with mashed potatoes, side dish of green beans. Apple pie for dessert," she recited.

"Meatloaf." Red looked down at his knife. "Meatloaf."

"That what you want?" Dotty looked around the table. "Meat loaf? All of you?"

"No. We was just talking about him," Beanie said. "I don't feel like meat loaf. What else you got?"

"Liver and onions. Chicken-fried pork chops. Chowder."

"The chowder fresh?" Red asked.

"You know it is. Dojan Minnowfish brought me a bushel of quahogs last night."

"He outta jail?" Beanie asked Shipyard.

"He didn't do nothing. Tied one on is

all. Had him in there until he dried out."
Shipyard handed the menu back to Dotty.
"Chowder. As long as it's not that New
York stuff you served couple years back.
Watery vegetable soup was all it was."

"I made this with milk, potatoes, onions,
lots of clams, and salt pork. A half cup of
quahogs in every bowl."

"Yeah, I'll take that."

"Same for me," Red said.

"Same here." Beanie passed his menu to
her.

Shipyard looked up as a siren sped past.
"There he goes again, back the way he came.
Looks like he's about to have a stroke."

"Who's he know lives this way?" Beanie
said.

"That selectman — selectwoman —
selectperson — whatever you call them
now — has a place on Hatch Road."

"Hatch Road? Where all the beautiful
people live?"

"Where does she get the money to live
there?" Beanie asked. "I'm in the wrong
business, that's for sure."

"They paying selectmen that much these
days?"

"Could be. That town's crazy enough,"
Shipyard said. "Wanna run for Oak Bluffs
selectman, Beanie?"

"No way. I ain't that crazy."

"Ex-husband's money, I think," Red said.

"She's a cold fish. He's lucky to be rid of her. Butter wouldn't melt in her mouth."

"She feels the same about you, Beanie," Shipyard said.

"Here you are, boys." Dotty had three heavy white china bowls of chowder lined up along her left arm, and a larger bowl of chowder crackers in her right hand. She set the bowls in front of the men, the chowder crackers in the middle of the table. "Anything else? Salad? Coleslaw? Apple pie?"

"More coffee." Beanie held out his mug.

"A slice of pie later," Red added.

Allison heard heavy footsteps on the stairs outside her third-floor room over the Sand Bar, and she opened the door a small crack, to see a red-faced Chief Medeiros on the other side.

"Where's Liz Tate?" he demanded, tugging off his sunglasses.

"I don't keep track of my aunt." She held the door open a crack, one hand on the knob, the other flat against the door.

"I need to find her, kid, immediately."

"How am I supposed to know where she's at?"

"Let me in, kid." He pushed the door open against her hands, backing her into the room. Allison tossed her hair out of her eyes and set clenched fists on her hips as he strode into her space. Her aunt was the only person she'd ever let see her room.

Allison had been working at a small rickety table under the window. She had stuck a paintbrush behind her ear; a daub of blue paint flecked her cheek.

A hot plate on the floor under the table was plugged into a tangle of extension cords. The Raybeez blared at top volume from the stereo. The TV blasted discordantly.

Much of her floor space was taken up by an unmade futon. Her teddy bear sat on a shelf above it.

She had taped up on the wall her watercolors and pen and ink sketches of Oak Bluffs scenes, most of them views around the harbor — boats, the Harbor House, the harbormaster's shack, the gingerbread houses.

The chief stood in the middle of her floor and glanced around. "Your aunt do those?" He spoke above the cacaphony, nodding at the drawings on the wall.

"They're mine." Allison kept her hands on her hips.

He looked around her room, his eyes

poking into all her stuff. "I need to find her, kid. Your aunt."

"You don't see her here, do you?" She tossed her head, her hair swinging away from her face.

"I've got business with her." The chief's face flushed an unhealthy red. He spoke loudly, trying to be heard above the noise. "Where is she?"

"How am I supposed to know? Try the Town Hall."

"She comes by here, call me. Understand, kid? Here's my card. That's my pager number. Reach me anytime."

Allison took the card.

"You understand, call me?"

"Maybe." Allison looked down at the card.

"Maybe, nothing. Call."

"Sure, sure." Allison held the door open until he stepped into the hall and clumped down the wooden stairs to the ground floor, his footsteps shaking the building as he descended.

She made a fist and shook it at his back.

When the phone rang, Victoria answered. Howland and Liz sat silently at the table, Liz staring at her coffee mug, turning it around in circles on the cloth. Howland had gone through his act, telling

371

Liz his tale of drug smuggling and murder. She'd protested, demurred. Acted angry and hurt and puzzled.

Howland had been courteous and distant. Victoria followed his diplomatic maneuvering, a side of him she had never seen before. The fencing had gone on for a half hour before the call came.

"Domingo, I'm glad to hear from you," Victoria said.

Liz and Howland both looked up.

"Allison called you?" Victoria glanced at Liz. "Yes, she's here. Do you want to talk to her?" She waited for Domingo to finish what he was saying. She looked at her watch. "I imagine he'll stay until Elizabeth gets home." She looked questioningly at Howland, who nodded, and then she hung the phone back on the wall.

"That was Domingo. Allison called him just a few minutes ago. The chief is looking for you, Liz."

"Well, I guess that settles it." Liz Tate stood. "Show me to my room."

"After we finish our little talk," Howland said.

"I don't want to hear more." Liz moved toward the kitchen.

"Perhaps you don't want to hear more, but I have one hell of a lot more to tell

372

you." Howland's high cheekbones had bright spots of color. "Sit down and listen to me. You're in serious trouble, lady."

Liz sat.

"You have a choice." Howland pushed his chair back slightly. "Prison, on the one hand, or the wrath of two powerful enemies you've made, Rocky, with his subtle ways of handling problems, and Chief Medeiros, who is less subtle."

"I have no problem with Rocky," Liz said sulkily, tracing a line on the tablecloth with her finger.

"You think not?" Howland fixed her with a bright stare.

"I have no problem with Rocky," Liz repeated.

"More coffee?" Victoria asked, getting up from the table.

Liz Tate shook her head. Her hair swirled around her face.

"We know where you got the atropine you put in the fudge. Nightshade berries. We collected the plants from your garden and can identify where berries were detached from the stems. The decorative swirls on your fudge are your own unique touch. The ladies who run the church fair identified the fudge as resembling yours. We've traced the chocolate, the sugar, and the cream you used to the market on Circuit Avenue, where they know you and recall your purchasing them. We found the man to whom you gave the shopping bag, the man who gave the bag with the fudge in it to Louie. Whether you intended to kill the chief's son or not, this is murder."

Liz Tate spoke softly, still tracing her fingernail along a pattern on the tablecloth. "It wasn't meant for Manny. What do you want me to do?"

"Testify against Rocky," Howland said without emphasis.

"My God! Never." Liz stopped running her fingernail along the tablecloth and looked up. "You know what he'd do to me?"

"I can imagine," Howland said dryly. "Care to think about what the chief will do to you?"

Liz Tate put her head in her hands. Her hair cascaded over her face, hiding it.

Howland said nothing.

Victoria fiddled with her cup.

McCavity stalked into the room and began to wash himself, one leg high in the air.

Victoria looked down at the cat with a faint smile.

Howland folded his arms over his chest. "Dare I say you made your own bed?" He leaned back in the chair. When he saw Victoria's expression, he set the chair back on its four legs. Liz stood, paced the small room, sat again. McCavity stopped cleaning himself long enough to stare at her. He stretched, yawned, investigated the wastebasket, leapt into it, and curled up, a ginger-colored mound.

"What do you have in mind?" Liz said in a small voice.

"I have a typed confession." Howland rummaged through his green canvas briefcase and brought it out. "In this, you explain in detail how you attempted to kill Dojan, believing that he knew you were involved in the drug-smuggling scheme, and how you killed Fatso Medeiros instead."

"I didn't mean to kill him." Liz lifted her head.

"You intended to kill Dojan, didn't you?"

Liz put her head in her hands again.

"You intended to kill, and you did kill. You killed the chief's son in a most unpleasant way. Doesn't matter who you intended to kill; someone died as a result of your actions." He put the typed confession in front of her. "It is against the law to kill people. Read this."

She lifted her head again.

"Make whatever corrections are necessary. I'll call the notary up at Alley's store, ask her to come here to witness our signing it. You, Victoria, and I will sign."

"What are you going to do with it?" Liz looked up, face contrasting whitely with her black hair and carmine lipstick.

"Use it if I need to."

"What about Rocky?" Liz spoke so softly, it took Victoria a second to understand what she'd said. "I would never do anything to hurt him."

"Rocky got you involved in this, didn't he?"

"He trusts me. I would never harm him, will never testify against him, no matter what."

Howland went on as if he hadn't heard her. "I have a typed affidavit explaining your relationship with Rocky, and your role in the drug operation."

"And I'm to read it, make corrections, and sign."

Howland said nothing. He held the pen out to her.

"I can't do it. He loves me." She put her head down on her arms. "And I love him. He asked me to marry him."

Victoria stared at her cup, eyes half-closed, her wrinkled face a topographic map of disapproval. "He's not likely to marry you if you're in prison for murder."

Liz lifted her head. "What do you plan to do with this affidavit?"

"We use it in court with other evidence to lock up Rocky for a long, long time."

"My God!" Liz paled.

"I can recommend a lesser sentence for you on the basis of your cooperation."

"When I get out, my life won't be worth a damn."

"Probably not," Howland said. "However, it's likely that Rocky will get a life sentence. The chief will be spirited away to some unknown place in a witness protection program."

The kitchen door opened and Elizabeth came in. The American flag stood out sharply on her starched uniform sleeve. She stopped when she reached the cookroom door.

"Sorry. I didn't mean to interrupt."

Victoria saw Elizabeth's puzzled expression as she glanced from Howland, whose face was grim, to Liz, who was staring, white-faced, at her folded hands, and then to Victoria.

Victoria pushed herself away from the table, got slowly to her feet, and said to her granddaughter, "We need to get the downstairs room made up."

\\ Chapter 18 //

"Mr. D. trusts you alone in this place?" Louie had come into the shack where Allison was working with a pile of receipts.

"He put me in charge for a couple hours. I'm hardly alone. Have you looked around the harbor lately?"

"I'll be glad when the president's outta here." Louie slapped a handful of receipts on the desk in front of Allison. "Here are some more."

Allison shuffled through the receipts Louie had given her. "When are you going to learn how to write? I can't read any of this stuff, you know?"

"So what?" Louie slumped into the chair in front of the computer, entered something, and moved the mouse around. "They forgot to take off the games when they installed the harbor stuff. I'll bet Mr. D. plays Minesweeper when no one's here."

"Leave it alone," Allison said sharply.

"Listen to you now. Little Miss Lawsuit."

The radio crackled, probably a boat needing a slip. Louie answered, gave the skipper a slip number, then hung up the mike.

An angular man wearing an earphone and a button in the lapel of his blazer came to the window. "I need to use your radio," he said to Louie.

"I'm in charge here, not him," Allison said.

"Sure," Louie said. "Anything for the president."

The man turned his back on Louie and Allison while he talked in semicode to a vessel. Then he hung up the mike and left.

"You could say thank you," Allison shouted after him, but he was already off the catwalk.

An elderly woman came to the window. "Would you know, miss, when the president will be arriving?"

"No, ma'am. Today or tomorrow, I guess."

"Will he come here to Oak Bluffs?"

"I'm sorry, ma'am, I don't know what his plans are. Maybe for the fireworks tomorrow."

"Thank you so much, miss."

"At least I been doing important stuff." Louie wadded up a piece of paper and tossed it at the wastepaper basket. It missed and fell on the floor. Allison kicked it.

"Yeah? Like what?"

"I did stuff for Meatloaf. He paid me. A lot."

"So what are you doing for Meatloaf now? Planting grass?"

"I don't know why I bother to talk to you." Louie clicked the mouse on the game. "I been doing stuff for the selectmen."

"My aunt, I suppose. Her errand boy."

The phone rang. Allison answered, took a message for Domingo, and hung up.

A sailboat came in through the channel, and Allison went out on the deck with her clipboard. She called out a slip number and pointed; the skipper nodded thanks.

She stepped back inside the shack, finished sorting the receipts, and took them over to the computer. "Mind if I do some real work?"

Louie's face flushed. He exited from the games program, stood up, and stretched. Allison took the seat he'd vacated and opened up the reservations program.

"You're wasting your time. You know that, don't you?"

"So?" Allison continued to enter data.

"Mr. D. thinks he's so smart, computerizing everything." Louie put his hands in his pockets and sauntered over to the window that overlooked the parking lot. "He's making a lot of enemies is what he's doing."

"Why don't you shut up and let me do my work, you know?"

"You wouldn't talk so smart if you knew what I been doing."

"What've you been doing? You're just dying to tell me, aren't you?"

A call came over the radio. The phone rang. Allison took the radio call while Louie answered the phone.

"You know that big tree limb that came down in Elizabeth's driveway?" Louie said when it was quiet again.

"Yeah?"

"I did that."

"Well, whatever you were trying to do, it didn't work."

"Yeah it did."

"I'm not impressed." Allison held up a receipt and stared at it. "What does this say? What's this boat name?"

Louie looked at it. "*Night Hawk*? I don't know. *Right Stuff*?"

"Is the boat still here?"

"Probably."

"Go back and write the name so we can read it, will you?"

"Furthermore, you know that accident she had? On Barnes Road? I set that up."

"Let me work, will you?" Allison pushed her hair away from her face with her shoulder. "I don't want to hear this stuff."

"It scared her shitless. Scared her old lady, too."

"Mrs. Trumbull scared? I don't think so." Allison waved her hand in front of her face. "I suppose you left those notes, too?"

"That's right."

"Whoever thought that up was stupid."

"I thought that up." Louie stood. "That was hardly stupid. Mr. D. was pretty worried about that, too. Still is."

"Not really. You finished bragging? How about going away and doing your job, you know? Here are a couple more receipts no one can read."

When Louie sauntered off, whistling, batting his receipt book against the railing as he went, Allison called Domingo and told him what Louie had said.

Dojan pulled his lobster boat up to the floating dock at the foot of the harbormaster's shack, where Victoria waited, sitting on a chair Elizabeth had put there for her.

Dojan's wooden boat was not large, maybe eighteen feet long, had a small cabin forward, a large cockpit aft, and an outboard motor patched with black vinyl tape and shiny aluminum duct tape. A long tiller led from a large red-painted rudder dotted with barnacles. The rudder had a cutout near the stern of the boat for the outboard motor. Most of the boat's paint had flaked off, and what remained was mostly green, with touches of black and red. The flat, broad gunwales were worn and splintery, as if over the seasons Dojan had pulled his lobster pots aboard there.

He shut off the motor, tied the lines to dock cleats, and leapt nimbly onto the dock. His bare feet splayed out.

"You came!" His grin showed his missing tooth.

"Did you think I wouldn't?" Victoria rose, holding on to the railing, and picked up a basket that was next to her. "I brought lunch, roast chicken and hard-boiled eggs."

Dojan rolled his eyes.

"Napkins and orange juice." She looked up at him and smiled. "I decided not to bring fudge for dessert."

His mouth formed a pink O in the middle of his beard.

"You gonna be warm enough?"

"I'm layered." Victoria showed him the windbreaker Howland had lent her. Under that was the heavy Canadian sweater from Fiona's parents, then the gray moth-eaten sweater of Elizabeth's, under that a down vest that didn't quite close, and then a stretched-out red turtleneck shirt. She started to lift that, and Dojan hurriedly held up his hand.

"If you get cold, I have jackets and blankets and hats."

"I have leather work gloves so I can haul pots." Victoria held up her gardening gloves, a hole in the thumb mended with masking tape.

Elizabeth came down the ramp to the dock. "For heaven's sake, Gram, you'd think it was February."

"I expect to be outside working, not idling."

"Don't fall overboard. With all those clothes, you'll sink like a stone."

"They'll be full of air, buoy me up."

"Bring home a lot of lobsters. I'll get your lines."

Dojan helped the bulky Victoria aboard and leapt into the boat after her. She sat on a box he'd brought for her. He started the engine, Elizabeth tossed the lines aboard, and Dojan steered slowly out of the channel. Victoria, still seated, coiled his lines neatly.

When they were clear of the buoys at the mouth of the channel, Dojan opened up the throttle, and the boat lifted in the water, the engine humming. Victoria noticed him cock his head toward the sound of the motor, as if listening to it, watched him steer with the slightest movement of the long tiller. The wind ruffled his hair, blew his beard away from his face, and sent his skull scarf streaming behind him. His bare arms, tattooed with eagles and roses, were dark brown, sun and dirt combined.

Victoria shed some of her layers. First the windbreaker, which she rolled up and tossed into the cabin, then the heavy sweater. Soon she was down to the red turtleneck, and the cabin floor had a heap of clothing on it. Dojan nodded. His eyes were clear; his mouth was open in a wide smile.

They turned right toward Cape Poge, the same route the whale-watch boat had taken. Gulls trailed after them, mewing. The motor hummed quietly, and small waves slapped against the bow. Before they reached the cape, Dojan slowed. Victoria could see the line of low shore and the lighthouse on the tip. Dojan pointed, and she saw his lobster-pot buoys bobbing in the water, yellow, with two blue stripes around them. He steered next to the first buoy, reached into the water, and pulled it on board. He hauled up the line fastened to the buoy, and Victoria saw the trap rising through the clear green water.

"Couple of keepers there." Dojan dumped the lobsters onto the deck and tossed the lobster pot overboard.

"Only a couple? It looks like a dozen to me, Dojan."

"See those marks on the gunwale? They gotta be that long."

Victoria moved her feet out of the way as lobsters scurried around the deck, claws clashing. Dojan grabbed the littlest ones by their backs and dropped them overboard. He reached into a coffee can for a handful of wide yellow rubber bands and fitted them over the claws of the two largest lobsters, then dropped them into a white plastic bucket of seawater. He shaded the bucket with a piece of dirty gray canvas.

The boat rocked gently. Dojan pulled his pots, dumped out lobsters, and dropped the pots overboard with a smooth rhythm. Victoria sorted out the smallest lobsters and tossed them overboard. Her work gloves were soon wet and coated with slimy green algae. The masking tape disintegrated, exposing her thumb.

Gulls cried and dived at schools of small fish; the sun wheeled overhead. Neither Victoria nor Dojan spoke.

Finally, Dojan stood erect, stretched his arms out to the side, and said, "That's all."

Victoria counted the lobsters. "We have a nice mess, at least fifteen."

Dojan grinned.

Victoria looked at him. "It's a nice picnic spot."

They tossed their gnawed-on chicken bones into the Sound. Cracked eggs against the gunwale and flicked the shells overboard, where large fish rose to the surface to snap at the remains. Gulls fought and squabbled and cried over their picnic leftovers. Victoria dipped her hands into the water, washed off the chicken fat, reached into her pocket for a napkin, and dried her face. She grinned happily at Dojan, who grinned back. The boat rocked gently, waves lapping against its wooden sides.

"When does the tide change?" Victoria had been watching trees on the shore pass them as the boat drifted slowly toward the arc of Cape Poge.

"Full flood now." Dojan's mouth was full of chicken, his beard full of crumbs and dripping fat. He tossed the bone he'd been gnawing overboard, and a fish snatched it and dived with a silver flash. "Slack tide in two hours. Change, a half hour after that." He wiped his forearm across his mouth.

Victoria watched the shoreline drift past. The near trees seemed to move faster than the distant ones. Dim objects approached, became rocks or boats pulled up on the shore, or tree trunks washed in from far places. The objects faded behind them as they drifted slowly. When they neared Cape Poge, she could see what looked like an array of slender poles. At first, she thought they were fishing rods stuck in the sand, but as they came closer, she saw they were tall masts on the other side of the spit. They drifted toward the cape. There were six or seven large sailboats clustered together beyond the breaking surf along the straight east shore.

"Are they at anchor?"

Dojan turned and stood up. "They're big."

"Are they rafted up? Seems like an out-of-the-way place for an overnight stay."

Dojan ducked into the cabin and came out with a pair of binoculars. He held them to his eyes and adjusted the focus.

"They're not from here. Saint Croix, Saint Thomas, Grand Turk. I can't read them all."

"That's unusual, isn't it? After making a long cruise, don't boats like that come into the harbor?"

Dojan scratched his stomach and burped.

"May I look?" She held out her hand for the binoculars, and Dojan passed them to her. They were greasy where he had held them. "There's only one anchor out. No, two. They're rafted together. They must know each other."

"Not much room in the harbor. Full of law vessels."

"If there's no room in the harbor, why wouldn't they anchor outside, where they can row their dinghies into shore? There's nothing here. No houses, no stores, no people, no nothing. Even the lighthouse is automated, no lighthouse keepers." She handed the binoculars back to Dojan.

"My great-grandfather was the Gay Head lighthouse keeper," Dojan said. "He lighted the kerosene lamp every night. He used to wind the clockwork that made the light go around. He lived in a house next to the light."

"That would have been your father's grandfather, wouldn't it? I didn't know him, but my big sister did."

"They didn't have electricity then. My grandmother remembered when the electricity came up-Island."

"I remember, too, Dojan. That wasn't so long ago."

Dojan gazed at her. "I wasn't born."

He stood in the stern, next to the tiller. The wind had picked up and his hair blew back from his face.

"Dojan." Victoria settled herself on her box seat with her back to the cabin. "I want you to do something for me." She looked up at him soberly.

"Yes, ma'am. I'll move the sun and the moon for you."

"As I recall, you're the Wind and the Rain."

Dojan grinned. "Yes, ma'am."

"What do you think of the tribal council?" Victoria put her hands beside her, her right hand resting on the coiled line.

"The tribal council." Dojan scratched under his arm and thought. "Good people."

"If you did something wrong, would you tell the council?"

Dojan stared at her, motionless. "Yes, ma'am."

"Would you tell them even if you knew they would punish you and the punishment would be harsh?"

"I am a Wampanoag from Aquinnah." Dojan stood up straight, his hand on the tiller. His eyes settled firmly on Victoria's somber face. "I can take what's due me."

Victoria took a deep breath. "You know it was wrong to harpoon that man."

Dojan swallowed. He looked over at the large boats anchored behind the curve of the spit. "Yes, ma'am." He swallowed again and looked at Victoria. "There was nobody I could tell. I couldn't tell the police chief, after I saw what he'd done."

"You could have told me," Victoria said quietly.

"Yes, ma'am. I trusted you. I should have told you. I was ashamed." He slapped his hands on his stomach. "There's been a thing growing inside me since that night. I tried to sweat it out. I tried drowning it out. I told Domingo." He lowered his head. "I keep seeing that man fall into the water. I still remember that red-hot anger I felt. I hurt bad."

"Who's the head of the tribal council now?" Victoria asked.

"Chief Hawkbill," Dojan said.

"He's your father's second cousin, isn't he?"

"Yes, ma'am."

"Go to him tomorrow and tell him what you told Domingo. The tribal council will deal out the punishment they believe is right. Will you do that?"

"Yes, ma'am." Dojan bowed his head.

"We'd better go. The breeze is picking up."

Dojan pulled the starter cord, the motor cut on smoothly, he steered the boat into the wind, and they headed home. The wind had stirred up whitecaps. Waves slapped the bow, spraying salt water over Victoria, whose back was to it. She blinked the spray out of her eyes. Her eyebrows and eyelashes were crusted with salt.

"We need to tell Domingo about those sailboats." Victoria reached into the cabin for her warm clothes. She put on the down vest and Elizabeth's gray sweater over it. "It seems strange to have boats from such a distance clustered so far from anything."

Dojan steered with the tiller tilted up so he could stand. His black beard, his hair, his eyebrows had turned white, rimed with salt. He had aged. Victoria laughed. She had not.

"Will you go with me?" Dojan asked.

"I will if you give me a ride and take me home again."

Dojan nodded his white-tipped head.

They cut straight from Cape Poge to Oak Bluffs, crossing the wide-open bay that surrounded the beach. Whitecaps sparkled as far as they could see. Dojan stood straight, his shoulders thrown back, his head up, and began to sing a sea chanty that Victoria knew. She joined in the chorus with her strong voice: "Look away! Look away, you jolly, jolly boys, look away!"

When they reached the lee of East Chop, the water was calm. Dojan turned into the channel and slowed to bare headway.

Elizabeth came down the ramp to the floating dock. The long muscles in her slim tan legs flexed smoothly as she walked.

"See what I brought back for our supper." Victoria held up two lobsters for her granddaughter's inspection.

"Did you have a good time, Gram? Was it rough out there? Were you warm enough?"

"I was glad I was prepared. You never know, on the water."

Elizabeth helped her grandmother out of the boat, and Dojan took off again toward the liquor store. He turned to Victoria as he left the dock. "Tomorrow morning." He held up his hand to her, and she returned his salute.

"What was that all about?" Elizabeth asked.

"They buy his lobsters at the liquor store," Victoria said.

"But —" Elizabeth started to say.

"Domingo!" Victoria interrupted. "I'm back."

"So his boat didn't sink after all." Domingo was waiting at the door of the shack.

"I'll be right back," Elizabeth said, striding up the ramp. "I need to help that sailboat with lines."

Victoria paused at the top of the ramp, out of breath, and watched Elizabeth run toward a boat that was pulling into a slip. Victoria carried the two lobsters by their backs; they flipped their tails and flailed the air with their unbound legs.

Once she had seated herself on the chair in the shack and had taken a couple of deep breaths, she turned to Domingo, who was leaning on the railing outside the shack.

"Before Elizabeth gets back, I wanted to tell you that Dojan is going to the tribal council tomorrow. It's poisoning him. He needs to get it out of his system."

"You did the right thing, sweetheart. You're a better man than either Howland or me."

"Something else," Victoria said. "What would you say if someone told you there were seven boats anchored on the other side of Cape Poge, all big boats, all from the Caribbean?"

Domingo gazed at her.

"When the harbor is teeming with police of all kinds?"

"Sweetheart, I'd say you found another piece of the puzzle." He reached around inside the door for the phone. "Atherton needs to know about this."

Howland was walking his dogs on the beach below his house when his cell phone rang. It was Domingo, telling him about the sailboats off Cape Poge.

Howland immediately contacted DEA and the Coast Guard. They dispatched the two Coast Guard cutters from the Oak Bluffs Harbor to the far side of Cape Poge, along with two spotter planes and a DEA helicopter from Otis National Guard Base on Cape Cod.

The pilots reported activity on the deck

of one of the sailboats. The crews from all seven boats seemed to be baiting and setting a dozen or so lobster pots.

The aircraft pilot reported this back to her lieutenant, who reported back to Howland, who told them to photograph everything. He requested that the Coast Guard cutters circle the sailboats until the DEA paperwork and people were in place.

"They're not likely to run for it," Howland said to the lieutenant. "Top speed for those sailboats is six or seven knots. They may try to jettison drug packages. Get the pilot to spot where they drift, if she can. They probably plan to hold the drugs in lobster pots until someone can retrieve them."

"When you're ready, we'll escort the boats to the harbor," the lieutenant told him, "and you guys can take over."

"There are at least two dozen law-enforcement officers there. This will give them something to do." Howland disconnected and headed for home with his dogs.

Elizabeth dropped her grandmother off at Domingo's on her way to work the next afternoon, and Victoria met with Domingo and Howland.

"Chief Medeiros is going to get away with committing Bernie's murder, isn't he?" Victoria asked Domingo. "I'm sorry for him, in a way, and somewhat sympathetic, but justice won't be served if he gets off."

"Sweetheart, Chief Medeiros is going to have the worst-possible punishment." Domingo gazed out the window. "He is going into the witness protection program. His daughter will go to live with her mother and the diesel salesman out west, and he may never see her again." Domingo turned slightly, and Victoria examined his profile, curved nose, large lower lip, bright eyes. "He will lose his identity completely as a police officer. He'll lose his roots. He will never again be able to be with family on birthdays or Christmases. He will start a new life in a place he probably doesn't want to be. If he breaks free of the program, Rocky's people will get him. If they don't, the DEA will."

"He didn't kill Meatloaf. Dojan did. I don't want to see Dojan put away somewhere, but . . ." Victoria left the rest of her sentence unfinished.

"You went with him to the tribal council?" Domingo asked.

"This morning. He wanted me to go

397

with him while he talked to Chief Hawk-bill, and I did."

Howland whistled. "Nice job, Victoria."

"The tribal council knows how to deal with this." Domingo took out a cigarette and lighted it.

"He's not as crazy as he appears," Howland said.

"Of course not," Victoria retorted. "He and I went to the tribal chief. Dojan told him everything, the murder he witnessed, his fight with Meatloaf. Dojan is wild with guilt. The chief is going to discuss it with the tribal elders."

"I wonder what their idea of punishment is," Howland murmured.

"I don't know." Victoria looked down at her hands, green-streaked from pulling weeds. "Chief Hawkbill said something about sending Dojan to Washington as tribal representative."

Howland put his hand on top of Victoria's, a strong square hand on top of her knobby one.

\\ Chapter 19 //

The fog bank held offshore for most of the day, a thick ominous gray mass that loomed on the horizon. Late in the afternoon, it began to move. From the beach, the fog looked as if it was rolling steadily toward the Island across the water, a woolly fleece, sucked inland by the rising warm air in the center of the Island. Tendrils and wisps of fog drifted across the sun, veiling it, making it a pinkish yellow disk.

On the beaches, the last of the sunbathers and swimmers tugged sweatshirts over their heads, wrapped towels or terrycloth robes around them, gathered up the remaining children, and headed back to rented cottages and hotel rooms.

In the Sound, foghorns intermittently wailed a mournful warning of shoals and rocks. The ferries sounded their higher-pitched whistles as they inched their way toward the Island.

Streamers of fog wafted past the harbormaster's shack. A boater came to the window, his hair and yellow slicker beaded with moisture, and Elizabeth slid the window open.

The boater wiped his face with the back of his hand. "It's thick out there." He unzipped his jacket and took his wallet from an inside pocket. "Any slips available?"

"The slips are all taken. There are a few moorings still." Elizabeth waved a hand toward the center of the harbor, which neither of them could see. "Are you at the fuel dock now?"

He nodded.

Domingo was standing with his back to Elizabeth and the sailor. "There should be two or three places left. Four boats to a mooring." He turned. "Think you can find it okay?"

"Yeah. We came over for the fireworks last year." The sailor laughed and indicated the thick fog.

"It might clear a little by this evening." Domingo shrugged. "You never know with Island weather."

The sailor took a bill out of his wallet and handed it to Elizabeth. "One night."

She filled out a receipt, gave him change, and watched him disappear into the murky cloud. Another figure materialized.

"Damn, Domingo. Here's that arrogant Secret Service guy again." She turned away from the window. "You deal with him."

The agent came into the shack without knocking and propped himself against the edge of the desk, folded his arms across his chest, and stared sullenly at Elizabeth. He was a tall, hefty, dark-haired man.

Domingo started to say something to the agent, but Elizabeth interrupted, flushed with irritation. "Don't you guys believe in manners?"

"May I please come into the harbormaster's office, ma'am?" he said without unfolding his arms. "So I can guard the president of the United States, if you don't mind."

"Funny," Elizabeth said sourly.

He was there for only a few minutes when a state trooper came in. "Need to use the radio." Domingo pointed to it. While the trooper was talking on the radio, a Coast Guardsman showed up at the door. "I'm supposed to check your radio against ours."

"As soon as that guy gets off," Domingo said.

Two women in yellow rain slickers came to the window. The phone rang. A voice on the radio asked to talk to the trooper. The Coast Guardsman picked up the mike and responded. The Secret Service agent crossed one ankle over the other, unfolded his arms long enough to take a pack of gum out of his pocket, unwrapped a stick, tossed the rolled-up wrapper toward the wastebasket, fed the stick into his mouth, and refolded his arms over his chest.

"You know, guys, we need to use our radio, too," Elizabeth said. "Believe it or not."

"Won't be a minute," the Coast Guardsman said apologetically.

Elizabeth went over to the desk, where the Secret Service agent lolled. "Move out of my way, buster. I need to get into that drawer."

He slid over, arms still folded. She opened the drawer, took the receipt book to the counter, and started to thumb through pages.

"Where's your grandmother?" Domingo asked her.

"Reading to the elderly at the hospital. . . . Sixteen, seventeen, eighteen . . ."

"Don't you think you should pick her up?" Domingo put his hands in his pockets and stared out at the grayness.

Elizabeth held her place in the book. "She'll be fine." She went back to counting. "Twenty-five, twenty-six, twen—"

"It's hazardous driving."

"She'll be fine, Domingo. Really. She's a big girl. Thirty-two, thirty-three . . ."

"She going to watch the fireworks tonight?"

"Yes. Thirty-four, thirty-five . . ."

"With this pea soup, there won't be much to see. Only a lot of racket. We'll shoehorn her in with the boys." Domingo nodded at the crowded shack.

Elizabeth slapped the book shut. "Damnation, Domingo. I lost count. Noreen's driving my grandmother here to the harbor. You, Domingo, are driving me crazy." She looked around at the law-enforcement people cluttering the small office.

Domingo turned from the window. "When's she due here?"

Elizabeth sighed and looked at her watch. "She'll be here any minute."

"I don't like her out alone." Domingo stared at the fog.

"Come on, Domingo. She's with Noreen."

Domingo stepped outside, lighted a cigarette, and paced. He tossed the cigarette overboard. "I'm going to look for them."

"Give them another couple of minutes."

The parking lot had disappeared. The catwalk seemed to be suspended in space over a bottomless void. The planks of the walk appeared and disappeared in eddies of fog.

"You there, Mike?" A second Coast Guardsman rapped on the door frame and entered the shack.

"Yes, sir. I'm waiting to use the radio."

The trooper, who was speaking into the mike, held up his hand in acknowledgment.

Domingo checked his watch. "Something may have happened."

A diver in a blue-and-black wetsuit with scuba tanks on his back and swim fins on his feet slapped into the shack.

"Why don't you guys have your own radios?" Elizabeth snapped.

"Ma'am, I wondered if you had a Band-Aid?" the diver asked.

Elizabeth opened the first-aid kit and handed a couple to the diver. He took off one of his swim fins and looked up sheepishly at her. "Blister."

"Here they come now, Domingo." Elizabeth straightened up and peered through the fog.

They could hear Noreen's high voice, Victoria's deeper one, and then the two women appeared out of the silvery mist. Victoria's white hair glistened with droplets of moisture.

Victoria leaned over the railing. "You can barely see the harbormaster's launch through the fog." The launch was tied to the shack's pilings. Beyond it, Elizabeth could vaguely make out the shape of a Coast Guard cutter with its diagonal red slash across the bow.

"What kept you?" Domingo said crossly.

"Nothing kept us." Noreen looked around. "Jesus, this is like a commuter bus."

Victoria wiped moisture off her face with a napkin from her pocket and sat down. "Will they still have the fireworks?"

"It's on the president's schedule. It will take more than fog for them to cancel," Domingo answered.

"You guys hanging around all night?" Noreen asked the agent leaning against the desk.

"Yep."

Elizabeth scowled at him.

The phone rang. Elizabeth pawed people aside to answer it. The agent's beeper went off. He looked at the number on it.

"Let me have the phone," he said to Elizabeth, who was taking a reservation. "Hang up."

Elizabeth glared at him, excused herself to the caller, and handed the phone to the agent. A customer had come up to the window, and she pushed past the state trooper, who, in stepping aside, bumped into her.

"Sorry, ma'am."

Elizabeth snapped, "Clear out, all of you! You." She pointed to the agent, who had hung up the phone. "Outside. Guard the president from that bench out there. Out!"

The shack cleared, and Domingo looked at Elizabeth with respect.

A powerboat entered the harbor, cruised around slowly, and departed again.

"Who let them in?" Elizabeth said. "I thought someone was keeping boats out of the harbor."

"That's a police cruiser making its rounds," Domingo told her. "As we speak, divers are checking the harbor for anything out of the ordinary."

"Like explosive devices stuck on boats," Victoria said.

The radio on the Coast Guard cutter came on with a crackle of static and an announcement that consisted mostly of numbers.

Elizabeth put her hands over her ears. "I'll be glad when this day is over."

Domingo went out onto the deck, and

Elizabeth heard the click of his Zippo. He took a few puffs and tossed his cigarette over the railing, then went back inside. On his way, he patted the shoulder of the Secret Service agent, who was sitting outside on the bench, his collar turned up against the steady drip of condensed fog spilling off the eaves onto his back.

Darkness crept in, filtered by the fog. As soon as Elizabeth hung up the phone from one call, it rang again. The scanning radio locked onto channel 16, then channel 22. Somewhere out in the foggy night, the Coast Guard was trying to assist a disabled vessel and an injured crew member.

"There seem to be a lot of people gathering," Victoria said. "You can hear them, even if you can't see them."

Elizabeth was aware of the soft murmur of voices, heard an occasional word she could almost identify.

By 8:30, the activity on the radio had quieted, and a half hour later, they heard the opening salvo of the fireworks.

Each time a rocket was shot off, the entire sky lighted up with a glow that lingered for a few seconds before the next was set off. Fog droplets reflected and refracted the light in a milky way that left no shadows and lit up the night softly. It was more magical than the displays would have been on a clear night.

Victoria turned to Elizabeth and gestured to the Secret Service agent sitting on the bench outside. "He looks miserable. He's welcome to have my seat."

Elizabeth rolled her eyes, then invited the agent back into the shack. He rose from the bench and shambled inside. The back of his jacket was wet.

With each detonation, the shack shuddered. No one talked over the noise. The display went on and on, lighting up the fog, blue, yellow, red, gold, green. Combinations of color were enhanced by the eerie drifting fog. It was difficult to tell where the explosions came from. Sound seemed to surround them; color engulfed them in swirls and eddies, the inside of a light-bulb, the inside of a milk bottle.

"This must be the finale," Victoria said as the fog was pierced with galaxies of light, explosions of color and sound, a tattoo of quick reports, a thunderous blast, a series of pops like firecrackers, the smell of gunpowder. Then everything seemed to be detonated at once. Red and orange flashed in the fog to the west, yellow and green overhead, blue and purple to the south. A rainbow of soft colors shimmered in the opalescent sky. And then it was over.

Victoria applauded. So did the Secret Service agent.

"My name's Joshua." He offered Victoria his large hand, which she shook firmly. Elizabeth stared in astonishment as he stood and politely told Victoria, "It was real nice meeting you, ma'am. I'm afraid I've got to get back to the boss. He'll be leaving before the crowd does."

Car horns and boat horns honked, and boaters blasted their canned air horns. Hundreds of footsteps swished on the bulkhead. Elizabeth heard the single voice of a pleased crowd.

"They were smart not to cancel it." Victoria turned to one of the men next to her. "This was one of the most beautiful displays I've ever seen."

"You must have seen quite a few, ma'am."

"We used to burn punk sticks when I was a child. The only fireworks I remember were all white, like white rockets."

"I'll make the rounds of the harbor," Elizabeth said. "Where did you put the launch, Domingo?"

"Right there." Domingo went outside and pointed to where he'd tied the launch to the piling. The boat was gone.

"I'm sure it was there. I saw it when we came back from the hospital." Victoria was puzzled.

"Some watchdogs," Elizabeth muttered. "Two Coast Guard cutters, the Secret Service, the marine police, the state police, a conservation officer, the Oak Bluffs police, and visiting firemen. And someone walks off with the harbormaster's launch. I hope you do a better job of watching the president."

She looked up as she heard pounding footsteps on the catwalk, and one of the dock attendants stumbled into the shack.

"Liz Tate," he gasped.

Domingo looked up. "What about Liz Tate?"

"She was parked," the kid said in between gasps for air, "Harbor House."

Domingo grabbed him by the arm. "What about it?"

"It's gone!"

"What are you talking about, the launch?"

"No, no," the dock attendant said. "Liz Tate!"

"Out with it." Domingo released his arm.

"Let him catch his breath, will you?" Elizabeth barked.

Domingo cut his eyes at Elizabeth. "You

410

sound like my wife."

"Sure, Domingo," Noreen said from her seat on top of the desk, where she'd been sitting throughout the fireworks.

Domingo stepped back. He stared at the teenager. "Well?"

"She parked in front of the Harbor House." He was shivering. "She was watching the fireworks from her car with Louie."

"Who?" Domingo demanded.

"Louie, the dock attendant. The kid with green hair. I seen them sitting in the car, and the next second it disappeared."

"What!"

"There ain't nothing left," the kid said. "A hole is all."

"It exploded?" Victoria asked.

"Yes, ma'am. It blew up. Like a fireball. I seen them sitting there, and I seen it blow up."

"How long ago?"

"Right at the end. The finale. When the fireworks were going crazy. At the end. It vaporized."

"Did you report it to the police?"

"Somebody musta. There was a cop car there before I left to come here."

"You said Liz Tate and Louie were in the car when the explosion took place?"

The kid nodded.

Victoria stood up. "Let's go."

When they reached the Harbor House, both lanes were blocked with cars and people leaving after the fireworks. No one seemed to be concerned about an explosion involving a car.

The fire truck was held up by the stream of cars flowing away from town. Someone had witnessed the blast; someone had called 911. A small crowd was gathered around the space between a truck and a rusty Volvo, but no one in the passing cars seemed to notice the space in the line of parked cars or the pit where a car had been, or the damaged cars on either side.

It made no difference that the equipment could not get through. There was nothing anyone could do. The dock attendant was right: The car had vanished, leaving strewn debris, a deep pothole, a blue pickup truck with its bed blackened, and a rust red Volvo with its snout skewed.

While Victoria and Domingo were standing to one side, Howland arrived, disheveled from running.

"Heard it on the scanner," Howland said. "Who was it?"

"The dock attendant, Huey or Dewey, said it was Liz Tate's car. She was in it at the time of the explosion," Domingo informed him. "With Louie."

"Hell." Howland slammed his hand against the blue truck. "There goes my case. My chief witness. All I've got now is Medeiros. I should have anticipated something like that. Goddamn!"

"Liz was still at your house, wasn't she, sweetheart?" While he spoke, Domingo stood with his feet slightly apart, hands in his pockets, staring down at the hole. To Victoria, the hole didn't seem big enough for what had happened.

"She was staying in the downstairs room."

Howland paced. The small crowd of people looked and pointed and moved on, one by one or in groups of two or three.

"Should someone get yellow tape from the shack?" Victoria finally asked. "We need to keep sightseers away, don't we?"

Domingo shrugged. "It's not up to us. It's up to the police."

"Are they likely to find enough to identify anyone?" Victoria asked.

Domingo gave a macabre grin, white teeth flashing against his dark skin.

"Is it possible there was some mistake?" she said. "That there really was no one in the car?"

"I don't think so, sweetheart."

"I had invited her to supper this Saturday," Victoria said. "Boston baked beans. I'd invited Rocky, too."

"Didn't you think that might have been a bit awkward for them under the circumstances, Victoria?" Howland asked. He paced back and forth in front of the hole.

"I wouldn't do that," Domingo said, stopping him. "You'll mess up whatever evidence the Crime Unit might find."

Even in the darkness, Victoria could see Howland's scowl, the lines of his face heightened by the lights along the harbor.

"She loved him," Victoria said. "She hadn't made up her mind to sign anything, and Howland couldn't force her. She wanted to be with Rocky at least one more time."

The three stood silently for long moments. Cars streamed by slowly. An occasional passenger would lean out the window and look at the small knot of people still around the place where the car had been. Victoria could see the fire engine working its way slowly through the oncoming traffic, its red light flashing.

Howland spoke first. "When I heard it on my scanner, I called the Crime Unit. They should arrive on the next boat." He looked at his watch. "By then, the traffic should have cleared."

"What can they possibly find?" Victoria said.

"They'll vacuum up everything inside a wide circle, if our friend here" — Domingo slapped Howland on the arm — "hasn't trampled it into the ground. They'll examine every blade of grass, every grain of sand microscopically."

"Surely you don't think Rocky had anything to do with this," Victoria said, sweeping her arm around the area. "Do you?"

There was a long silence. Finally, Howland spoke. "This is the way Rocky works. We've been trying to get evidence and witnesses against him that will hold up in court, but every time we get close, witnesses disappear, evidence vanishes. This isn't the first time he's used explosives."

"How can you destroy a car, every last bit of it, without damaging everything else around it?"

"Plastique," Howland said. "You can be surgically precise with the stuff, mold it like modeling clay, and stick small pieces where you want it to go off."

"Liz and Rocky were close." Victoria wadded up the damp napkin she had been holding and put it back in her pocket. "She didn't have the least suspicion of him. Just this afternoon, he gave her a jewelry box." Victoria sighed.

"A jewelry box?" Howland said.

"He was so romantic, she said. He told her not to open it until the grand finale of the fireworks." Victoria suddenly realized what she had said, and she put a gnarled hand up to her mouth. "She thought it was an engagement ring and a necklace."

"That's how he did it," said Domingo.

"Thank goodness she didn't open the box in my house."

"Nothing would have happened," Howland said. "The box was only the detonator. The explosives were inside her car."

"So when she opened the jewelry box, the detonator set it off." Victoria stared thoughtfully at the hole. "Wonder why Louie was with her? What a pity he was killed, too."

"Apparently, he and Liz had some kind of deal going," Howland said. "She was siphoning off drugs for Louie to sell, according to my sources, and Rocky knew about it. He must have told Louie to deliver a message to Liz in her car, and to wait with her until after the fireworks were over."

Victoria thought a minute. "I'm going ahead with the bean supper," she said firmly. "He has to eat, even if he's grieving, and he won't suspect me. Perhaps he'll let something slip."

Howland nodded.

"Would you like to join us for supper? Either of you?"

"No!" Howland and Domingo said together.

"Ah, wait!" Howland held up his hand. "I believe I'd like to accept. Who else will be there?"

"Rocky, Elizabeth, and me. Elizabeth invited someone she met at the harbor, so there'll be five of us, including him."

Howland shoved his hands into his pockets and stared at the grassy strip between the road and the paved walk. There was not much to be seen in the dark. "A thousand damnations. I should have known. All we have now is the chief, and I'm not sure we've got a strong enough case with only his testimony. We have to go with it. Goddamn it to hell."

\\ Chapter 20 //

"So kind of you to ask me to dine with you." Rocky handed Victoria a large bouquet of late-summer roses. "This is a difficult time, as you can imagine."

"I'm so sorry. I knew you and Liz were close." She buried her nose in the velvety pink blossoms. "They're like the ones my grandmother used to grow. I haven't seen any like this for years." She lifted the silver teapot from the corner cabinet.

"Our gardener taught me everything I know about roses. He could make anything grow." He held out his hands. "I'll carry that. Where would you like it?"

"In the dining room." Victoria handed him the arrangement and led the way into the parlor, where she had laid a fire earlier in the day.

"There'll be only five of us tonight." She held on to the mantel and started to kneel.

Rocky quickly moved to her side. "Let me light the fire for you." He struck a match, then waited until the kindling blazed.

"Who are the five? You and Elizabeth and me, I assume."

"A friend of Elizabeth's, someone she met at the harbor."

"We can exchange sea stories, then. And the fifth person?"

"Howland. You know him, of course." Victoria glanced over at Rocky to see if his expression had changed.

He coughed and took his handkerchief from the pocket of his beige jacket. "Excuse me, Victoria, pollen. Howland and I have computers in common. This should be a most interesting evening."

"Howland can be difficult," Victoria said, gazing innocently at Rocky. "You seem to be able to handle him so tactfully. He's quite vain, although I can't imagine why."

Rocky smiled faintly and stared into the fire.

"You knew, of course, I had invited Liz. I'm so sorry." She smoothed her worn corduroys over her knees. "She was such a vibrant person. What a tragedy."

"A great tragedy," Rocky replied. He leaned forward, his hands clasped between his knees.

"Does anyone know how it happened?" Victoria asked.

"There was speculation that because she was selectman and had access to the fire-works, Liz borrowed some for a private display. They're quite dangerous, unless you're trained to handle them, I'm told."

"You must miss her terribly."

"Her loss hasn't sunk in yet," Rocky said solemnly.

He looked at the flames. "So pleasant. Comforting."

"There's nothing like oak for steady burning. Locust, too, but that tends to snap."

"I read your sonnet on Prometheus, bringer of fire," Rocky said, still staring into the flickering flames. "A lovely poem."

"I'm flattered that you remember." Victoria changed the subject abruptly. "The fireworks were spectacular the other night. The fog actually enhanced the display."

"The water droplets in the fog give it a wonderful soft quality," Rocky said. "In a physicist's terms, diffraction and diffusion." He smiled.

"Do you know where they set them off?" Victoria asked.

"In one of the parks in a roped-off area. Our gardener, the one I mentioned, used to design fireworks displays for the Holy Ghost celebrations. As a child, I was fascinated. They require great skill, and a knowledge of explosives."

Elizabeth entered the room with a tray of sherry glasses and a platter of cheese and crackers and set it on the coffee table.

"Not quite as elegant as *Dawn Chorus*," Victoria said, "but the thought is there."

Rocky made a demurring sound.

"My friend should be here any minute," Elizabeth said. "I told him I'd pick him up at the harbor, but he's hitchhiking."

"Is he a local man?" Rocky asked.

"He's from New Zealand, quite nice." Elizabeth blushed.

"Ah, I see," Rocky said, smiling. "Obviously a man of discrimination." He lifted his glass of sherry to Elizabeth, who blushed even deeper, and then to Victoria, who tilted her head.

"There are quite a few New Zealanders on the Island," Victoria said. "The Vineyard seems to attract them."

"People who live on islands are great travelers," Rocky said. "Think of your whaling grandfather."

Someone knocked at the kitchen door.

"That must be Horace." Elizabeth unwound herself from the small chair she'd set next to the fire and went to the kitchen. She returned, followed by a chunky, tanned man with clear deep blue eyes, hair so blond, it was white, and a beard to match.

Rocky stood, towering over Horace. Elizabeth made the introductions.

"My grandmother."

He bowed stiffly to Victoria. "Elizabeth tells me your grandmother came from Australia. A long way, in those days."

"It's a long way today," Victoria said. "Sailing here still takes as long as it did in the whaling days."

Elizabeth introduced Rocky. "My grandmother's and my friend, Rocky. He has a boat, too."

Horace turned from Victoria, and when he saw Rocky, he looked startled. He recovered immediately, but Victoria had glimpsed the expression.

He held his hand out. "How d'ya do, Dr. Folger."

Rocky seemed surprised at being addressed by name and title. "Please, Rocky," he said.

"A nickname derived from your family name no doubt," Horace said. "I understand 'Rocky' is what your students call you."

"When I was teaching," Rocky corrected. "I'm not doing much teaching these days." He seemed puzzled, as if he should know Horace but couldn't quite place him.

"I understand you're consulting," Horace said.

"You seem to know quite a bit about me," Rocky said. "I'm afraid I'm at a disadvantage."

"The disadvantage of an international reputation." Horace bared large teeth and bowed to the taller man.

Victoria sensed an undercurrent she couldn't quite pin down. Elizabeth seemed slightly embarrassed by Horace. Rocky continued to look puzzled. When there was a knock on the door and Howland entered, Victoria was relieved, but only briefly. While the tension seemed to ease between Rocky and Horace, it was even worse between Rocky and Howland. The two men faced each other like cats defending territory, Victoria thought. As she began to regret having invited Howland, Elizabeth rang the dinner bell.

Victoria made her Boston baked beans in the traditional New England manner, soaking dried beans on Friday night, boiling them Saturday morning, and baking them all day with molasses and salt pork. Her grandmother had used the same bean pot every Saturday during Victoria's childhood.

Victoria had set the table with the sterling silver, the good china, the crystal goblets. She had polished the brass candlesticks and melted new candles into place so they stood straight. The silver teapot with Rocky's roses was in the center of the old damask tablecloth. She'd ironed the heavy linen napkins that morning, and they lay next to the forks at the left of each plate.

Elizabeth poured the wine and set the bottle on the floor next to Rocky, who nodded, as if to say he'd be pleased to take care of refills.

Horace held Victoria's chair for her, and she sat at the head of the table. Elizabeth came into the dining room from the kitchen bearing a great rectangular platter heaped with steaming baked beans, hot dogs set along the side. She set them in front of Howland, who was at the end of the table, opposite Victoria.

"You have the honor of serving, I see," Rocky said to Howland, slightly easing the tension between them.

The conversation touched on world events, on boats and sea stories, on computers. It skirted the deaths of Bernie and

Meatloaf. Avoided, at first, the demise of Liz Tate.

Rocky sat at Victoria's right, Horace at her left. Elizabeth sat between Horace and Howland.

It was her granddaughter who stumbled into the subject Victoria hadn't wanted to introduce herself.

Elizabeth turned to Horace. "What did you think of our fireworks?"

Victoria watched Rocky's face. He stiffened slightly.

"Marvelous good show," Horace said. "Especially the finale."

"Do you have fireworks displays in New Zealand the way we do here to celebrate nothing?"

"Christmas, the queen's birthday, that sort of occasion," Horace said. "Usually a special event, not simply for the fun of it." He looked at Rocky again. "Where they really put on a good show is in the Caribbean, isn't that so, Dr. Folger?"

"Rocky," Rocky said automatically.

"You spent quite a bit of time in the Caribbean on your astrophysical work, didn't you?" Howland asked.

"I did much of my research at the radio telescope in Puerto Rico," Rocky said carefully.

"You spent time, too, around the islands as a child, isn't that right?" Horace said.

"You seem to know a great deal about me." Rocky smiled grimly. "May I ask how you do?"

"I'm interested in the famous." Horace grinned.

"I'm hardly famous," Rocky said.

Victoria watched as if she were at a tennis match, Rocky to Horace, across the table, back and forth.

"You're famous all right," Horace said, and grinned again. Elizabeth looked from him to Rocky to her grandmother, a perplexed expression on her face. "These beans are delicious, Mrs. Trumbull," Horace said.

"An old, old recipe," Victoria replied. "Simple fare."

"Served in the most elegant manner," Rocky said, obviously relieved to have attention shift from him.

"A good traditional meal," said Howland. "It emphasizes the pleasure of good conversation."

Rocky darted a quick look at Howland. Horace smirked. Elizabeth looked uncomfortable. Victoria watched them all and wondered where this was leading.

Rocky turned back to Horace. "I gather

you've spent time in the Caribbean yourself."

"Righto," Horace said.

"Did you spend much time there?" Victoria asked.

"Bought my boat there. *Clotho*."

"Clotho," said Victoria. "One of the Fates.
The one who spins the thread of life."

"That Atropos snips," Howland added.

"You sailed from New Zealand to the
Caribbean with someone, didn't you?"
Elizabeth said.

"Right." Horace looked down at his
empty plate. "My much younger sister."

"Where in the Caribbean?" Howland
asked.

"The Turks and Caicos," Horace said.

"Isn't that where you keep your boat,
Rocky?" Victoria asked. "I seem to recall
your saying you sailed *Dawn Chorus* up
from Grand Turk."

Horace was looking at Rocky in an oddly
expressionless way.

Rocky nodded. He had bitten into a
piece of brown bread before Horace mentioned the Turks and Caicos, and he
seemed to be having trouble swallowing it.
He avoided Horace's pale eyes.

"Where's your sister now?" Elizabeth
asked Horace.

"She was killed." Horace never took his eyes off Rocky.

Silence thundered in Victoria's ears. Elizabeth stared at her new friend. Rocky stopped chewing his mouthful of brown bread. Howland sat up straight, put his hands on the arms of his chair, and watched Rocky.

"Killed!" Elizabeth said weakly. "How awful!"

"What happened?" Howland turned to Horace.

"Howland . . ." Victoria began.

"She'd got into drugs in New Zealand," Horace said, his eyes fixed on Rocky's face. Rocky chewed, shifting his mouthful from one side to the other, like a cud.

"I got her away from that scene. Took her with me on my boat. She sailed with me and dried out, cold. You can't imagine the agony she went through."

The others were silent. Victoria heard the house creak. Bicyclists went by on the road in front of Victoria's house, laughing. The sound of their laughter was jarring.

"There were days and nights when I had to hold her while she screamed and thrashed. Let the boat drift. She hated me, she did. We went through nightmare storms together, when every bit of rigging

428

shrieked and moaned and sang, high-pitched, like a banshee. Where the waves rose as high as the spreaders, breaking. Sometimes we'd ride over the tops of the waves and get caught on a steep slide on the backside, and plunge the bow into a trough and keep going down and down. Sometimes the waves would break over us, fill the cockpit, start a regular waterfall into the cabin. We'd throw the door boards off, and use a toilet plunger in the scuppers to get the water to drain out before the next wave swamped us."

Victoria stared at him, her mouth open.

"The boat would heel over fifty, sixty degrees to starboard, then in an instant whip over to port. I never knew whether it was my sister who was screaming or the wind. Or the boat, or me, or all three Furies. You know what I'm talking about, Dr. Folger?"

Rocky took a sip of wine from the goblet and swallowed. He continued to stare at Horace.

"She came out of it. The sea does that. When we reached Grand Turk, she was clean. Strong and brown and healthy. She was beautiful, wasn't she, Dr. Folger?"

Rocky stood abruptly, and his wineglass toppled over, spilling merlot over Victoria's damask cloth. "That's why you look familiar," he said in a whisper. "Arabella's brother."

"You thought you could dodge me forever, eh?"

Victoria felt the hair on the back of her neck lift.

"I must say, mate, I didn't expect to find you here at this supper table." Horace put his chunky hands on the table and looked up at Rocky, who loomed over all of them. "I'd traced you to the Island, mate, and I'd have traced you to hell."

"This is neither the time nor place to discuss this," Rocky said. "Why don't we meet tomorrow at my boat."

"I don't think so, mate."

"What do you want of me? I never intended to harm her," Rocky said. "In fact, I didn't harm her. She did it to herself."

Horace made a strange choking noise and stood, both hands flat on the table, his back hunched like a gargoyle, his mouth twisted in a snarl.

Victoria felt the violence build.

"I'm not a fighter," Rocky said. "Come to my boat tomorrow, and we can talk like civilized people."

"Civilized!" Horace spat. "Heroin. Cocaine. Crack. Speed. Civilized?" His voice rose. "How many people have you slaughtered so you can live like a bloody emperor? Look at your fine threads." He reached across the table and seized the lapels of Rocky's cashmere blazer, knocking over the arrangement of roses in the silver teapot. One of the candlesticks fell over. Elizabeth picked it up quickly and snuffed out the flame. Howland stood at his end of the table and glanced from Rocky to Horace. He held his hands tensely at his side. Victoria lifted herself up from the table and got her grandfather's cane from beside the bookcase.

"Stop this minute!" She shouted over the two raised voices. "Stop! I won't have violence in my house."

Horace glanced at her, briefly distracted. Rocky reached under the table and brought out the half-empty bottle of merlot.

In that instant, Victoria was aware of the smells around her: the baked beans that had been cooking all day, the lavender hand lotion Elizabeth used, the camphorwood sea chest in the front hall, the fear scent of Rocky.

Victoria moved around the dining room table, one careful foot after another, until she was in back of Rocky. Howland twisted his head slightly to look at her. His mouth turned down in his faint smile.

Rocky drew his hand back in a wide arc to avoid the low ceiling, and started to swing the bottle, full force, at Horace.

Victoria moved as quickly as she had ever moved in her life. She held her grandfather's cane by its tip and brought it down smartly with all her might on Rocky's uplifted arm. The merlot bottle dropped onto the table with a crash, rolled onto the floor, and broke, spewing shards of glass and red wine over Victoria's worn carpet. Rocky stepped back and slipped on the broken glass and the spilled wine. He grabbed at the tablecloth, which came off in his hands, scattering dishes and silverware and glasses over everything with a huge crash.

Victoria felt a surge of anger at the destruction. She lifted the cane as high as she could and thwacked Rocky on his head, stunning him.

From out of nowhere, Howland brought out handcuffs, and snapped them onto Rocky's limp wrists.

Victoria checked her grandfather's cane to make sure she hadn't damaged it.

Rocky put his tousled head in his cuffed hands. Sitting among the debris of Victoria's bean supper, his elbows on his knees, he shook his head over and over again.

Horace stood up straight. "You're a fed, eh?" Howland nodded. "I've got enough bloody documentation on that devil to seal him up live in a bloody tomb forever." He jerked his head at Rocky. "Put me on the stand. I'll testify against him if it takes the rest of my bloody life. Shake on it."

Howland thrust out his hand.

"To Washington? They're sending that crazy Indian to Washington?" Beanie pushed his baseball cap back and scratched his head.

"Hey!" said Shipyard, covering his coffee cup with a beamy hand. "Keep your cooties to yourself."

"Whose crazy idea was that?" Beanie straightened the visor of his cap and put both elbows on the table.

"The tribal council," Red said. "It was unanimous. Pass the sugar, will you?"

"Where's Dottie?" Beanie checked his watch. "I ain't got all day."

"Sorry, boys." Dottie bustled in with three bowls of chowder and chunked them down on the table. "This is the last of Dojan Minnowfish's quahogs. You heard about him going to Washington?"

"Yeah. To negotiate for a casino," Beanie said.

"No!" Dottie said.

Shipyard laughed. "Don't believe what Beanie tells you."

"What'd he do to deserve such an honor?" Red reached for a chowder cracker, broke it into his bowl, and shoveled a spoonful into his mouth.

"Musta been something bad," Beanie said.

"I can see him working over some senator." Shipyard laughed. "Scare anybody into doing anything."

"The guy's not stupid," Red said.

"Where he's going, who'll know the difference?" said Shipyard.

"Seems more like a jail sentence to me," Red said.

"Speaking of jail, I hear they nabbed the professor," Beanie said. "I told you there was something fishy about him."

"They ever find out who killed Bernie?" Red asked around his mouthful of soup and crackers.

"I hear they're trying to blame that on Meatloaf." Beanie reached for the pepper shaker and shook it over his chowder.

Dottie, who was passing the table with her hands full of an order, bent and nudged him with her elbow.

"What's the matter? Not seasoned right for you?"

Beanie flung his arm over his head and ducked.

"Who are they saying killed Meatloaf?" Red asked.

"They're trying to blame that on Medeiros," Shipyard said.

"I hear he's testifying against the professor." Beanie stirred the pepper into his chowder.

"Christ, I wouldn't be in his shoes," said Shipyard.

"He's going into a witness protection program. We've seen the last of Medeiros, that's for sure," Beanie said.

"Surprised the hell out of me when Atherton turned out to be a drug agent. I thought he was a computer nerd." Red reached for another cracker.

"Speaking of that, you heard some company offered to buy his computer program? Pass the crackers, will you?" Shipyard took one and spread butter on it.

Dottie, on her way back with dirty dishes, scowled at him. "You guys are animals."

Shipyard brayed.

"The harbor program?" Red said. "No kidding."

"How much they offering him?" Beanie asked, potatoes showing in his full mouth.

"I hear it's a million dollars," replied Shipyard.

"No shit!" said Beanie.

"How'd you find out about it?" Red asked.

"He got a registered letter from some computer company." Shipyard bit into the buttered cracker, and flaky crumbs dropped onto his shirt front.

"You reading other people's mail again?" Beanie asked.

"Wasn't me. It was my wife's sister," said Shipyard.

"A million dollars?" Red shook his head.

"That's what she said," Shipyard said. "He turned it down."

"What!" Red and Beanie said together.

"Says he developed it on government time."

"Jee-sus," Beanie murmured.

"I hear Mrs. Trumbull beat shit out of the professor," Red said.

"Broke his arm with her grandfather's gold-headed cane."

"Teach him not to mess with our senior citizens," Red said.

"They don't make old ladies like they used to," Shipyard added.